Before I Say My Vows

I0685981

MACH PERSON

ISBN: 978-0-578-48509-6

Any references to historical events, real people, or real places are used factiously. Names, characters, and places are products of the author's imagination.

Front cover art by David Thomas
Back cover image by Sam Trotman

Printed in the United States of America

First printing, 2019

mperson@machperson.com
www.machperson.com

For Tra'von

Thank You...

It was you that kept me pushing forward. From the first day I thought, 'what if', to the very day you hear these words aloud: you have been the primary force behind my will to write. So, thank you, to myself. You are my toughest critic and had it not been for you, this story and many others wouldn't exist. Thank you to my biggest fan, my son. You are one brilliant little human. Through this entire process, you rooted for me in ways that kept me anxious for you to ask again. To see you so involved and interested in my writing has been a motivation. To my husband and sidekick. I have never met another person like you. Thank you for waking up in the middle of the night to answer my questions. For picking up the phone at work and even listening for countless hours to Mark read to us. Most of all, thank you for being my "motivation" and taking care of me during this entire process. I know it was not easy. To my beta readers, Brittney, Caroline, Marisha, and Suzanne! I am thankful to each of you for taking the time to read my story. Listening to my progress and asking for updates. Your feedback, honesty, and advice meant so much to me. I can't begin to express my gratitude to you ladies! Thank you, David, for bringing my vision to life with such a beautiful cover. I never imagined it would have turned into such a magnificent piece. Dude, you're pretty awesome. A special thanks to you mommy. For encouraging my writing, spreading the word, and being amazing support. I have talked your head off for most of my life and you always listened and complained only sometimes. You tell me all the time that you can help me with anything that doesn't involve computers. So, you will forever be my best "consultant". I love you, Queen.

Before I Say My Vows

Prologue

"This can't be." I whispered breathily. My heart pounded like a drum as the woman sat behind her desk, mouth partly opened. Her eyes darted between my mama and me as if unsure who the information would destroy more. I shook my head in dismay and closed my eyes. Willing myself to wake up and see my suitcases packed for the ride to new student orientation. The office didn't fade away though. Neither did my mama's shaky voice.

"There has to be something you can do." Mama whispered with her hands gripping her purse. The plea in her eyes tore at my chest like a bear clawing at its prey. The nauseating taste lacing my mouth constricted my throat. Pregnant. Scholarship. Revoked. The woman's words rang like a siren in my head as I silently repeated them. Struggling to make sense of something that didn't require further explanation.

"I'm sorry Mrs. Sandbrook. Because Nhoell was accepted into a special program, those terms and conditions cannot be overturned. There is nothing I can do." Her brows crinkled together as her eyes flickered with pity.

"Nhoell, you are a brilliant young woman," The doctor turned to me. "There are so many other schools out there that will accept you. You may have to put off time for now, but don't give up. I'm truly sorry, and I know the school will be, too."

"Thank you, doctor," Mama nodded tersely, then rose from her chair and stormed out of the office. I bustled behind her. The hard strut down the hall as she gripped her purse underneath her arm, kept me a few feet away. The rippling clacks from her heels that bounced off the

1

walls kept me quiet. She continued with her head raised and I did so with my head down. In a matter of seconds, my hopes fell off a cliff along with my dreams and aspirations.

Finally, in the car, she pounded her fist on the steering wheel. Fighting a battle I didn't see but felt. I pressed myself into the door while my eyes glistened with tears that trailed down my cheeks. My teeth clenched, holding back the sob rising in my throat, then I squeezed my eyes shut. The sounds of her fist still working at the wheel, then her piercing sob drowned me into submission. No longer able to stifle my own cries, my body shook uncontrollably as I cried with her. Once her callused hands moved slower with each scream and her sobs eventually turned into hiccups, she heaved with her head against the wheel. Turned away from me.

#

It only took my grandma forty-seven seconds to bust in my room after we made it home. Switches in her hand, she came at me fast, swinging in all directions. I jolted upright and positioned myself on the bed against the wall. Grandma's eyes bore into me so hard that I stilled and held my breath. Behind her, mama entered the room and watched with tear-filled eyes.

"How could you do this to us? After all we did for you!" Her lips perched together quivering as her wrinkles grew deeper between her eyes.

"You could've been something. Instead, you let that boy give you a baby! You a child, Nhoell! That boy don't want no baby. He got his life, he got football and scholarships! Now what you got?!"

"I'm sorry!" I cried out.

"Don't you dare!" Mama yelled. "I spent my life trying to protect you. To keep you safe. How could you?"

The door of a car closed shut. My head turned to the window and my immediate thought was what he would think. What would the guy that helped me create another human think of this dire situation? They both followed my gaze. Grandma scurried to the window, lifting with little effort and screaming at my child's father and his dad.

"Hey, you! Boy! We got a bone to pick with you! You stay there and don't you move!"

Greg hunched his shoulders at his dad.

"Com'on girl!"

Me and Mama followed her. Keeping my mouth closed, I wiped my tears away as best I could. But they kept coming.

Across the street, Greg and his dad stood waiting as we approached. Looking past my mama's shoulder at me, his dad narrowed his eyes. But it was the fear that crossed Greg's face that sent chills up my spine. I looked away.

"What's this about?" His dad questioned tightly.

"I will tell you," Grandma started, but Mama cut her off.

"Mr. Rehevas, can we please step inside? This doesn't concern our neighbors." Greg hadn't turned away for one second. Had he seen the look his dad had given him, he may have done more than turn away from me. Mama cleared her throat, pulling his dad's attention back to her.

In their house, Greg and his mom sat opposite my family. Mr. Rehevas stood with his arms crossed over his chest. His large frame towered over everyone and the room. Had Greg stood next to him, he would have matched his father in height, but not in weight.

"Now, what is this about?" His rough voice vibrated through the floor. I slumped back into my seat, wiping the few tears that lingered.

"We just came from the doctor, Mr. Rehevas. Nhoell is carrying." Mama replied evenly. Greg's mom gasped. His brows furrowed as the color drained from his dark complexion. But I had no answer for his unspoken questions.

"That can't be," He whispered.

"Are you saying that this child can't be yours?" Mr. Rehevas shouted. The grumble in his voice shook me, and Gregory too. His back straightened as he faced his father's commanding voice.

"N... no, sir." Greg stammered.

"No what, Greg! Which is it?" His father took a step toward him, his fist balled. Gregory gripped the armrest of the couch and my heart lurched as he focused in on his dad.

"Robert, please." His mother pleaded.

"Hush, Karen! Is it or isn't it, Greg?"

"Yes, it is, sir. The baby is mine." His voice trembled.

Mr. Rehevas yelled out. "I knew it was a mistake," He paced the floor for a few seconds. "putting you and this girl in the same room. You are not about to have a child. You have your whole life ahead of you, and I'll be damned if I let a mistake like this ruin it!" He pointed his finger at Gregory.

"The damage is done," Grandma spoke. "Nhoell's scholarship was revoked, and she will not be attending college right now."

Gregory's mouth hung as he shook his head faintly. My vision clouded with tears again as I wiped them before they touched my cheeks.

"And you think my son is about to give his up to babysit? Hell no! Abort the child now before it's too late! Don't worry, she'll forget it soon enough!"

"That's enough!" Mama yelled.

"Now don't you go there." Grandma rose.

"No!" My reaction surprised me. "I'm not killing this baby,"

"If you don't, what are you going to do? Gregory will be at school, you'll be home taking care of this child by yourself. And we aren't supporting it. Do you think he will give it all up for this? He doesn't have time for a kid!" His words pierced through me like sharp needles.

"It doesn't matter! I'm not killing it. You can make decisions for Gregory, but you will not make decisions for me!"

Mama grabbed hold of my arm and gave me a gentle squeeze. "Nhoell, that's enough."

"Mama, I'm so sorry I did this to you. I'm sorry about the scholarship. I never thought this would happen. I'll make it up to you, but I can't kill it. I can't." Gregory sat next to his mother in silence, staring off at the coffee table that created a bridge between us. Somehow, his dad felt like the guard.

"I know," Mama whispered.

"Whether you keep it or not. Gregory won't be here. He's leaving tomorrow and won't be back for a while." His dad said as a matter of fact.

"Is that true, Greg? You're leaving tomorrow?" I sat at the edge of the couch and waited. His eyes burned red as if wanting to cry but not one tear fell from them.

"Nhoell, no."

"Tell her, Greg! We just left the signing!" his father ordered.

"The signing?" I asked him. "You didn't tell me?"

"Why would he, he didn't plan to stay." Mr. Rehevas said again.

"Dad, com'on!" Gregory yelled out.

"I am talking to you!" I stood abruptly up from the couch. My mama's touch did nothing to calm me. So many things ran through my mind in a matter of seconds. Was he planning on telling me at all that he was leaving? Did he know I was pregnant and planned to leave me and the baby? My heart drummed in my ears. I wasn't sure if it was for Gregory or because I feared his answers.

"Are you leaving," I sobbed, "Do you even want this baby? Me?"

"Yes. I mean, no." He stood up to come to me, the table still bridged us. His hands shook and my body trembled. Gregory tried reaching out for me, but I stepped back. I fooled myself for years, believing that I had a chance with someone as amazing as him.

"Which is it, Greg?"

"Nhoell, I'm so sorry about this. Everything. We can figure this out."

"Figure what out! The baby? Us? You're leaving me. You promised me you would be here. You promised to marry me no matter what happened."

Gregory reached out to me again, I slapped his hand away. "I hate you!" I took off running out of the room. My heart thumping against my chest. Embarrassed and confused. I hated him. I hated how humiliated he made me feel in front of our parents. How he toyed with my feelings then left me stranded with a child he helped make. I ran down the steps of their patio, then through the yard. Once I reached the street, the squealing tires against the pavement and the blaring horn of a car was the last thing I remembered before it struck me.

#

My vision was so blurred I thought I was going blind. Mama slept curled into a fetal position on a lounge couch next to me. My tongue felt thick and dry against the roof of my mouth. I took a moment and eased my arms as much as I could when a sudden pain shot through my shoulders and down my back. My eyes widened in alarm as I groaned, trying to remain still again. The beeping increased and, in a flash, mama hovered over me eyes wide with relief. Thinking back, the image of a car and a blaring horn reminded me of how I ended up in the hospital.

"Nhoell?" She whined.

My eyes closed shut as her words echoed through my ears.

"My baby." I forced out. Mama's eyes closed for a moment then reopened with a sadness that washed the smile off her face. My nose and head burned as the tears rolled slowly down my cheeks, tickling me. I tried to lift my hand to my stomach again, and the pain returned. This time, with an emptiness I never felt before.

"Greg?"

Mama wiped her nose and gently held my face. She kissed me on the cheek. "I love you so much."

"Where is Greg?" I repeated in a mumble, my swollen tongue making it harder to speak. But I didn't want water. I wanted my baby. I wanted Greg.

"He's gone to play football, baby. You been in here four days now."

"No. No, no, no." I sobbed through the ache that started in my chest and the pain that rushed through my body. The monitor's beeping increased as my mama used her hands to wipe the tears from my face.

"Why, mama? He lied. Why did he lie? He said he loved me."

She laid her forehead against mine and cried with me. But I pulled her in, ignoring the pain that felt like shards of glass stabbing at my skin. Mama held me as I cried out my hate for Greg. He had stolen my baby and my soul and left me without a word. Chasing his dreams while mine had plummeted into the ocean from the cliff they'd fallen from. It was the same cliff I fell from too.

Chapter 1

It was nine o'clock on Sunday morning when nudges and pokes hit different spots on my body. My thigh. My stomach. My arm then my breast. Then another poke on the butt. I moved around the bed with the constant coolness from the satin sheets surrounding me. Another hit in the side and my body jerked away. The pokes were turning into tickles and I let out a giggle then swatted at the culprit.

"You missed." He chuckled and kept poking at me. I swatted again and again until he laid over me with his large body and attacked more.

"Get off of me you mountain!" I laughed out, jerking from side to side. He laughed with me, continuing his assault until I screamed for mercy.

"I'm getting rusty," his arms on either side of my head, he leaned over me. "you took way too long to surrender." A sexy grin tugged at his lips.

I stared into his deep gray eyes and watched the smile spread across his face forming natural creases. When my heart suddenly fluttered, the large window on the other side of the room overlooking the city became my escape from the unfamiliar feeling. For two months, one week, and five days, Jake Vaughn had been my beau.

"Do you really think I would give in so easily Mr. Vaughn?" I bit my lip to stifle the laugh rising. "Those attacks are nothing. You must not know me."

"Oh, really." His brow went up, and the creased lines vanished from his face. I stopped biting my lips in time for Jake to attack me.

This time with his teeth. He growled and shook his head into my neck as I screamed and laughed like a maniac. I used my arms to push him off but the tickling sensation shooting through my body made me weak.

"You had enough?" He bellowed.

"Yes! Yes, I had enough you beast! Get away!"

"Good," He laughed again and leaned back over me. "took a lot less time this go around."

"That's because I let it."

Jake leaned down and kissed me then began sucking and nibbling on my lips, making me coo into his tease. I relished in the warmth of his mouth and the taste of him was fresh. Suddenly, I stopped kissing him then threw my hand over my mouth. Shoving him to the side, I escaped from the bed and scurried to the bathroom to brush my teeth. His bellowing laugh followed me.

"It's okay, sweetheart. I love your morning breath! I wish I could wake to it every morning."

Shoving the toothbrush in my mouth I rolled my eye and smiled.

"Don't take long, Nhoell. I have something for you downstairs."

"No," I said, with a mouth full of toothpaste before it fell onto my chin. "No Jake, no more surprises!" He didn't answer back. Looking into the mirror, I gently touched my lips then my chest where the light flutter happened. Jake Vaughn was a man of many qualities. Funny, considerate, kind. Especially generous. I knew that firsthand. Since signing a contract with him four months prior, the number of things he'd done for me had been in the teens. Our initial relationship was business but that ended almost as soon as the job did. Jake's assistant contacted my company, Sand's Designs, requesting an on-site quote. I wasn't aware that my client was *the* Jake Vaughn, owner of Vaughn Incorporated, a billion-dollar security company. Once I learned of his identity, I pushed harder than I ever had because I wanted referrals. In a sense, I got what I wanted. Because that led to him asking for dinner once the job was complete. Refusing him led to offering his client list as a bargaining chip, which I kindly accepted. There was no way I would've turned that down. What I didn't expect was the interaction with influential people or trips across the country to visit galleries after hours. The last thing I expected to feel was my heart fluttering from a simple look.

I spat and quickly rinsed my mouth. After a quick shower, I dressed in jeans that insinuated the hips my mama gave me and a sleeveless blouse. I brushed my lush coils into a large bun before applying light makeup.

Downstairs, Jake sat at the marble island with his laptop open and papers in different stacks. The rising sun beamed through the floor-to-ceiling window into the living room, hitting Jake's fair skin at various angles. I kissed him on the neck and sat my purse, phone and keys at the end of the island. I tried to pretend not to pay attention to him watching me so seriously. That alone was difficult because of the remnants of the feeling from earlier.

"You look gorgeous. Any plans today?" He asked, directing his attention back at his computer.

"Thanks," I grabbed a bottle of water from the fridge. "I'm going to see Carla. With Sands so busy, I haven't had time to hang out. I expanded and hired more people, but it's always so much more work to do."

"You know, I can always help with that."

"I can handle it," I grinned from ear to ear. "I didn't says it was too much. Speaking of work, I'm surprised you're here and not at the office. Clearly, you still aren't taking time for yourself. Like I suggested."

"It seems I have realized that I enjoy being here with you, instead."

I stilled, caught off guard by his reply and that stupid little feeling in my chest again. I cleared my throat and ignored it. "So, about this surprise."

"You're standing in it."

Jake rose quickly, then made his way to the living room and stood in front of the window. New York's cityscape behind his six foot two inch toned frame was something to look at. The tailored suit he wore made me want to just bite into him just to see what he taste like. And good god his gray eyes were the most alluring part of him. I felt weak just looking at him. It was the waves of pink, orange, and purple on the horizon that made me want to paint the scene before me.

"Okay," I shook off whatever fog he put me in, then followed him to the living room with a raised brow. "What do you mean?"

"Nhoell, I didn't buy two floors of this hotel just to build a prototype for the new condominiums. And I sure as hell didn't ask you to stay here for a few weeks just to give me your honest review."

"I don't follow." My heart already started beating faster than it should have. Because I did follow. I knew where this was going.

He stepped closer. "Nhoell, I'm saying that this high rise is yours. I want you to move in." He held out the keys and dangled them. I didn't reach. Hell, I couldn't reach.

"What? I can't. Jake, I can't just move in here, " I stutter a bit, trying to gather any coherent thought. "I mean, asking me to stay for a few weeks is different."

"Did you love being here?"

"Well yeah. But I still can't take it. It's too much, this is too fast." I shook my head. "I'm sorry."

"You may think this is too fast, but you and I both know life is too short. I have never met a woman like you. You're strong, smart. Beautiful no doubt. But the way you take charge and face everything head-on. I want that. That and a lot more." He rested his palm on the side of my face and I closed my eyes at his touch. "I wouldn't forgive myself if I let you slip away. Surprisingly, you've made me feel things I have never felt in my life. I don't want to lose that, Nhoell. Not now."

"Jake, " I whispered. It was all I could do after hearing those words. I don't know if I'm ready. I... I think I have to think about it."

"I'm not asking you to marry me yet." He smirked, and I raised my eyes.

"Marry? Why in the hell would you want to marry me?"

"Why not? I can't ask for your hand?" He grabbed hold of my hand and kneeled. My mouth opened in shock. Because clearly he lost his mind. Or I lost mine.

"No, I'm not saying you can't. Not right now. Get up, Jake! Stop playing with me." I attempted to pull him up but he didn't budge.

"I have to ask for your hand right now, Nhoell, so you'll believe me. Since you won't take the condo, I have to resort to desperate measures."

"What? Are you kidding? Get your ass up Jake. This isn't funny."

"I know. I'm very serious. Do you want to see the ring?"

" What! No! Okay, okay. Don't ask. Please." I covered my face, trying to hide the utter embarrassment, but the excitement that was also written across my face. "I accept, now get up."

Jake rose and picked me up with him as he planted kisses across my face and neck. Instead of putting me down, he carried me toward the guestroom on the other side of the kitchen.

"Where are you doing? Com'on, put me down." Once he opened the door to the guest bedroom, he put me down. "You crazy ass man."

Jake grabbed my shoulder and turned my body around. I took in a sharp breath and my hands flew to my mouth. I was speechless. Various canvases adorned the large room and paintbrushes, oil paint and charcoal sat on top of the newly installed shelf. In the corner sat a carved oak easel and a beautiful matching stool. My heart beat steady against my chest and my fingers trembled slightly over my mouth. Jake's hands massaged my arms and that flutter in my chest returned.

"Do you love it? As much as I love you?" he whispered in my ear. I swung my body to face him.

"What? What did you say?"

"You heard me."

I took a beat before responding. "I really love it, Jake. I don't have any other words to express that."

"Neither do I." He held up the keys again. I smiled and grabbed them from his hand while he pulled me in by the waist, kissing me. I took him all in and melted into his snug embrace. My heart warmed at the feeling he lit in me as I relaxed in his arms.

"I guess I can let you explore a bit more. I must make a quick phone call. Thank you for accepting, Nhoell."

"No, thank you."

He placed another sensual kiss on my lips before leaving.

Going through everything and rubbing my fingers across the beautifully carved easel almost caused me to lose track of time. I left the guest bedroom to find the kitchen empty, apart from Jake's stuff on the island. Grabbing my purse, cell, and keys, I looked around the condo. The sun made its way above the cityscape, casting light throughout the open floor plan. Gray, polished stone covered the dining room floor. Plush carpeting and white contemporary furniture graced the living room. Vibrant vases and art made from stone and crystal adorned both rooms, giving it an artsy setting. Just next to the large fireplace, a metal staircase led to the second-floor master bedroom and a very spacious and well-secured closet. That too was designed by Vaughn Inc. We flew the bathroom marble from a West African country and the tub from Persia. Even though I didn't design the condo for Jake, I had some say in the products he chose. It was a replica of what the other condos would look like once construction on the new building began.

I let out a soft chuckle and shook my head at the lengths Jake went through to make me smile. Allowing me to help design the rooms for his condominiums had only been a grain of salt compared to the success my business garnered. I partly had him to thank for that. After contacting only three people from his contact list, there was no need to reach out to anyone else. They came knocking at my door with checkbooks in hand after seeing my work.

Grabbing my water last, the red ink scribbled on papers near Jake's computer grabbed my attention. I picked up the stack and flipped through them. They were mid-year financial reports. Crinkling my brows at the ink plastered on most of the pages, I went through the rest of them and finished up just when my phone rang. Replacing the report with my phone, I answered. Jake appeared from around the corner.

"Hey Jessica, give me a second," I grabbed the papers. "Jake, this report has a few errors in them. The gross should be a lot higher. Page one and nine. The ink was useless by the way."

"You checked this?" He took the papers and flipped the pages "Just now?"

"Yes. I think it was row ten on page nine that makes the biggest impact. Sorry I have to take this." I put the phone back to my ear.

"What are you, a genius or something?" He chuckled.

"Some people call it that." I winked. "Hey, Jessica. What's up? No, that's Mr. Penn. He will change his mind eight times before finalizing if you let him… it's okay, I will call him and drive to that location for the new client first thing in the morning… okay. Later."

Jake was still going through the report after I hung up.

"Nhoell, can you look over this one before you leave? I'm having a hard time believing I caught myself a mathematician."

"Mathematician? Really. Alright, but I'm charging a fee."

"Trust me, it'll be more than I pay the last person." He said underneath his breath. I watched him go through the rest of the report.

#

Carla Dunn, my one-of-a-kind best friend since college, sat across from me with a Chester cheese grin on her face. I finished telling her about the morning's events and her response was, 'I knew it was something, how you came up in here glowing and shit.' I expected nothing less from Carla. We sat at a restaurant that became our go-to place. She was on a first-name basis with the owner after trading a piece of art he fancied. In return, her own special table and free dining were available whenever.

In college, we pushed each other at everything we set our minds on. Sand's Design was my priority. I scraped up every penny, sold my art, won grants just to purchase a lot for my business. After graduating, my passion had only intensified.

Carla's thirst for success intensified too. She worked her ass off to build Westwind Gallery. Just as she promised, she became an art dealer. One of the best at only twenty-nine. After researching endlessly and saving money for a down payment, she later found and purchased an old textile factory on seven acres of land. She renovated the entire building that comprised of three levels to her gallery. Even though I sold some art in college, it was Carla who helped put my art on the market. At that very gallery. It was only after she begged me for three weeks that I finally agreed, though. Her opening night featured a collection of paintings I made specifically for the occasion. We put the artist as Unknown to bring more mystery to other work that shee"ll be carrying. That night, all of my paintings were purchased. The next morning, I retrieved the names of the buyers to thank them. By the time I got ahold of them that afternoon, they had already sold them to another buyer.

"From the look on your face, you agreed. To be honest, I'm surprised you said yeah." Carla said.

"I'm surprised I did too. I can't tell you the last time I felt this way." I replied, as I absentmindedly stirred my straw in my cup.

"I'm surprised because I've never seen you into a guy like this. You usually cut them loose as soon as they show some feelings. It must be the money."

"Says the woman who runs off every guy after three months. And it isn't about the money." Carla rolled her eyes and looked the other way.

"They run themselves off because they can handle what's on the outside, but not what's on the inside. Trust me, none of them are worthy enough anyway if they can't keep up with little ole me. So, are you really doing this thing with Jake Vaughn? I hear he isn't everyone's favorite person."

"Yeah, I hear that about me too. Besides, everyone has an enemy or two. Besides, he's the nicest man I've ever met. And I'm actually happy. Nervous too, because I don't want to get hurt. You know, if things don't work out." I put down my straw and toyed with my fingers instead. Carla placed her hand over mine.

"I think it's alright to be a little apprehensive. Especially of love."

"Who says I love Jake?" I cut my eyes at her.

"Then why are you moving in?" I softened my expression.

"Exactly. But seriously, everything won't always be perfect. You're smart enough to know that. I haven't been around him enough to peep him out, but I'll fuck a rich white man up over you, Nhoell."

"Oh, my goodness Carla. Keep it down," I snickered under my breath. "I know you'll be the first one beating at my door. So here is the key." I held my hand out with two keys dangling on a key chain that read, *I love you, girl.* She grabbed them.

"I love you too. You better had given me my own set." Carla winked her eye before putting the keys into her purse.

Chapter 2

The following Monday, my phone's blaring ringtone jarred me from my sleep. Grabbing it from the nightstand and shielding my eye from the morning light, I answered. Carla's voice shrieked through the receiver.

"Are you fucking kidding me! Nhoell, I know you feeling this dude, but your business? Why in the hell didn't you mention this last weekend? Or how about when I talked to you the other day?"

I sat up in bed and let my feet touch the plush carpet and turned on the lamp. The room had suddenly chilled around me.

"Carla, what the hell are you talking about?" I cleared my throat then looked at the time on my phone, squinting. "It's eight o'clock in the morning."

"Which means you should be up getting ready for work and not merging your business with Jake Vaughn. What the hell."

"Excuse me? Why in the hell would I merge my business?" Now alert, I stood up and went to the restroom.

"That's what I want to know. Hold on,"

I put the phone on speaker then rinsed my face with cold water, allowing it to completely wake me.

"I just sent you the link." She said.

A notification popped up, and I clicked it. The news article opened, and it read, *Booming Small Business, Sand's Design to merge with Vaughn Incorporated.* I quickly scanned through the article about the merger and a new direction of Sand's Design. The journalist called it

Vaughn Design Group instead and elaborated on how Vaughn Inc. was investing in smaller businesses. At the bottom was an old photo of Jake and me shaking hands, making the article appear legit. My fist tightened over the phone and my screen flickered colors.

"Nhoell, did you read it? What is this about?" Carla yelled through the phone.

"I don't know. I'm going to find out, though. Thank you, Carla, I'll call you later with updates."

"Nhoell? Be careful. If he did this, and you knew nothing about it… just call me if you need me."

"I will." As soon as she hung up, I slammed my fist into the sink and tried my damnedest to calm myself before calling Jake. When I finally steadied my mind and nerves long enough to make the call, I didn't get an answer. Then I tried his office. Not there. I called repeatedly and left message after message, and not a single one was returned. When I finally called my own office, Jessica picked up the phone.

"Sand's Design. I mean, Vaughn Design Group, how may I help you."

I grimaced, and a wave of anger rolled through me all over again. What the holy fuck!

"Jessica? Why are you answering the phone this way?"

"Ms. Sandbrook? I'm so sorry." She whispered. "I arrived this morning and there are new people everywhere. I mean, I figured when you said you were coming in late, well. We heard about the merger."

"There is no merger, Jessica. I will take care of this. I'll be in the office later, I have an errand to run.

I arrived at my errand around noon. Jake's building was one of the tallest downtown. After getting past security and onto the elevator, I pressed the 53rd floor and waited. My skin flushed, and my chest burned like hot coals. I clenched down onto my jaws enough that morning to know a dental visit would be needed in the future. Jake Vaughn had a lot of explaining to do, and I wasn't leaving until it was all said and done. I would be damn if I let a man take what I built right from under me. The more I thought about it, the angrier I'd become. Once the elevator opened, I was met with a large bulletproof glass wall and an intercom speaker and scanner next to it. I pressed the button and waited. To get through those glass doors and many more throughout the building, you had to be granted access. Jake's entire building was an advanced prototype for others around the world. Not even their in-house developers could hack the mainframe.

"How may I help you?" A woman's voice said over the speaker.

"Hi April, it's Ms. Sandbrook."

She buzzed me in. I made left and right turns until I was at April Crowe's regal reception desk, the gateway to Jake's office. She was a tall woman, with an athletic build, slanted eyes, and a small scar underneath her earlobe. When I first went to Jake's job as his associate, April and I chatted a little each time. Based on our past conversations and her body language, I was sure she held a military background. Once I approached the desk, April stood and smiled back.

"Hi, Ms. Sandbrook. I'm sorry, but he still isn't here yet. I expect him back, but he has a meeting as soon as he gets in."

"It's okay April, I will wait. In his office." I walked to Jake's door.

"Wait, I'm not sure if I can let you in there. I hope you understand."

"I do." I kept walking until I reached his office and let myself in. April didn't follow.

Jake's one thousand square-foot office was designed to barricade himself in and keep others out when necessary. Behind his sleek black executive desk showed a beautiful landscape of the city through a floor-to-wall window. The other side of the room had a built-in bar and luxurious lounge chairs made from fine leather. Another large oak table sat on the opposite side for private meetings. From the touch of a simple button, walls built into the ceiling could close off the area for privacy. I recalled first coming to his office and meeting with him at that very table. Then being in awe of the mechanisms in which the walls shut us in the room together. Being in such proximity to him raised my temperature that day. I felt the attraction between us and I was sure he'd felt the same. But sitting and waiting for him to arrive, I was no longer certain.

By the time Jake strolled in some forty-five minutes later, I was far from the edge he'd driven me to. I was livid. Being in his office surrounded by memories of his smiles and teases made me feel even more naïve for having believed that he cared for me. He walked into his office talking on his Bluetooth earpiece with April fast on his heels. From the surprised look on his face, she didn't have time to tell him I was waiting. I stood, my hands folded tight behind my back as my face flushed. He ended the phone call, then excused April. Smiling, he walked over with his arms outstretched.

"Hey, sweetheart. I didn't expect to see you here." I pushed his arms away from me and stared up directly into his eyes.

"What in the fuck is going on, Jake? With my business. What did you do?"

"I see, you found out about the merger. That was my next surprise."

"I don't give a damn about surprises, Jake. You cannot take something that doesn't belong to you."

He bit down on his lip, nodded, then sauntered past me to his bar as if he didn't know what to say. The glass made a loud clank when he sat it down. Then he poured in the dark liquor.

"I honestly thought you would be happy about this. The merger, more clientele. International clients at that."

"I don't need your name to make it, Jake. I don't know if everything you said last week was a lie or not. But it's starting to feel like it. I can't understand what would possess you to do something like this, knowing how I feel about my business. You need to make this right. Go to the news station or magazine. Do what you have to do to let them know it was a mistake."

"But it wasn't a mistake. I have taken nothing that doesn't belong to me." He replied coolly.

"My business does not belong to you! That is mine and only mine. I built it, I created, and I do the goddamn work. Don't treat me like I'm stupid!"

Jake moved to his desk and pulled out a manila envelope and

walked it to me.

"What's this?" I asked suspiciously.

He tilted his head, motioning me to open it. With almost shaky hands, I pulled out the documents and glanced over them one by one, shaking my head. I could feel my face twisting into a grimace and my jaw ache.

"No. I didn't ask you to do this."

"Just think of it as transferring a loan. So now, you can pay me instead."

"Are you fucking kidding me? You cannot do this. I won't allow it!"

"It's already done. Sweetheart, please understand that this is the best possible move right now."

The sound of his voice. The way he spoke to me. It was like what was happening wasn't an issue at all, so I grew angry all over again.

"Not without a fight, you lying, scheming piece of shit. I'm calling my damn lawyer. And you can keep the condo and everything in it. I can't believe I fell for your bullshit."

Again, I turned with the copies of paid off loans and a contract that named Vaughn Inc as the owner tight in my grasp and hastened away. It was his grip around my forearm that stopped me from moving any further. Glowering at it, I snatched away, but his grip only grew tighter.

He gritted, "Do not play with me, Nhoell."

I stared at his eyes, startled to see that I didn't recognize him. Instead, they darkened from the beautiful grays that always smiled at me. Eyes that were filled with kindness and generosity bore in me with impatience and rage. With all the force I had, I pushed him away, expecting him to let go. But he didn't and the grip on his hand burned my arm like rope tearing at dry skin. Before I could speak another word, his hand slapped me hard across the face, sending a loud popping noise throughout his office. Reflexively, I yelped but swung just as quick back at him. He caught my wrist mid-air and his mouth curved into a sinister smile.

"Let's try this again. What belongs to you is mine. I already have your signature. Just as I promised last week, you will marry me. Then, we can share what belongs to all of us. Understand?"

"You're insane." I gritted. He released my wrist and slapped me again. I inhaled a sharp breath and shook my head, my eyes watery from the stinging.

"No," I whispered. "You can hit me as much as you want. I'm not giving you my business. I'm not marrying you." He slapped me again, and the tears flowed down my face. Then again. And again until I finally screamed out. My face was burning raw and the tears that flowed over my cheeks felt like acid burning away what was left. I felt defeat as my heart plummeted to the floor at the realization of what was happening.

"I was right. It won't be easy to break you." He leaned down and kissed the spot he'd hit. I turned my head away.

"I figured I would need leverage." He released me and the rush of blood flowed back through my arms and into my fingertips. "You're free to go. Call the police. Call your lawyer and tell them all about it." He walked back to his desk and sat down. "Keep in mind that anything you say will leave your blood on the sidewalk. There is a good chance it'll be your friend's blood too. I'm sure I can come up with something interesting."

"This has nothing to do with Carla."

"It didn't. Now that you refused my offer, she's in it as much as you. You leave me no other choice."

"You can't do this! You sick bastard!"

"A sick bastard that you love, right?" He chuckled. "Now go. I understand how big of a decision this is." He turned to his computer and ignored me. Snarling, I rushed from the room and past April, bleeding the fumes I brought in with me.

Chapter 3

My legs moved fast, dragging me through a crowd of people hurrying in both directions. Sweat trickled down my back as I maneuvered to the right, nearly tripping over a little girl kneeled over. I gripped my purse, moving it closer to my body. The succulent aromas from the different directions made my stomach growl in response. But the adrenaline pumping through my endocrine system had erased any hunger I may have felt. Ten minutes and the plane was taking off, with or without me. I would be damned if I missed it. Up ahead, my gate number appeared in bright red. I was that much closer to being home, somewhere I hadn't been in three years. Not since my grandma died, and I didn't even stay the entire weekend with my mama. Home reminded me of a painful past I promised not to go back to. And I never did.

Walking to the departure gate, I handed my boarding pass to the woman, my hands trembling more than usual.

"Are you okay, ma'am?"

"Oh, yes. I'm nervous about flights." I replied with a smile, grabbing my ticket.

"Be well." She replied.

But I was already in the corridor, bustling ahead until the door of the plane entered my view. Two flight attendants stood waiting with beautiful smiles plastered across their faces. It was difficult not to return their kindness. So, I smiled when I passed them, then walked down the narrow aisle as the knots in my stomach loosened. Once I sat down, I peered to the front of the plane and swiveled to the back. Finally allowing my shoulders to slump and letting out a long sigh, I aired out my shirt.

I couldn't remember the last time I'd been afraid of a situation. Been afraid of a man or even sidestepped by one. I let my guard down and lowered the drawbridge and gave Jake Vaughn complete access. How could i be so stupid. Why didn't I see the damned flag. He was all too perfect. The man had done a complete one-eighty on me and I never saw it coming. I cursed myself for falling for him, for not trusting my instincts about the client list and moving in. Out of all people, why did Jake come after my business?

I kneaded my temples with my knuckles and drew in a long breath. Opening my purse, I pulled out my pocket-size sketch pad and a pen and I jotted down a to-do list: call Carla, find an excellent lawyer, block Jake's number. I thought about calling Carla as soon as my feet touched the pavement after leaving Jake's office. Instead, I sat in my car and cursed and screamed like a sailor charging his enemy. Jake's words circled my brain about her being in the same boat as me. How I was the one that got her into a shit storm. The last thing I wanted to do was call her and mix her up even more. Ultimately, it was the tenderness in my face from Jake's hits that helped me make the final decision. So, I sent her a text claiming an emergency at home and was getting on the next flight. Promising everything with my business was getting handled.

The overhead compartment slammed shut, startling me as a heavyset man sat and gave me a slight nod. Only then did I realize I held my breath. Giving him a terse nod, I finished my list and a quick sketch before putting my pad away. Moments later, the pilot came over the loudspeaker and greeted the passengers. Thinking of all my options, I leaned my head against the seat, resting my eyes until the engine came alive and the plane rumbled. My hands finally stopped shaking and my heart eased to an even pace as I listened to the flight attendant provide safety instructions in the dullest tone. In no time, we were lining up on the runway for takeoff.

"Looks like we have an emergency on the runway. Please

standby."

I opened my eyes and faced the window. I couldn't see a single thing ahead or behind us. After five minutes of anticipated waiting, a gust of wind rushed into the cabin. I sat back in my chair, trying to become one with the seat. Hoping it wasn't Jake entering the plane. From ahead, two male police officers spoke with an attendant as she pointed to the rear of the plane. They strolled down the aisle, one behind the other, their hand on either taser or gun. Their steps grew closer and finally stopped.

"Excuse me, ma'am?" a deep voice broke through the chatter on the plane. I lifted my head. "Could you come with us, please?" I looked between them both, neither appeared to be in a good mood. Neither was I.

"What for?" I replied.

"Please, just come with us."

"Again, what for?"

The second cop clenched his jaws when a beep sounded from the rear of the plane, catching his attention.

"We can discuss it off the plane. Right now, I need you to come with us."

"I'm not leaving this plane. You haven't given me a single explanation on why you need me to. So, no. I will not leave." I sat face forward back in my seat. My heart was beating like African drums now. Fast and hard. I didn't want to have a showdown with NYPD. There had been too many instances with law enforcement abusing their power. Especially with the black community. Last thing I wanted was to find myself behind bars, or worst. In my heart though, I knew it was Jake.

"Ma'am, we don't want to remove you from this plane with force. But we gotta do our job and what's necessary." The officer said.

"If you were doing your job, you would tell me why you're removing me from the plane. I'm sorry, officer, but right now I have a lot to lose and I'm not leaving."

"Are you threatening us?" The second officer asked in surprise.

"Seriously! Are you kidding me?" I sat up. From the corner of my eye, a light flashed. "You know what? I have nothing else to say. Until you can explain why your employer stopped a commercial flight for one person... I'm not leaving." With that, I sat back in my seat.

"We asking you nicely."

"Sir," the second officer spoke. "Could you please step to the side?" In no time, the seat next to me was empty and four large hands were grabbing at my arms and clothes.

"Don't touch me! No! Don't touch me!"

"Stop resisting!"

"I am not resisting! You have no right to do this!" They pulled me from my seat and dragged me down the aisle of the plane. I had an unobstructed view of a dozen bright lights aimed at us until we ended at the door. The officers released me and I stood up straight.

"I'm going to sue the hell out of all of you."

"You have to get down those stairs to do it." The second officer cracked a smile. At the bottom of the stairs were two more officers and two squad cars.

"Let's go. You've wasted enough time."

#

The two asshole police officers put me in the back of the cruiser, drove around the corner into a hanger housing smaller planes, then handed me to two men in a black on black Lincoln Navigator. No matter how many times I asked, neither one of them said a word. After twenty minutes of riding through the city, I recognized my surroundings and knew the condo was our destination.

The men stayed closer than necessary as they walked me through the foyer and into the elevator. Still, neither one of them made a single sound. I was okay with that because I needed to focus on how I would get away from the lunatic that stole my business.

At the entrance of the condo, both guys waited for me to enter and didn't look like they were giving me an option. I cut my eyes at them and went inside.

Jake sat in the armchair facing the large window with a glass of dark liquor in his hand. His expression was distorted in the reflection, but mine was very distinguishable. I didn't move another step.

"Did you honestly think it would be that easy to leave? Who do you think I am?"

"I don't know who you are, Jake. Or what you want from me."

"What I want?" he mused. "There isn't much that you can give me that I don't already have."

"So why am I here?"

Jake rose from his chair, his muscles flexing through the silk dress shirt. Only a few nights ago, I gripped those same muscles as he brought me to climax. My lip curled in disgust at the thought of how he made my body react.

"I've told you already. You will be my wife."

"Why?"

"Satisfaction, of course."

"I'm not marrying you, Jake. And I can't give you my business."

He cruised over and stood inches from my face as his eyes trailed from my eyes to my lips.

"Did you already forget," he touched the side of my face with the back of his hand. "What I can do to you and that friend of yours."

"You will not lay a hand on her." I spat, staring him hard in the eyes I thought I loved.

"Will you take her place then?"

I shook my head. Jake closed his eyes and pinched the bridge of his nose.

"I'm going to leave, Jake. I'm not marrying you, and I don't care about your threats. I won't let you take my business."

"Okay," he nodded his head repetitively. "Okay, Nhoell." He stepped back and extended his hand for me to leave. I watched him. Hesitantly, I took a step back, keeping my eyes on him. He stared as the space between us grew. When he was finally out of my line of sight, I sped to the door and gripped the knob. From behind, Jake's large hand gripped the back of my neck and pulled me back to the living room as I swung at him repeatedly. Once he let go, he struck me full force, knocking me to the white carpet where red spots dripped from my nose. I touched my face, feeling the warm wet liquid on my finger. He held back at his office. Probably because I still had to walk out. It was that, or he wasn't used to being turned down.

I balled my hand into a fist. When Jake grabbed me from the floor, I rammed it into his face as hard as I could, hurting myself. He stumbled back, then touched his lips and wiped away the blood that stained it. By then, I stood and receded far from his reach.

"I expected you to put up a fight. But not like this," he chuckled and marched toward me. "You're full of surprises aren't you, Nhoell! Oh, don't you run now."

He followed me fast around the couch as I dodged him left and right, hoping to make it to the front door. In one move, Jake shoved the couch in front of me, blocking it. But I jumped over it and ran to the door, screaming for help. As soon as I opened it, the two men from the Lincoln stood blocking my exit. Behind me, Jake grabbed my hair and pulled me into the living room. I screamed at the men for help. But the sound of the door closing told me neither of them would intervene.

Turning me around to face him, Jake grabbed my face and put his forehead against mine.

"You're going to be my wife."

"No!" I pushed him to get away. And again, he hit me, knocking me to the table, causing the décor to fall to the floor. Jake pulled me up by the collar of my shirt and I grabbed the decorative stone bowl from Berlin. Swinging my body around, I smashed it hard across his head and he fell back into a chair and let out a loud groan. I ran to the mantel and took another glass piece to attack again. When I turned around, a bloody Jake stood in front of me, eyes black as night and hands balled into a tight fist. One hit from him and the glass was breaking on the floor and me with it. I turned again to see him coming back, his hands raised. Before I could crawl away, his blows came in quick successions, targeting every visible part of my body. I stopped fighting and covered my head and neck, blocking few blows. Each hit took the breath from me and I no longer screamed sounds. The pain shot through my back and my head and dizziness came quick. Fear struck me as my arms weakened and my body numbed, and I could feel myself losing hold. Suddenly, he stopped and let out a loud cry. As the darkness consumed my vision, Jake's sobs faded away.

#

My vision was blurred when I woke up to beeping noises surrounding me. The chilled air circulated my face. Glancing down at the IVs in my arms, I wiggled my finger and the tingling sensations flowed through my veins. Trying to lift myself caused immense pain that made tears flow down my face. I tried calling out to my mama, expecting her to appear in my sight and tell me everything would be okay.

The sirens from an ambulance drew my attention to the drawn shades, but voices from outside the door pulled me back. Two women in scrubs passed the glass window just as an officer approached my door and stood guard. Only then did I recall what happened to me. What Jake did to me. My stomach turned and all over again the tears rolled down my face, tickling my ears.

Then, one man that guarded the condo stepped to the officer and shook hands. Just like that, the officer walked away and Jake passed the window and entered the room. My monitor beeped rapidly as I watched him approach. The few tears that left me earlier were followed by dozens more as I remembered the pain from his fist hitting my body and the fear that struck me when I thought I would die.

"Shhhhhh," He massaged the top of my head then planted a kiss on my cheek. "You're okay. They arrested the men that did this to you." Outside the door, the police officer reclaimed his position. Jake followed my sight as I scrambled to feel for the call button.

"Trust me, he's one of mine," he reached over my head, grabbed the call button, and handed it to me. "just like this hospital. Now, what were you saying about marrying me?"

Chapter 4
(Three Months Later)

It was the shadow of a man that kept me awake at 3 a.m. Ever since getting out of the hospital three months prior, that recurring dream haunted me most nights. Waking up scratching at my throat to breathe each time didn't allow me to remember anything. I didn't think it was a coincidence I was having nightmares ever since leaving the hospital. It was no one but Jake Vaughn haunting me in my dreams. Just as he had been haunting me in real life.

I lay awake in bed for hours until my phone chimed through the Bluetooth system. I grabbed it, then solved an equation to silence it. My routine of waking up and sketching before getting ready for work was history. Not only because I was awake most nights, but because it was something else Jake had taken from me.

Opening my text messages, I looked at the four names that glowed on the screen: Jake, Carla, Holly, and Nora. I was 84 contacts short of what I used to have. It took less than a week for me to learn that whatever I searched on the internet and whoever I called, Jake found out about it. I expected nothing less from the owner of the best security company out there. My search for lawyers and attempt at learning what I could about the Vaughns only garnered a warning from Jake. And that warning were continuous pop-ups on my computer screen of Carla sitting at her office desk.

Clicking Jake's name, I sent a quick text letting him know I was awake. Then I clicked Carla's name and sent a kiss and heart emoji, telling her I was ready for the day. For the past few months, there had been nothing to get excited about other than my dates with Carla. Which had become limited. What used to be five visits a week turned into one every two to three weeks. I blamed it on the planning of the wedding she didn't want me to attend and not the hospital visits she knew nothing about.

I tossed my phone on the bed and before I could get up, it rang. Checking the caller ID, I huffed, dropped my head back onto the pillow, then answered.

"Good morning, Holly."

"Yes, Nhoell. It is a good morning," she yelled into the phone and I cringed at her high pitch voice. "I do hope you are ready for tonight. My brother says you will be in attendance this time, mommy and I are expecting you to look the part, this won't be like those galas you're used to, this is my event and you will be on his arm,"

I massaged my temple as she continued.

"Also, don't embarrass us. I didn't appreciate you asking me stupid questions at Diane's party, so don't dare do it here, are you listening?"

"Yes. I'm listening."

"Good. Jake said you have a hard time doing that on occasions, so pay attention."

I pulled the phone away from my ear and gripped it so tight, my knuckles ached.

"I will be over this afternoon. Understand?"

"Yes. I understand, Holly."

She hung up. I took a few deep, steady breaths before regaining the composure I lost. Jake's younger sister truly had it out for me. Ever since introducing me as his fiancé, she made it her mission to control everything I did. The first time she attempted, I snapped on her so badly that she called Jake and show me just how much control she had over me. Needless to say, it was the last time I disrespected anyone in his family.

Fragrant vanilla and cinnamon coffee called my name and helped me to rise from bed. Without thinking, I grabbed my housecoat from my day lounger near the window, then walked down the open staircase. Even though it was the middle of June, I used the fireplace each morning. So reaching the bottom stair, I flipped the switch.

Already made was a fresh cup sitting on the coffeemaker. If I had nothing, at least I had my morning brew. Especially after many sleepless nights.

Grabbing my favorite mug, the one that reads "Let There Be Peace," I turned on the news in the living room. The first person I saw was Jake. *Vaughn Technologies to Build Downtown Luxury Condominiums* said the subheading at the bottom of the screen. He spoke about his plans and the elaborate designs coming from one of the greatest architects in the country. I changed the channel and another news station reported on gang-related robberies and vandalism and another reported on a gang leader that was being sought by the FBI. I switched it back to Jake.

"You are not really watching this horse shit, are you?" A voice blurted from behind me.

I spun around, wasting coffee on my hand and the floor.

"What the hell, Carla! Don't sneak in on me!"

"But I wasn't sneaking, darlin'," she said matter-of-factly.

I rushed past her to the kitchen, her eyes following suit.

"I have the key remember, and I was loud enough," She yelled out as I ducked underneath the kitchen cabinets grabbing what I needed.

"Don't you think?"

I reached Carla with a washrag in hand and looked at her as she stuck out her foot to display the metal-like bottoms of the high heels. "I'm good, honey, but not that good, not in these shoes."

I smirked, then got to my knees and sprayed the floor.

"You're right about that. I didn't expect you to be here so early. I texted you like five minutes ago." I replied.

"Well, I figured I would come by and jump on you in the bed. I was pissed when I saw you were already alive."

"You're quite the comedian." I shot her a nasty look before turning back to the screen and unconsciously scrubbing the carpet. I kept my eyes keyed in on Jake as he stood handsome and confident like he always did.

From the corner of my eyes, Carla moved. I could see her eyeing my hands as they flowed over the area I'd been scrubbing.

"I'll just put a note on the door for housekeeping."

Rising from the floor, I looked her up and down and folded my arms across my chest. It was the first time I took in her appearance since she'd walked in. The outfit she wore gave me an admiring pause. I stared at her flaunting figure as she stood model-like in a blue pencil skirt and yellow blouse, exposing just enough cleavage to tease the eyes. Her purse dangled in the crook of her arm, and her Bluetooth pulsed green on her ear. She had her course, amber hair pulled back in a twist out, drawing attention to those large hazel eyes. Carla's lips were lush and probably as soft as they looked, too.

"Any other plans when we're done? Looks like a date," I said, given her a raised eyebrow before finally embracing and kissing her on the cheek.

"Oh yes, I definitely have plans. Now hurry your ass up."

It felt like months since Carla and I spent time together, though it was only three weeks since we last went out. When Jake's mother, Nora, attended her PWNY (Prestigious Women of New York) meetings, she dragged me along with her. Since they never introduced me as Jake's fiancé, I never introduced myself as such. Always Nhoell. Holly's numerous events kept me busy more than anything. She was never the one planning them, but always took the credit. But the wedding always seemed to be front and center. Especially when it came to Nora. Everything seemed to be urgent with her. I was almost sure she didn't like me, only tolerated me because of Jake. It was the sister from hell that tested my patience over and over like a battering ram. Still, two months wasn't that far away, and I still hadn't figured out a way to get me and Carla out safely. After running two other times, Jake appointed two bodyguards/driver/prison guard to follow me. He stationed them across the hall and at the door when needed. Because they never spoke a single word to me, I named them Lee and

Jimmy. It was Lee who brought me back after I tried leaving on the Megabus. But it was Jimmy who stayed in the hospital with me that night.

It was Lee who drove Carla and me to a few boutiques and bookstores. One boutique had been her favorite shop since I'd known her. As many times as we'd gone to that store, the astronomical prices shouldn't have surprised me, but they always did. I didn't really want to buy any books when we made it to the bookstore either. Still, I purchased a meditation book and a book on herbal remedies. I didn't want Carla to think I wasn't having a good time, but I couldn't completely enjoy our outing. Checking in with Jake about six times a day was the usual. It was only eleven-thirty and I'd already made those six calls letting him know what we were doing and where we were headed next. I was certain Lee had been doing the same thing.

For the next few hours, we continued our excursion with laughs and jokes that reminded me of why I loved spending time with her. Carla amused me with stories about her job and the high school kids she mentored. The gleam on her face as she spoke about her work made me proud. I longed to be back in the art community. To get back to the things I'd neglected: interior designing, paintings, drawing... my business. I had the urge to paint again, but each time I picked up a brush, I froze. I didn't have it in me to visit the art store or to leave sketches around the loft anymore. That beautiful art room that Jake made for me; he destroyed it, and me, only mere weeks after my release from the hospital. His reasoning? For me, dressing like a whore when going to his office. That was my release. My only comfort from the Vaughn family. He'd taken that away from me, and I hadn't been able to paint or draw since.

Carla and I made it back to the hotel, swapping entrepreneurship stories. She nagged me about working again, but I dodged the questions that indirectly told her the truth about my position. Working again? Yeah, right. As much as I watched Jake on TV, at events, and when he came to the condo some nights, I still didn't know what his triggers were. Nor his limits. But I knew working or owning anything wasn't an option. Also, it had become difficult to keep up with the excuses I gave Carla.

"Like I said before, now is an appropriate time to get out there, Nhoell." Carla closed the door behind her and placed the shopping bags down near it. She started up our conversation from the elevator again.

"I wish I could, Carla. It's just been really busy around here." I dropped my bags at the steps, then made a B-Line for the kitchen and grabbed a kale and almond smoothie.

"Busy with what? Com'on. You can get any job you want out here. Don't let that asshole keep you from doing your thing. Hell, I don't see you enough as it is. You spend more time with the wicked witches of the west." Carla followed close behind me, placed her purse on the island, then sat on the barstool.

"Carla, it's not like that. I wish it was that simple."

"Help me understand what the problem is. Jake? If you keep letting him make these executive decisions in your life, then you'll become a doormat. If that's the case, just get your ass on a plane and go home. Reflect on your next move since you've partnered with this asshole."

I chuckled at her. Thinking I could simply jump on a plane and vamoose. It reminded me of the first time I tried to run and how well it worked out.

"It's funny to you?" Carla said, sounding hurt. I took a deep breath, put down my shake, and looked her square in the face.

"None of this is funny, Carla. I want to work, I want to design, and there is nothing more important than painting. But I can't. Not with him."

"You make it sound like this man is forcing you to stay here! Is he? I'm not stupid, Nhoell. I see how much you've changed since coming back from Atlanta. If you want to do something, just do it! You were the one telling me to push past my limits and shit. But look at you. You're making more excuses. This isn't like you."

Concern etched in her face and, it tugged at my heart. We rarely argued. The few times we did, we never had to scream. She was pushing me further and further into a corner, and it was harder to dig myself out each time.

"You are living on top of the fucking city wasting your goddamn life with a piece of shit man who doesn't care about you! I'm sorry to say it, but it's true."

"Don't you think I know that?" I screamed back at her. "You don't need to tell me what I know!"

"Then why are you here! If I don't tell you, then who will? His mama? That other sister? No, I'm sure it'll be fucking Holly telling you her brother is shit!"

Her words stung. The veins in her forehead and neck rose, and her eyes pierced me in a way that made me take a step back. My chest rose steadily as I bit my tongue to keep from speaking the truth. Because I wanted to. I wanted to put her pain and anger toward me to rest. I wanted to breathe. The click of a lock and slamming of the front door startled me. Heels echoing on the marble floor grew louder. Carla and I both looked in that direction, waiting to see who'd come in. Only Jake and his family had copies of the keys. Then it donned on me.

Dressed like everything she wore accumulated to fifty grand or more, Holly in her one-of-a-kind business attire veered around the corner with her purse dangling from her arm. Her brunette hair curled to the middle of her back, bounced with each step while the jewels casing her neck and arms shimmered. She stopped just in the living room and faced the kitchen where we stood, then shot a distasteful look at Carla.

"Oh, I would've thought she would be gone by now," Holly said, looking at me but referring to Carla. "You must've been awfully busy, Nhoell. I guess you didn't have time to check-in when you arrived." She raised her brow and glanced at Carla.

"Shit." I peeled to the stairs where I sat my purse with the shopping bags and pulled out my phone. It had only been five minutes. "Holly, I'm so sorry. I must've forgotten. I'll call him now."

"No need. I sent him a text," Holly replied.

"Seriously? And this is the shit you have to put up with." Carla blurted out. "Not only do you have to check in with that fucking psycho, Nhoell. The sisters from hell check in on you, too!"

"Carla!" Panic filled my chest once the words left her mouth.

"Excuse me," Holly looked at Carla from head to toe. "You should take a moment to think before you dare say another word."

"Or fucking what, you repugnant bitch?" Carla rose from the stool. "You'll call your brother? Do it. I dare him, you, or whoever else to step to me!"

"Carla, stop it!" I screeched at her so loudly, my ears rang.

"There is only one bitch in this room, you skanky whore, and it isn't me," Holly sneered.

When Carla took a step forward to Holly, I matched her steps and grabbed hold of her arm.

"That's enough, Carla!" My words didn't seem to faze her. Her eyes had narrowed in on Holly and the vein from her neck throbbed again. She cracked a lopsided smile.

"Let me hear you say that again," Carla whispered, but her voice came out so gritty, I didn't blame the look Holly gave before taking a step back and clutching her purse. Her eyes darted between me and Carla. Then she took another step back before speaking again.

"As you know, Nhoell... my brother will hear about this." She turned and left. Not realizing I still held a tight grip on Carla's arm, she snatched away. I exhaled.

"Why, Carla? Why did you do that?"

She laughed bitterly. "Did you see yourself? Did you see how fucking quick you went to that phone to call him? Telling that piece of shit sorry for not calling? This isn't you, Nhoell. Look at yourself before asking me why." The look she gave me twisted my heart. Just as quickly, Carla stomped away in her metal bottom heels. Seconds later, the slamming door shook me and the loft.

Chapter 5

After I shimmied into the sleek black gown Jake picked out, I stepped into my walk-in closet and entered the key code to access the jewelry cabinet. The wall slid open, displaying diamonds, jewels, handcrafted watches, and rings. Some were gifts of apology after Jake flipped out and did his worse one day or another. The one gift I needed lay in the center surrounded by the other jewelry. The day he gave them to me was the last day I wore them. We fought until it was only him doing the fighting. Afterward, he gave me an hour-long lecture on the importance of appearances. The next day, he gave me the pearl set and told me to wear them while we had sex.

I didn't question why he wanted me to wear them again. Instead, I put them on and left the closet to find him standing in the doorway of my bedroom. Still, after all he had done, the way he looked at me sometimes made my heart flutter. I hated myself for the way my body reacted. But I hated him more. I replayed the entire day in my head, picking out everything that went wrong. It all included Carla.

"Are you ready?" he asked. His deep, commanding voice sent goosebumps down my arms to my chest. He took one stride to me, then placed his palm over my cheek. I held my breath when his thumb touched my lip. In a slow sensual motion, his fingers trailed down my neck until they reached my cleavage.

"I asked you a question." He repeated.

"Yes," I breathed out, then inhaled. My chest rose against him.

"You're more beautiful this way. Come on."

Just like that, he hurried away. I leaned back into the door frame and held it tight. My eyes shut, I took one deep breath, counted to three, then I exhaled. I repeated the ritual once more, then reopened my eyes and pushed away from the frame. Shaking off the uneasy feeling that came from being around Jake, I looked at my reflection. I was beautiful, but not in the way he wanted me to be.

We pulled up to what looked like a three-story building with intricate designs adorning the exterior. From the outside, it mirrored a beautifully carved marble box. But once we entered, the entire scenery was an open space that glowed in a golden hue. Down the long hallway, the bright crystals that hung from the ceiling seemed to reflect off each other. Once inside the grand ballroom, the elegant chandelier casting sparkling lights on the walls reflected off the eight golden columns. The columns surrounded the room evenly with more of those carved designs. I squinted at the closest one, trying to get a better look. Once Jake pulled me along, I finally paid attention to the low hum from the other guest. Like Jake and I, men and women wore their variation of black. From the shimmering to the suede and glittering specks, to the fine jewelry gracing the necks of many of the women.

Making our way through the crowd, one person after another approached Jake with a handshake and a beaming smile. Each one hoping to get past a greeting, into a meeting. Near the stage, Nora and Holly stood in white dresses, talking with another woman. Jake's mother's oak complexion stood out compared to the other women with her. Had it not been for Nora herself, telling people Jake was her son, no one would've known.

The white gown she wore shimmered with each movement, making her the grandest woman in the room. Her dark hair was curled at the nape, touching the beautiful black diamonds around her neck. She was radiant, but there was a tiredness in her eyes as she stood there. But when Jake and I approached, those same eyes lit up.

"Hello, mother." He kissed her cheek. "You look beautiful. So do you, Holly." He turned to Holly and gave her a quick kiss as well.

The fitted mermaid-style gown embraced her curves. A few loose brunette curls fell from her updo hairstyle down the sides of her face. Holly broke necks as she stood out amongst every single person in the room. It was a pity that she was so meanspirited, though.

"You're just in time, Jake. This is Julie Gentry, her father owns most of the land further east."

"It's nice to meet you, Ms. Gentry," he shook her hand.

"I am honored to meet you. Holly has very nice things to say about you, and your mother is the most stunning woman in here. Hopefully, we can talk later. I hear you may be interested in some land." She batted her lashes.

Internally, I rolled my eyes at them. It was just like Holly and Nora to act as I was anywhere but near. I preferred to be anywhere but near. But learning from a past mistake, I stood quietly by Jake.

"Thank you, Ms. Gentry, I will keep that in mind. Oh, mother, I will be back in a moment. There is someone I need to have a word with." Finally turning, Jake leaned down and kissed me on the cheek.

"You know what I expect from you." He whispered, then was gone just like that.

I faced Nora and the others, each of them looking as if waiting for me to do something.

"You all do look amazing. And this place," I looked around once more. "Holly, this place is gorgeous."

"Yes, I know. It's why I chose it."

"Do you know who the architect is?"

She stared daggers at me as the color in her pale face turned red.

"Now why would you ask me a rediculous question? Gosh, Nhoell, you never learn, do you?" Holly turned on her heels and walked away. Nora glared at me, then followed suit. There went trying to make nice after what happened this afternoon.

They left me in the presence of Princess Julie who held her wineglass to her lips as she watched me intently.

"Seems you two aren't very cozy. You're not at fault, even I know who the architect is. They put it in the program. I hear he's in town too. So, what is it that you do…" Julie started.

"Nhoell." I doubt she'd forgotten my name so quickly. "I'm... an artist." I continued looking into the crowd as Holly laughed with another guest.

"Umph, my sister tried to become an artist, so my parents sent her to a psychiatrist. She's a doctor now. Well, you know what they say, there's a job for everyone right. So, what are you to Jake Vaughn?"

"Business partners. Sorry, Ms. Gentry, but I need to go to the lady's room. It was nice meeting you."

I hightailed before she could ask me anything else. I was used to getting cornered by women demanding to know about our relationship. Men too. So, I was an expert in leaving those conversations.

For the next ten minutes, I walked around the ballroom talking with one person or another. While some people held genuine conversations, others only wanted to know if I was their bridge to Jake Vaughn. Once they learned I wasn't, their presence became nonexistent.

I kept my eyes on Jake as he made his rounds. First with the commissioner, then with the state senator. It irritated me at how everyone fell at his feet when he approached. He held a cloak over their eyes just as he did mine. Still, I watched him like a hawk. Paid attention to the people he spoke to and the things he did. The sociology and psychology classes I took for two years weren't for nothing. Jake had habits, and he had triggers. Most of all, he had a weakness. He'd become my target, just as I'd become his. Even though he had the advantage, if I knew nothing, I knew it would be a matter of time before Jake let his guard down.

Finally making it to the carved columns on the far side of the room, I traced my fingers over the ridges and dents. Inspecting, there were symbols, not at all what I originally thought. I pulled out my phone and took a photo, then Googled the name of the building to read about the architect. Hearing Nora's name in hushed whispers pulled my attention away, though.

"It was because of her episode a few months past. Why else would she allow such a girl into her family?" An older woman spoke. 'Her voice was raspy and low.

"I hear that's just a rumor. She's his mistress, not his fiancé. Besides, a doubt Nora would let just anyone have her grandchildren." The older woman responded.

My heart beat fast as I stepped closer to listen.

"Either way, she isn't well enough to have a seat on the board. And it'll be a crime if she let that daughter of hers take her place. She isn't worth a grain of salt. I don't care how much money that child raised. It wasn't her doing, anyway." She let out a hacking cough. Ahead of me, a server walked in my direction. I lifted my hand and shook my head. He retreated.

"She'll die first before giving up her seat, you and I know that."

"I know. I don't care if her family started the organization. The entire family is dysfunctional. Especially that first one," another hackling cough. "the black one. She's been screwed up since the husband passed. We can't leave it up to them to manage."

"That's why I'm here. I'm hoping we can be allies when the time comes."

"Don't worry, you have my vote." She coughed out again.

I retreated away from them, careful not to be seen. My heart was racing as I soaked in the entire conversation all over again. Was there a possibility that Jake only wanted me to have an heir? And did he rush to marry me because something happened to Nora? I considered the idea, then thought back to the weeks leading up to the merger. I couldn't remember if Jake ever said anything that hinted his mom was sick. Or even the fact that he was interested in children. No. That couldn't be it. If that was the case, why take my business? Why beat me?

Far away from the gossip girls, I grabbed a glass of wine from one of the passing servers, then took a gulp. On the other side of the room a brown-skinned woman in a beautiful black fitted gown, draped down the center of her back, caught my eye. I didn't know why, but the wide smile that crossed her face warmed my chest and eased my racing heart. Only able to see her from the side, she was a tall shapely woman with long dark coiled hair reaching her shoulder blades. I stood watching in envy at the way she laughed with the woman standing with her. Suddenly, she stopped and turned toward me as if she knew I'd been watching the entire time. My breath caught in my chest as I realized who the woman was. She turned more to the left and the tight look that washed over her face shook me. No longer the joy-filled woman that caught my eye, but an angry black woman killing someone with just a stare. I followed her glare across the room until it landed on Jake. Confused, I turned back to Marilyn, Jake's older sister, but she no longer stood in the crowd. She was gone.

#

Walking through the foyer to the elevator, my palms dripped in sweat and my legs seemed to wobble with every step. The heels I wore didn't make walking any easier. The phone call Jake answered occupied his attention as we followed his two bodyguards to the door. I went upstairs and took the quickest shower I'd ever taken, not allowing the steam a chance to surface. Once I heard his elated voice through the walls, I moved faster, hoping the phone call didn't piss him off. I dried off while paying close attention to the sound of his voice.

"… make sure you get the best we have in the company for the presentation. Once the plans and the figures are laid out, he'll be sweating to sign those fucking papers… this isn't just any designer!"

I oiled my legs and dabbed perfume around my neck. After letting my dampened hair fall down my shoulders, I applied a bit of gloss to my lips then took one last look in the mirror. My makeup smudged under my eyes and had given me a sexy, edgy look rather than the sexy, classy one. Slowly, I could see the doubt in my own eyes as I looked at myself in the mirror. The probability of Jake resisting me reached the ceiling. I never initiated sex since before our engagement and, right then, I thought of everything falling apart. But deep down inside, a part of me knew he wouldn't turn me away once he saw me in my birthday suit.

Finishing up his call, I hurried to the nightstand and lit the candles, adding the finishing touches. As if on cue, his heavy footsteps grew louder on the metal stairs. Slow and steady. I dimmed the lights and disappeared from sight. The heavier and louder his steps became, the more my stomach turned. My fingers trembled as I stared at the ceiling with my eyes closed, listening. I didn't know if he would reject me, then beat me, or just lay me across the bed and fuck me. But once I saw him step into the room and his back faced me, my nipples grew hard from arousal and determination. He had taken off his jacket and his dress shirt fit his broad frame and defined muscles enough to send a tickle to the spot between my legs. I pushed everything he had ever done to me out of my mind and focused on the human man that stood in front of me. A few gentle steps and I eased behind him, placing my warm, nude body against his back. A soft moan escaped my lip as I massaged his shoulders and rubbed my breast on him, wanting to feel every hard part of him against me.

"What are you doing?" he said with a strain in his voice.

"Hopefully you," I replied in a whisper.

He spun around and with a tilt of his head, he looked at me from head to toe. I kept my hands roaming him, touching him. Scared to stop and lose confidence or give him time to decide. I eased one of my hands down his chest, then to his hips and watched him as his eyes fluttered. His brows furrowed. Once my hand reached its destination, my lips curved into a wicked smile. I grabbed his tie and pulled him down for a kiss. Jake moaned in my mouth as soon as we connected, and our tongues danced with one another. Still throbbing in my hand, he grew harder with every movement and nibble. I, too, could feel the throbbing between my thighs. Yes, I thought to myself. I pushed him closer to the bed, then broke our kiss. His jaw clenched, seeming partially enthralled and, well, something else that I couldn't describe. I wanted to say something, to tease him more. But I didn't trust myself to speak and risk changing the atmosphere. Instead, I unbuttoned his shirt, licking my lips and nibbling them gently, giving him the most seductive look I could muster.

I unbuckled his pants, and another moan escaped his mouth, and once again, I could feel the gushing flow in me. He sprung free, and I let my hand run over his smooth, hard length before looking at him and dropping to my knees.

"When you start, don't stop until I tell you to." The words left his mouth, and I dove in, taking him almost completely. He collapsed on the bed, legs tensing, hands gripping my hair. Jake didn't last ten minutes before pushing me away from him. As soon as he did, I climbed on top of him and rode him until the volume of his grunts and groans matched mine. After a while, he came, and I came with him. But I started up again and ripped him out of his shirt and shoes. Because Jake didn't come to the condo unless he wanted something, my goal remained the same. Do what's needed to keep his hands off me. Though exhaustion took over four orgasms ago, I fucked Jake until well after two o'clock in the morning when we both passed out.

Chapter 6

I woke up the next morning from another nightmare of shadows surrounding me. My nose stung as if I'd been drowning, and I struggled to catch my breath. I looked over to find Jake watching in silence as if I hadn't awakened fighting for my life. He simply removed the covers, then disappeared into the bathroom. Apart from the dream, the uneasy feeling that came over me once I laid eyes on him was disturbing. Especially when he usually left before the sun rose.

After calming myself, I searched for my phone then sent Carla a quick text apologizing. I wanted to know if she would be at the cake tasting. I hoped she opted out because of the incident between her and Holly. Sure enough, she assured me she wouldn't leave me to hang for anything in the world.

Jake and I arrived ten minutes after. As expected, Nora and Holly waited with Carla. It surprised me to see Marilyn waiting too. She was even more beautiful up close. But it was her familiarity that made me hesitate when we approached. Quickly recovering, I smiled and greeted Nora first, then Holly. Everyone seemed in good spirits. Even Carla, seeing as she greeted Jake. Still, the relief I felt knowing she didn't let our tiff keep her away uplifted me.

The owner, a slim white man with an oddly thin mustache and overly pointy nose, greeted us with smiles and open arms. He and Jake shook hands, and we all made our way to a tasting room in the parlor's rear. Inside sat a table large enough to seat eight. Assortments of flowers and cakes decorated the room. Silver, crystal, and golden platters, drink ware, and utensils sat on display for all who entered to see. The drink ware highlighted the room, as it sat in a beautiful glass case on top of a table. I could hear Carla's approval as she also looked around the room.

We'd taken our seats, and I sat between Jake and Carla while Jake sat between his mother and me. Holly sat on the other side of Nora, and Marylin made her way to the opposite end with Carla. I couldn't help but take stolen glances at her. Not only was the previous night on my mind, but she also reminded me of someone I attended school with.

The baker presented us with his first platter of cake, delivered by two women. First, a chocolate-lemon-strawberry cake, which sat beautifully on silver sampling platters. I nearly gasped after taking the first bite and tasting the multi-flavored goodness as it melted sweetly in my mouth. I smiled at Carla, raised my brows in excitement, and nodded my head. Carla and Marilyn both agreed with me by finishing the entire plate. It bothered me we were at a cake tasting, enjoying the food for a wedding I didn't want to attend. To have Carla so close to me knowing that Jake held her over my head unsettled me the most.

"Marilyn, you've never had any taste anyway. Jake, your guests would be appalled if you chose this one. Trust me, I know," Holly said, after pushing the cake away.

I stared, stunned at her blatant disregard of the chef as he stood watching, also astounded. Jake put his fork down and called for the next cake. As Nora questioned Jake about work and his wellbeing, Holly kept herself included in their conversation. When Marilyn began casually talking with Carla instead of shutting herself off, I listened in. Her behavior from the night before and a sense of familiarity piqued my interest. I was certain she saw me in the middle of the floor, yet, she didn't seem the least bit unfazed. She asked Carla about pieces of art that she just acquired. Clearly, Marilyn knew her work. And Carla didn't brush her off like she had done with Holly so many times in the past. Since being with Jake, she was the Vaughn I saw the least.

The chef walked in again with his assistants. As the two of them distributed the samples to each of us, this time on the crystal platters, he described the cake.. I politely placed my fork down and placed my hand back in my lap. Carla took her bite and moaned into the cake.

Carla gently nudged me. "I figured I'd try it anyway, right?"

Jake took another bite of the cake before setting his fork down and dabbing his mouth with his napkin.

"Very nice. But Nhoell has a nut allergy, so we couldn't possibly have this. Paul? Can you explain to me how this cake made it to the top five?"

"I do apologize, Mr. Vaughn. I thought we received a call regarding the changes. We must have gotten our order mixed up. Honest mistake. We will get the next one out."

"I'm sure," Jake replied coolly.

Paul disappeared to the back. Nora leaned forward just enough to see me from around Jake.

"Nhoell, you're quiet. Is everything okay?"

"Yes, everything is fine." I returned her smile with a vibrant one of my own.

"Good," Next to me, I could hear Carla's annoyance through her low scoffing. Jake continued to sit back in his chair, relaxed as he kept a preoccupied eye on his phone. As busy of a man as he was, it was never like him to be so consumed with his device around Nora.

"Once we leave from here, we'll be meeting with the florist again to finalize a few things, and I'll have to start on the seating chart." She added.

"That should be easy," I chuckled. "I only have my mom and Carla."

The room grew eerily quiet. Even Carla didn't say a word. I glanced at Jake, who stopped texting on his phone and stared at me. I replayed the conversation in my head, trying to decipher what I said in error.

"But, I don't mind helping with the list... that's no problem at all." I spoke in the sweetest voice I could muster. Carla's hand lightly touched my leg, and I nearly jumped. I silently counted my deep breathing ritual in my head in quick succession. It's didn't ease my anxiety of fucking up.

Paul entered again with his assistants close behind him, their hands filled with gold platters. I exhaled I sign of relief.

"This here is my rendition of the world's most famous and most delightful, a Sachertorte," he said with so much assurance. "Please, enjoy."

Again, I waited for Jake to taste the cake. For a moment, I thought I heard him make a sound. For a man who only saw food as a weakness, a requirement for good health and living, it seemed strange. Yet, he ate some of the fanciest dishes one could ask for. Apart from my art, food also became my comfort. I owe that to my grandma's cooking, growing up.

Finally, listening to everyone agree on the cake, I took a small bite from the portion provided, relishing every bit. Almost immediately, the cake melted in my mouth and the flavors danced a calming ritual on my tongue. I thought I would cry from its scrumptiousness. I turned to Carla. Both she and Marilyn watched intently, waiting for my reaction. Carla nodded her head repeatedly as she pointed to the cake with a full mouth. I laughed at her for going for another bite.

"I love it. I've never had anything like this," I said, still filled with excitement. I turned to Jake, who seemed to have the same relaxed expression. I knew he enjoyed it. With only a few crumbs left on his plate, there was no doubt.

"I'm sure there are many things you haven't had, Nhoell," Nora said in a cutting tone.

It was such a contrast from the sweet, sincere voice she'd given me only moments before. As if everything was too good to be true, her comment had taken all the excitement out of me. I didn't respond. Instead, I placed the fork down and hid my frown with a smile. As much as the rebuttal on my tongue stabbed at my lips to open, they didn't. Fuck. You. The voice in my head yelled. But not even those silent assaults changed the fact that Carla witnessed how I allowed them to speak to me.

"Yes, Nora. One is having some low-down coward for a fiancé."

Once the words left Carla's lips, my heart sank, and my head turned to her so quickly, I thought it would snap. It seemed as though the room, the entire earth, had all stood still for that moment. Carla stopped looking at her plate and gave me the most disappointed look. Her eyes trailed above me, to Jake I assumed, and cut him a look that wished him more than death. Never in my years of knowing Carla had I seen her look at anyone the way she looked at Jake that day.

"That is, until now, Nora." Carla raised a brow, daring Jake to say something.

"Jake!" Nora screamed a hoarse cry as if unleashing him.

"Carla…"

So many different outcomes circled my head that no other form of communication was available. I turned in my seat to face Jake. I immediately wished I hadn't, because his face told me that I should haul ass and run. Jake was about to unleash. The look he'd given Carla already marked her dead.

"Jake, I-"

"Close your mouth, Nhoell."

I closed my mouth so quickly that I nipped my tongue. I knew something terrible was going to happen. The last time Carla had done something that upset Jake, I suffered the punishment. This time, Carla sat only feet away from him.

"You will not sit here and silence her, Jake," Carla said, firm.

"You… will not disrespect my mother. And you will not question me about my wife." He said coolly.

"Fiancé, Jake. She isn't bound to you yet, and I'll be damned if I let her make such a stupid mistake."

"Please, Carla!" I blurted out before I could think of anything else. Everything that left her mouth was more and more insulting. Jake placed his arm around me and leaned to whisper in my ear.

"Dead women don't speak, Nhoell. They are easier to deal with." My throat tightened, and I could feel the cake turning in my stomach. My back became rigid and my hands shook uncontrollably as they lay in my lap. My shame didn't allow me to look her way. I wasn't the woman who'd preach to her and talked all day about her aspirations.

Not even the woman who stood up to asshole men that felt they'd owned me after the first night. I felt it in my heart every time he laid his hands on me, I wasn't that woman.

"What have you done to her?" Carla said.

"Get out!" Jake yelled to the owner of the bakery. The door opened and closed. Jake's arm hung over the back of my chair and my stomach ached again.

"What do you suppose someone like you is going to do to stop me from marrying her? Huh?" He slammed a fist on the table. The plates clanked and wine glasses almost tipped over. I flinched, but Carla did not.

"I will do whatever it takes," she said resolutely.

"Even if it means your life?" he replied almost comical

"I don't take threats lightly, Jake. Especially not yours."

"You should never take anything I say lightly. Now, leave before someone gets hurt." His voice so intense, yet calm. She rose from her seat slowly.

"Are you threatening me, again?"

Jake smoothly placed his hand on my shoulder and softly rubbed the back of my neck.

"Not you. Not at all you."

He squeezed the back of my neck and the surging pain that shot through my shoulder blade caused me to scream out. His grip held on. Tears flooded my eyes as my breathing quickened. I took deep breaths, my hands in my lap, careful not to move his. Careful not to speak.

"Let her go! Now!" Carla screamed and Jake released me. I let out long breaths and sniffled, trying to gain my composure. Internally, I begged Carla to leave. I prayed and hoped that my only ally, my only friend, would hold her tongue for once. I didn't know how I would respond if Jake put his hands on her in front of me. In my mind, I saw myself doing nothing. But in my heart, I saw myself fighting for her, just as I had for the past three months.

"Now, are you going to walk out that door and leave us to finish our day?"

Silently, Carla weighed her options. He began to massage the back of my neck again. I stiffened.

"Jake Vaughn, you will get yours... and your family, for letting this happen. You've chosen the wrong woman. Nhoell, I will pray for you..." She grabbed her purse. "Because this man is a demon and I will not let you go down with him." Then she was out the door and gone. Next to me, I felt Jake turn to his mother.

"Satisfied, mother?"

"Of course, Jake." She kissed him on the cheek. There was no doubt in my mind anymore that Nora Vaughn and his entire family knew he beat me as often as he could.

Chapter 7

The only person I knew that put a smiley face on pancakes to cheer me up was Carla. It was the smell of food that got me up because breakfast was never prepared unless I made it. So when I made it to the kitchen, a freshly made cup of coffee and the smiley face breakfast gave me my answer.

"Come out,"

I tried holding back my smile. When she stepped in from the hall, her eyes saddened, my smile faded completely. I reached out my arms and she extended hers and we met each other halfway. Her warm embrace reminded me of the many embraces we shared.

"I'm so sorry, Nhoell. I don't know what I was thinking. I just... saw the way you were around them. And that... that bitch... I'm so sorry."

"Don't worry about it. It's okay."

"But it's not," she pulled back. "look at you, you're still here."

She looked around the kitchen and over into the living room adorned with charming art pieces and elegant décor we replaced. For the second time. "You are living like a queen... yet, you are being treated like a slave. He put his hands on you."

"I know," I whispered, returning her grim expression. I glanced around the rooms as if expecting someone to appear. "Sorry, I didn't tell you. I'm sorry you had to find out."

The army of tears marched behind my eyes and lit torches that burned. Carla stared at me with that same army appearing in her beautiful hazel eyes.

"Why? Nhoell, how long has this been going on?" Her voice strained.

I shook my head as the lump rose in my throat. For as long as I could remember, Carla had never shed one tear in my presence. But the hurt in her eyes made me grab and pull her into my arms. Letting out a loud sob, my grip tightened around her as her shoulders shook. The lump in my throat grew bigger, but I held back my army that sat waiting. As much as I wanted to believe she was crying about the situation, I knew she was crying because I didn't tell her. Moments later, when she'd calmed, I pulled her face up.

"Please, talk to me." She said, pulling away and sniffling, using her fingers to dab at her eyes. But I didn't release her arms.

"Not here."

"Can you get away for a couple of hours," she rolled her eyes. "I can't even believe I'm asking."

"It's okay. It's best if we get out of here. I have to head downtown later anyway." I didn't mention dropping off Jake's completed financial reports he left me. The same reports I corrected when I accepted the condo.

"Good, I want you to see something. First, I need to get to the office and take care of a few things."

She bit the bottom of her lips and narrowed her eyes as if apologizing.

"It's okay. When was the last time I went to your gallery, anyway? I'll go get ready."

I took my exit. Getting her out of the condo was the first thing I needed to do, and she opened that door for me. Now that Carla made it on the banned list, it was the last place I needed her to be. She had become more than Jake could handle. Usually, it was like that with her. Few men she dated didn't stick around to deal with her, for one reason or another. The way I saw it, young, ambitious, and aggressive, she was a woman to be reckoned with. So I imagined Jake using his company's software to apply facial recognition throughout the hotel. I even believed he installed something like that to find me each time I ran.

Lee drove us uptown to Westwind Gallery. The sight of the beautiful brown textile building sitting on lush green land reminded me of a scene out of a painting. Memories of Carla and I walking the same steps dozens of times flowed through my head like a movie reel. She rushed ahead, and I followed slowly behind, taking in the sight. The last time she and I met up multiple days in a row hadn't happened in months. As calming as it was to be around her, it made things more difficult to handle and unpredictable. Though Jake was never predictable either.

Lee parked the car in the lot adjacent to the building and I sent a quick text to Jake. Once I entered, Carla had already disappeared behind a door that led to the offices. In the lobby sat a reception desk and a large painting hanging behind it. Pamphlets of information on the land and building sat on the desktop. From behind the door, a familiar face walked through.

"Hey Ms. Sandbrook, it's nice to see you again." A young black girl with coarse hair and a freckled face skipped over then embraced me. She was one of the high school kids that did community service and joined the mentor program for the gallery. Showcasing young talent to the neighborhood kids around the city had been one of Carla's primary focus when she thought of the area. The girl that stood in front of me was a troubled kid when the school counselor contacted Carla. She'd been house-hopping and taking care of her kid brother. That was something Carla paid attention to.

"Hi, Lalei. It's nice to see you too. How's school? And your little brother."

"Good, my grades came back up and I'm on the debate team too. Ms. Dunn said if I keep it up, I'll have a job here after college if I want. You know we miss you around here?" She beamed and shifted to one foot after another.

"I know. I missed you all too. I'm glad school is going well. Make sure you keep it up though. It's easy to lose focus."

"I will. Or Ms. Dunn will strangle me." She said seriously.

"You got that right," I laughed. "I'm going to take a look around, okay."

"Okay, we have two new exhibits. I bet you'll like them."

I entered the door leading to the gallery. There were three total floors, and it took me twenty minutes to view only a quarter of the first floor. My mind warped itself in the paintings and drawings showcased. Each one speaking to me a different story and giving me a bit of light. Then there were some filled with darkness and pain that I stared at longer. Thinking about what I had to do about Carla. About Jake. More than anything, I was afraid of the outcome.

There had been three-dimensional art of faces and figures sitting on intricately carved stands I couldn't help but touch. Some art hung from the ceilings and others stuck out from the wall. No matter where I stood, I was surrounded by life everywhere. It warmed my chest to the point of clutching my shirt to ease it. The beauty that surrounded me and those unspoken words helped me forget all my worries for just a moment.

Once I entered the third floor of the gallery, my heart swooned and before I realized it, tears were flowing down my cheeks. Hanging from the ceiling as the largest art piece in the room was a mural I painted back in college. I gifted it to Carla after she received a call home and had become unnerved for a couple of weeks. I never knew what happened or what she'd done with the mural afterward, but seeing it hanging opened all the emotions I'd put into it that day. My love for her, our bond, our promise. Forever is what the message on the back said. Forever. I sniffled and stared for a long time until my tears dried on my face.

"It's beautiful," Carla said from behind. I didn't turn to face her. "I didn't know how much I needed you until the day you gave me this. It spoke volumes, Nhoell. You have been there for me every step of the way. You've changed my life too. You probably don't see it, but you have."

She touched my shoulder, turning me around to face her. My eyes were swollen with tears.

"I want to be there for you. I was so focused on myself that I didn't say anything about your behavior change. I knew something was wrong. But I excused it by telling myself you would tell me if you need me." Her face was relaxed, not gearing up to cry as she had at the condo. I couldn't say the same for myself.

"But you didn't, you went through this by yourself. As smart as you are, I don't know why you're still there with him. But I am here. Forever. I didn't have anything to do at the office," She turned back to the mural. "I wanted to bring you here and show this to you. You haven't been painting. You are wearing your emotions on your sleeves. And that family is draining you. Nhoell, this is your strength. I will help you take it back."

#

"I didn't go home, that day," I whispered, using the fork to play around my food. "That day you called about the merger."

"I thought-"

"I know. Jake lied, so did I." I took a deep breath and my hands shook a bit. Jake had never put his hands on me in front of anyone. I knew he despised Carla, but why do it in front of her? What triggered it? From our agreement, I was to tell no one about anything. Especially not Carla. I didn't know what Jake's next move would be. But it couldn't have been anything beneficial to me or Carla now that she knew.

It was a welcome solace seeing her seated across from me on the floor in her office like we'd done hundreds of times. The aroma emitting from the bags of takeout told me it was long overdue. My go-to dish: the catfish and grits with a side of bacon. I loved my bacon. Carla went with her usual, the spicy shrimp and grits.

"I was in the hospital."

"What?" She put her fork down. "Nhoell, are you serious? You didn't call me?"

Clearing my throat, I gave her a look that said, listen. She retreated and picked her fork back up.

"I confronted him, he paid off my loans, pretty much forged my signature, then threatened me to marry him. After he hit me, I left," I took a bite of my food, not wanting to eat anymore. "I didn't leave because he hit me. It was because he was threatening you."

"Me?"

"Marry him or he hurt both of us. He means to draw blood. So, I thought if I ran, he wouldn't have a reason to go after you. But then he stopped the plane and had me brought back to the condo. We fought, and I lost." I put my fork down, seeing my hand tremble unsteadily. "I've never been so afraid in my life. What he did to me... and he's everywhere. I try to look up information to learn something at least. Anything. But he knows when I do that. Who I call, who I text. Everything and nothing set him off. I can't read him. It's like he's two different people." I took an exasperated breath. "Still all I can think about is what he might do to you if I don't agree. Hell, at this point it doesn't matter if I don't agree. I can't get away from this man."

"Nhoell?" she whispered, touching my arms, grabbing my attention. "I need you to listen. He won't do anything to me."

"He will. I know he will."

"You can't stay there and take what he's doing. You can't put your life on the line like this. He may be rich, but rich men bleed too."

"I know. But I've tried. I have nothing on him. No one on my side but you. He paid the fucking police off, Carla. Police report. What police report? Now I can't get near a precinct without him knowing. He has the senator in his back pocket and the commissioner eating out of his hand. I am an ant going against a mountain!" I exhaled heavily. She sat quietly for a moment. Just staring off.

"Ants are strong too, Nhoell. It's amazing the things they can accomplish together. I'm going to help you. I don't give a damn about him. I don't care what it takes. I won't fuss at you for not telling me, because I should've said something in the beginning. You are my sister and we are in this shit together."

Those words gave me goosebumps. I always saw Carla as my sister, being the closest person to me and all. Closer than my mama, even. But the thought of putting herself in front of Jake's bulldozer frightened me. It was true, I'd never seen him hurt any other person, but regular people didn't use the police to stop planes. Wealthy criminals that thought they were God did that. Carla was no safer than I was, and I needed to figure out another way. I couldn't see her cry again. And I wouldn't see her hurt because of me. Years ago, I asked her why she acted so tough. She chalked it up to growing up with five older brothers and left it at that. It was my first time hearing she had siblings, but she shut down once I asked about them.

We went on for another hour or so, and before I knew it, I had 30 minutes to get to Jake's office with his report. Carla would wait at a coffee bar near his building. Our shopping plans for later would be a cover-up to discuss a plan. She swore she had a strategy that would release me from Jake. That, I wasn't so sure about.

Chapter 8

He knew I would drop them off no matter what. Before he left me with Nora and his sisters after the cake tasting, Jake instructed me to bring back the reports he left behind. His blasé demeanor after his confrontation with Carla hadn't surprised me. Nora and Holly carried on as if nothing happened. Marilyn, on the other hand, drew closer to me once Carla had left. That comforted me more than I wanted to admit. It had become a requirement, and I'd done them at least twice a week. I still regret not keeping my nose out of his business that day.

Riding the elevator to Jake's floor, I always enjoyed the view of being able to see outside. But it didn't distract me from my nerves. I told myself things will go smoothly. I was on time, I wasn't wearing anything revealing, his documents were in my purse. I forced myself to believe he didn't know I told Carla. All was good.

I stepped off the elevator and waited for April to grant me entrance to the main area. Once I approached the desk, she stood and smiled.

"Hi, April. Is he in his office?" I asked.

"Yes, ma'am. He's waiting for you now."

At his door, I waited until I heard the click before entering. Jake sat behind his desk talking on the phone. His furrowed brows and protruding veins in his forehead made me keep my distance.

"I don't give a damn about him declining the proposal, and I don't give a damn if he's an honest man or not!" Jake scribbled something on a piece of paper then slammed the pen down. "there is no such thing. Everyone has a price. Find out what it is and get him in here!

This is my goddamn city!"

He slammed down the phone and finally motioned for me to have a seat.

"What are your plans for today?"

I held tightly onto his report in my hands as I imagined them wet with sweat once I handed them over. I cleared my voice before answering. "I'm going to have a cup of coffee."

"With Carla?"

His question seemed innocuous, but I learned to not let my guard down with Jake.

"Yes."

"Then?"

"I want to check on some things for the wedding ceremony," I lied, hoping he couldn't tell.

"Carla will not be part of my wedding, nor will she be in attendance. Understand?"

"Yes, Jake."

"You've been spending more time with her these days." He glanced at his watch again, then at the door. "You have five minutes to look over these."

He slid a stack of papers to me from across his desk, then clasped his hands on the table, looking at me watchfully. I handed him the financial reports, eyeing to see if sweat ruined them. It hadn't. So I picked up the new stack and took them to a lounger near his bar. As I flipped through the pages, my eyes zeroed in and my hands marked with accuracy and speed. The vast majority of the reports I reviewed had various errors. Each time, I made a note of how to reconcile them. I always expected the next sets to be close to perfect, but they never were. Whoever ran the numbers didn't deserve the salary, I assumed Jake paid them. The issues were too obvious not to miss.

It took me three minutes to find all errors and correct them. In less than five minutes, Jake's office disappeared behind me. From the moment I sat down and got to work to the moment I walked out the door, I didn't hear another word from him. I couldn't help feeling used, toyed with.

April stood again as I walked past her and waved goodbye. Outside the double glass doors, the wait for the elevator seemed like an eternity. My heart rate slowly sped up and pulse-like drumbeats hummed throughout my body. Tightening my grip on my purse, I checked my surroundings. There was no one around. I hit the elevator button four times in rapid succession. Nothing. With my hand against my pounding chest, I counted my breaths. Still, my heart nor my mind calmed. When the elevator bell finally rang. I bolted in once the doors opened, bumping into people coming out. The group spoke loudly in the hall, but it sounded more like a hum as the drumming continued. Closing my eyes again, I tried to take deep breaths as the sound of the hums grew distant. Leaning against the back of the elevator, I clutched my shirt, needing to get to my chest. The bell sounded again, signaling the closing doors. Right before the panels met, my spasming body stole every single air from my lungs before I collapsed to the floor. Crashing waves beat at me one after the other until I was hyperventilating. With shaking fingers, I quickly pressed the lobby button before the doors opened again.

Floor by floor, the hum in my ears decreased and sound became recognizable. I focused on the clouds until the drumming eased. Pulling myself from the floor and wiping the sweat from my forehead, I adjusted my clothes. The doors opened moments later, and I rushed through the two rows of security and out of the building, trying to figure out what was wrong with me.

Carla waited for me with a Spiced Chai Latte at the coffee bar, her face skewed with worry. I'd walked the block from Jake's office, which didn't help the rapid heartbeats. When I told her what happened, her questions came at me like darts.

"You were on the elevator, Nhoell. Maybe the drop caused your heart to flutter or something."

"Trust me, it wasn't a flutter." I took a deep breath before speaking again. Instead of facing her, I looked out the window. "I can't explain what it felt like."

"Do you think being around him after what happened got you

feeling this way?"

Watching the traffic of people pass, I thought of her question. All the physical, emotional, and psychological experiences drowning me came from being with Jake. Paranoid. Always apprehensive that I would say the wrong thing. If that wasn't enough, dreams haunted me each night, and it was becoming difficult to function during the day. My body was no longer my temple, but his to trample on.

I whispered, "Maybe."

I brought my latte to my lips for another sip. A sudden jolt in my heart stunned me, and the ambient noise from the coffee shop hummed. I grabbed at my chest as the cup fell to the floor, splattering tea everywhere. Carla scanned me, her mouth as wide as her eyes. When she spoke, it gave me an underwater feeling.

Tearing away from her, I rushed quickly to the restroom. Finally, behind closed doors, I breathed as deeply as I could, trying the focus on counting or breathing. But the crashing sensation coursing through my body overpowered me. I hugged myself tightly, waiting for the feeling to subside. Though it wasn't pain exactly, the prickling needles wreaked havoc on my heart. I needed to see a doctor. A cardiologist. Something.

Carla's panicked voice broke through. "Does it hurt? Nhoell? Talk to me, please."

"Constricted." I managed.

"Nhoell!"

Then it stopped. The tightness in my chest went away. My throat relaxed as I breathed steadily. My entire body felt normal again, apart from some residual heaving.

I looked at her, perplexed. "It stopped."

"Just like that?" Carla sounded as confused as I was.

"I don't know what's wrong with me. I need to see a doctor."

"I agree. I don't need you running downtown having heart attacks and shit."

I shook my head at her complete change in tone. Only Carla found humor in such a dire situation. I rinsed and dried my face and gathered myself together as she watched closely with concern. I didn't blame her. Because I was concerned too. With no time to waste, we left the restroom. I needed to see a doctor.

My latte sat at the bar waiting for me. Not wanting any more to drink but not wanting to appear ungrateful, I picked up the cup and followed Carla to the door. Her tall, curvy stature blocked my view when it swung open. At the same time, my phone rang Jake's ringtone. I rummaged through my purse with one hand while holding it open with the other and balancing my cup.

"Nhoell!" Carla yelled out my name. I peered up just in time to keep from crashing into a few people entering. Then I went back to searching, my heart racing faster with each second. Side pocket!

"I am so sorry, sir. I wasn't paying attention. Did I get anything on you?" I went for the side pocket in quick, jittery movements as I listened to the tone approach its ending.

"Nhoell!" Carla yelled again. I grabbed my phone from the side pocket and snapped my head up.

"What!" The phone stopped ringing. "Shit."

"Leave the damn phone alone and apologize to this nice-looking brotha."

With her hip out and purse dangling from her arm, Carla's gaze turned to the man's feet and trailed to his face. Clearly she wanted to take a bite out of him. So, following suit, I started at his impeccable brogue oxford shoes and worked my way to his slim-fit dress pants. His beautiful, dark, hands rested at his side and the suit jacket fit his frame nicely. Good god he was ripped. When I reached his face, I felt mine turn to stone. He smiled like he waited for me to lift my head. It was a smile I knew all too well. My heart fluttered, and my body oozed a slow, warm hum, unlike the heavy pounding it had given me beforehand. Only then did I recall the many moments I felt this uncontrolled feeling. The drumming in my heart, my body, in my fingertips, and even between my legs. It felt like my soul eased its way back into its vessel. But resentment tainted the pleasure I felt building in me. All I had now for the man that stood towering over me was seething anger. My soul throbbed again. And the memories of the last time I saw him came storming back like a blizzard. I despised him all over.

"Nhoell." He spoke in a heavy voice so enthralling, I thought I'd cave in. "How have you been?"

I still didn't respond. My only thoughts were of hurting him as painfully as I had for the past ten years.

"Nhoell?" Carla said hesitantly. "You know this guy?"

I blinked a few times to keep my equilibrium, then forced a smile.

I spoke to Carla, not breaking eye contact with him. "Yes… I'm afraid I do. I've been well, Gregory. Yourself?"

"I can't complain. You look wonderful. Oh, you're married."

"What?"

"Your ring."

His shift in tone confused me.

"Oh," I placed my hand at my side, away from view. "Not yet."

"I see." His shoulders eased, and the gleam in his eyes made my heart drum in my chest again. I had not seen him in ten years, but there he was. Staring back at me, with a light in his eyes I never saw before. He didn't deserve that light. He didn't deserve to be happy.

Jake's ringtone startled me and brought me back to sensibility. I looked at my phone, concentrated on not missing his call a second time.

"I have to go." I pushed past Gregory and out the door. As soon as the wind encased itself around my body, cooling me off, I took a deep breath and answered the phone. "Hi, Jake!"

"Why didn't you answer?" he asked casually.

"I'm sorry. I was searching for it in my purse. But we're just now leaving the coffee shop." Damn, Carla. I turned around and she wasn't there. I kept walking, trying to add more distance between Gregory and me.

"Is that so?" Jake's even tone continued.

"Yes. But we won't be going out today. I'm thinking about heading home."

I didn't think my feet were moving fast enough. I had yet to call Lee to pull the car around, and I walked in no particular direction. I was rattled and on edge. Most of all, I couldn't screw up the phone call with Jake.

"' Thinking', Nhoell?" he said flatly.

"No, not 'thinking'. I'm headed home."

"I expecting your call later."

He hung up the phone before I could respond. I punched in a few keys, then pressed the send button and realized that I stopped walking. I finally looked behind me to see Carla walking over, looking more curious than concerned. She should have been concerned.

"Nhoell, what the hell is going on? Who was that guy?"

Lee pulled to the curb and got out of the car. I turned back to her.

"The man I was supposed to marry," I whispered, looking back as if expecting to see Gregory come around the corner.

"You'll be alright getting home?" I asked, looking at Carla with a mix of shock and confusion.

"Of course." Carla grabbed my hand, clung to it, then slipped a small cell phone to me. "This is for you. We'll talk later. Check the contact numbers." She whispered.

Lee pulled away from the curb into the busy street. My chest didn't stop aching, even with the distance growing between Gregory and me. As hard as I tried not to, Gregory occupied every inch of my mind. Those images of him stayed with me until I made it back to the condo and locked myself in the closet. After ending the quick call to Jake, I pulled out the small Nokia-like phone Carla gave me. Clicking the contacts option, I froze at the sight of Gregory's name.

Chapter 9

I stood by the bedroom door that night and listened to Jake's hushed whispers. It was the shutting door and his heavy footsteps that woke me. Then his whispers that made me tiptoe to eavesdrop.

"I know." He waited before talking again. "I'm at the condo. Where else should I be? She's will not be a problem? I'm asking you to stay out of it. When this is over, I'm going to prove just how wrong you are. I'll take care of him too. I said I would handle them."

I gently closed the door and tiptoed back to bed. Using the blankets, I covered my head and waited. Sleep would not come easily. I wondered if it was Carla that Jake spoke about. If so, what did he mean by taking care of them? Most importantly, who was on the other end of the phone?

Jake surprised me by climbing onto the bed and massaging my head. He did that until it was only the rhythm of his light breath breathing down my neck. It was unlike him to sleep over, and in one week he'd done so twice. That tight knot routine he had felt like it was loosening. If things kept up, the plan Carla and I concocted earlier that day had a high probability of success. Much higher than the plans I came up with on my own. Even though the thought of failing weighed on me, what would happen to Carla was front and center. It was a relief and a worry that she finally knew the truth. Because of that, I'd put her in even more danger. Still, we both knew there would only be one chance, and it was a chance we were willing to take. It was only a matter of time before Jake let his guard down completely.

I had to be ready.

#

Gentle caresses on my back and hips stirred me. Warm hands slowly moved from my hips to my ass, and the squeeze released a moan from my throat. A warm, throbbing sensation forming between my legs quickly washed over me. I knew the hands caressing my body belonged to Jake, but it was Gregory's face that popped into my head. Immediately shaking the thought away, I opened my eyes to see Jake sitting at the edge of my bed. Every time I looked at him, I had one or two primal reactions; fear or lust. Sometimes both at the same time because I never knew how he would respond. At that very moment, his hands searched my body hungrily, awakening me fully. I leaned over and planted a heated kiss on his lips, and he passionately took me in. Grabbing my hips and groaning into my mouth as his tongue ravaged mine, I gripped his head to take more of him. His lips met the nape of my neck and he bit down, cupping a handful of my breast. Another moan escaped as my back arched, and my neck exposed to the ceiling. I savored that rare moment he bestowed upon me. Another twice in one week. When he groped my breast with one hand and my hips with the other, he whispered my name.

"Yes?" I answered.

"Go get in the shower. You have five minutes."

So easily, he lifted me as he stood, placing me carefully on my feet. I was left heaving and empty, but I hid my displeasure. Although I didn't want him, I needed to feel him inside me. I needed to release the pent-up frustration I felt ever since I ran into Gregory. Right then, the only person who could relieve that ache was Jake Vaughn.

I glanced at his bulge, grabbed it, then stood on my tiptoes and offered my lips to him. He returned the favor by slapping me on the ass as if to hurry me along. I obliged and sashayed into the bathroom to shower.

Jake gave me five minutes, but I only needed three to bathe three times. The thought of him between my legs giving me release eclipsed all other thoughts. Even the thought of what he'd done to me. Getting out of the shower with a towel wrapped around me, I made my way back into the room. The sight of him fully dressed, sitting at the edge of the bed with his hands together as if praying, stopped me in my tracks. Confused, I didn't know whether to approach him and fall to my knees or lie on the bed and spread my legs.

"Is everything okay?" I asked softly, trying to sound as docile as I could.

"Drop the towel," he commanded.

Hesitantly, I did as I was told, my body shivering from the thought of the wet beating I had before. Jake's hands dropped from his face, and I could see his eyes slowly making their way up my body. He stood in front of me and grabbed hold of my hips again, pulling me closer to him. Leaning in, I closed my eyes as his stubble rubbed against my face and his lips brushed my ear. An intense sensation between my legs shot through my core. I moaned as his warm breath sent shivers down my spine to my knees.

"Meet me downstairs, sweetheart."

With that, he left me heated and confused while my hope slowly diminished once he left the bedroom. Jake was up to something. Teasing me like he used to, making me secrete from his touch. Grabbing my robe, I went downstairs to find Jake sitting at the island with his computer open and a stack of papers laid out. I approached him but remained a couple of feet away. He swiveled around in the barstool and pulled me between his legs. Grabbing my hips, he trailed his finger down my neck, then to the opening of my housecoat. I closed my eyes and allowed his touch to travel through the rest of my body.

"What are your plans for the day?"

I responded absentmindedly. "Mmm… the gym, then meeting with your mom."

"Cancel it," he replied.

I opened my mouth to respond right before he slapped me. The impact took the scream from my throat when I fell against the edge of the island, hitting my wrist on the way down. My housecoat open and my body exposed, I kept my eyes on Jake who rose from his seat. The sharp stabbing pain in my arm didn't allow me to get up as fast as my mind said to. He moved at a steady pace, his breathing controlled and jaws clenched tight. The look in his dark gray eyes seemed dead and so far from reality. I called out his name calmly, as I slid backward on the marble floor. He didn't respond and his eyes bore into me like my words were the last thing he wanted to hear. I thought about kicking at him, but instantly remember all the times I fought back. When Jake reached me, my pleas didn't matter anymore. He grabbed me by the arm, sending waves of pain back to my wrist, and pulled me to the front door.

I cried out, looking him into his eyes, pleading with him, begging him to stop, asking him for forgiveness for whatever I'd done. His face and his entire persona had transformed into what I grew to know all too well. The tenderness he showed me last night and all morning was nothing but a facade.

At the door, he snatched off my robe and pinned me against the wall. Letting go of my wrist, Jake squeezed my jaw and used his other hand to rub my stinging face. My legs quivered as tears trailed down my cheeks. He leaned in closer to my naked body.

"Shh."

I stiffened, preparing myself for another hit.

"Carla Dunn will not step foot in here again. Do you hear me?" he gritted. I nodded like a child and sniffled, swallowing my cries.

"Yes, Jake." I managed to say.

"If I ever hear her or you speak to my mother that way again, you'll both regret it. I still expect you to keep your mouth shut. Do you understand me?"

"I understand. I do."

"Good. Go clean yourself up," He kissed me again. "I'm glad we had this talk." I rushed past him and quickly upstairs. The front door closed shortly after. I didn't cry like I wanted to. I couldn't cry in case he hadn't truly left. My wrist swelled, making it a pain to wrap, but I managed.

Back downstairs, Jake's credit card lay on the counter next to a stack of papers. After double-checking that I locked the door, I went back to the bathroom and properly re-bandaged my wrist and iced it. I locked myself in the closet and cried until my eyes burned and my head pulsed a steady beat. But rather than sadness, it was the rage that I felt. I wanted to be rid of him, and he wanted to be rid of everyone in my life. Carla was the last thing I had left, and getting rid of her was his mission. I knew if I cut Carla off, Jake's lash-outs would increase. That morning, on the floor in my closet, I needed Carla in my corner. I needed her to tell me that everything would work out. That Jake would not hit me again. That I didn't have to marry him. But remembering Jake's words, I realized the more I involved her, the more I got hurt and the sooner he would go after her, too. I feared he would take care of her before we had a chance to escape.

Chapter 10

Cortina and Cordelia Sandbrook. They were the formidable women that brought me into the world and raised me to be a strong, independent woman. My mama, grandma and I moved to a house in Atlanta after my twelfth birthday. After living in Chattanooga for the past few years and many places before that, we all looked forward to finally settling down. My mama, Cortina, provided, but my grandma always brought in a little extra something. Their motto is, 'Anything presented to you is an opportunity to better yourself or worsen yourself'. I lived by that code because Grandma repeated it every morning, just like she had with my mama growing up. It also made me pay more attention to decision making. Grandma raised my mama by herself, and according to her, she would've preferred a tsunami. My daddy died on the job before my fourth birthday, and I remembered nothing about him. I never heard how it happened, but we moved soon after the incident.

I saw Gregory the first day we moved. From across the street, he looked in my direction, and I smiled. For a moment, I thought he was angry. He strolled over as I held a box of teddy bears and dolls. With each step he took, I grew nervous. I was surprised that my heart raced as fast as it did. I didn't expect him to walk over for a smile! He stepped on the curb but averted his gaze, looking anywhere but at me.

"Hey, my dad sent me over to help." His voice crackled, vacillating from a boy to a young man's.

"Well, that's nice of him," Mama said, stunning both of us. "You look like a strong, healthy young man. Think you can help me with some light furniture? The movers aren't here with the big stuff yet, so don't worry about that."

"Yes, ma'am."

I stared at him as Mama handed him a box and pointed to other items lining the yard. Letting out a deep breath I hadn't realized I held, my stomach suddenly felt ill. So I disappeared into the background, away from the nearness of him.

Throughout that day, I watched him go in and out of the house with one box after another. I thought he was cute. But it wasn't like me to think any boy cute. Especially not at my old schools.

On my way down for another load, we ran into each other at the front door. I expected him to say something. Speak or at least introduce himself. But we just stood there in silence. It was just my luck that we ended up in the same room and all I could do was stare. And I didn't understand and why my stomach became unsettled all over again.

He cleared his throat, snapping me from whatever warp-hole he sucked me into. Embarrassed, I rushed passed, leaving him standing at the door. I couldn't understand at twelve why I became so upset. What confused me most is the reaction he gave me when I saw him. He didn't like me.

In school, even though I always tested above grade level, my mama never let me skip a grade. She said it was because I needed to work my way through everything. I thought it was because she wanted me to stay with my peers. Even the bullies. No matter where we lived, she always protected me from them. But I didn't care one way or another what they thought. As long as I had my art, I didn't allow myself too.

I walked into the middle of a lecture on my first day of school. I didn't anticipate being late. Who does? But mama and I sat in the car and debated why she didn't have to walk me to class. After begging her and close to tears for fifteen minutes, she finally agreed to let me go alone. So, standing in front of the classroom, I didn't know if the debate was worth it. Everyone faced me, but it was Gregory's face that my eyes landed on. He turned his head away from me though. After introductions, I sat between a dark-skinned girl and another empty chair. Before I could get out my notebook, she leaned over and whispered.

"I'm Althea, where you coming from?"

"Tennessee," I replied.

"Really? What part? I have family in Tennessee."

I looked at the teacher and tried to pay attention to the math problems on the board.

"Chattanooga. I grew up in-"

"Nhoell?" Mrs. Malcolm called out. "Would you care to share the answer to the first problem? Seems like you're off to a wrong start."

"Algebra," I said, not realizing I spoke out loud.

"Yes. If you were not talking during my-"

"C equals negative ten."

"That's correct, next time-"

"The second answer is equal to fourteen, then thirty and five. Mrs. Malcom, I'm sorry for disrupting your class, it won't happen again." With my back straight, I waited for her response. I hoped it wasn't one that ended in mama turning her car back around. That would have been a terrible turn of events.

"I'm sure it won't. But, please," She turned to the front of the board and wrote.

"What is the answer to this one?"

She and the class looked at me with anticipation. I contemplated giving an incorrect answer but thought about what would happen if my grandma found out. Probably switches to the backside.

"Calculus?"

"Do you know the answer?"

I gave her an answer.

"Looks like you're further ahead, as I expected. I saw your transcripts. Your parents ever think about sending you to high school?"

"Yes ma'am, once I graduate middle school."

She chuckled. "I'm watching you both. Have a seat."

Gregory's popularity didn't go unnoticed as I kept my eye on him throughout the day. No matter where he appeared, someone always stood by his side. People even stepped out of their way to speak to him. Everyone admired him. With our different social statuses, I dismissed the idea of ever being friends. Having Althea, who later sat with me during lunch, filled that void of loneliness. She always seemed excited when she talked, and her outspoken personality never ceased to amaze me. Not only that, but she knew pretty much everything about everyone in the school. And her style was cool as hell. I wasn't as stylish and forward as many of my peers, but I wasn't a pushover either. Except for when it came to Greg, it seemed. But Althea quickly became a one of a kind friend, and I was grateful to have sat in that seat that first day.

That evening, I dashed down the stairs, passing my grandma in the kitchen. Thirty minutes and she would call out for dinner. We stored my art in the basement with other random stuff. I hit the light and many of my paintings hung on the wall, and the rest she leaned against furniture or set out on the floor. A long table extended from one end of the wall to the other with new paint and brushes. The basement looked like a real art studio, and my fingers tickled at the thought of using them. I heard the garage door open and Mama's car pulling in. On the other side of the room were two doors. One door led to the backyard and the other one to a set of stairs reaching the garage. I ran up those stairs and met my mama with a hug.

"I take it they finished the basement for you. I thought the contractors would be down there all day." Mama grabbed her purse from the back seat along with a stack of papers. Her cocoa complexion and the soft features in her face made me want to keep her smiling. I thought of nothing but making her proud and becoming a hardworking, Sandbrook woman. Growing up watching both my mama and grandma work their asses off to provide for me was motivation.

Like a puppy, I followed my mama to the kitchen. Grandma's meatloaf with gravy and her creamed spinach seeped into my nose.

She hugged Grandma and tasted the meatloaf and spinach as she talked.

"I met an artist the other day," she said, as she rinsed the spoon to taste more. "Then I ended up seeing some of your old work and thought I'd show him."

Grandma finally popped Mama on the hand with a wooden spoon.

"So, I took few things you were working on and showed him. He loved it! He said your talent at this age will land you in the right galleries as you grow."

"That's crazy! He liked it?"

Grandma interjected. "Not crazy, honey. Nothing like this is crazy." "You good at what you do. So, don't stop."

"I know, Grandma."

Gregory and I spoke for the first time during a math project we partnered on. I remember being under so much pressure from my mama and grandma, and my teachers. I found myself spending more and more time in the basement to escape from them.

Althea and I brainstormed different ways of approaching Gregory. Because he never looked at me, let alone spoke to me, I gave him equal treatment. Regardless of the facade I put on, I thought about him nonstop. Since the day I became his neighbor, my body had awakened and everything I felt became more intense. I never paid attention to my flat chest or small butt. I never cared. Seeing other girls around Gregory that wore bras two sizes bigger than me made me self-conscious. I didn't like it. And I didn't like that he distracted me by just being near. Gregory spent the next few days avoiding eye contact with me. That alone riled me.

After school on Friday, grandma already questioned me about the project. If there was one thing I knew about her, she didn't play when it came to schoolwork. She instilled in me a sense of duty to school, and eventually work. I credit her with developing my sense of responsibility. So, instead of chatting me up about my day, she went straight to the project. Once I told her Gregory and I were partners, I found myself walking across the street to his house. It was that, or my Grandma Cordelia would walk over there herself. After knocking, a few moments later his mama opened the door. Her eyes were like Gregory's. Not in the sense of being inherited, but it was the feeling it gave me from looking into them. They were soft and gentle, yet reserved and lonely.

"May I help you?"

"I'm Nhoell, we moved in across the street."

"Oh, right, the smart girl. Greg told me about you. Says you should be in college?" She smiled gently.

"Really? Well, I don't know about college though. I don't think I'm mature enough yet. You know, to handle that stuff."

"Listening to that come from your twelve-year-old mouth, I would think otherwise." She chuckled and her smile reached her eyes that time.

"Is Gregory here? We are working on a project together. I really want to get started."

"Really?" She seemed alarmed only for a quick moment, then recovered with a smile. "That's nice. That's great. Well, he's with his dad. I'll let them know when they're back. How's that?"

I didn't immediately respond. When I did, I smiled like an excited teen and thanked her for her time. Moments later, I scurried back across the street trying to catch my breath and thanking god Gregory wasn't there but asking myself why his mama looked the way she had when I told her about the project. It bothered me like an invisible gnat because I didn't want her to hate me either.

That night, as I painted a mountain-scape that came to me in a dream, a knock came from the back door. When I opened it and saw Greg, my heart beat so hard I nearly doubled over. He stood only inches over me as I looked at him, mouth agape. It was ten o'clock at night and I freaked out at the thought of my mama or grandma catching him.

"What are you doing here?" I peered up the driveway, then at the door behind me.

"My mom said you came by."

He spoke for a damn change. When he did, an intense wave crashed through my body like nothing I'd ever felt before. Greg took a step back. I made a hiccup sound and tried to keep myself from falling. Confused, but overwhelmed, I searched the ground.

"It's ten o'clock," I stuttered. "What are you doing back here anyway? Couldn't you stop by tomorrow?"

"I went to the front door. Your mama sent me around this way. I didn't think it was a big deal." He turned around to walk away.

"It's not," I blurted. "I just don't want to get caught if we don't have permission. My grandma would have a fit."

"Well, we have permission. She said I have five minutes and that came with a threat. Now, what you want?"

He was harsh, which surprised me. Because even though he ignored me, he was always kind to other people.

"Gregory," His eyes softened for a moment just before he glared again. God, I was relieved when my heart didn't beat uncontrollably. "You can't be serious. We have a project to do, right?"

"And?"

"What do you mean 'and'?" I snapped.

"We have two weeks until it's due. Calm down."

"Don't tell me to calm down. This is my grade and yours."

"We both know you will get an A, so what's the big deal?"

Whoa. We were getting louder than I intended. I stopped talking, took a deep breath and exhaled.

"Gregory,"

Again, he had what I thought was a wounded look on his face just before showing me his natural scowl. "So what if I know I'll pass? That's not the point. The point is that I'm expected to start tomorrow, no questions asked. If you can't help me with that, I'll do it on my own."

"You standing here talking like you somebody's mama," he scoffed.

"If that's what it takes to get you to act right."

"Act right? You can't tell me what to do, Nhoell. I don't need to 'act right' for you or anybody else."

Hearing him say my name caught me off guard. Butterflies fluttered in my stomach as the syllables from my name seemed to delicately roll off his tongue. For a second, my anger dissolved. I wanted him to say my name again, but that annoying scowl returned and changed all that.

"Greg, you do what you have to. I'm working by myself on this, because… because you suck you, stupid idiot."

The door slammed so hard in his face I felt the wind blow my hair back. My shoulders rose and fell as I stood in shock that I was even rude enough to do it. But, hey, I was pissed. Pissed that he was treating me like crap for no good reason. Angry because I gave a shit. And annoyed that I liked Gregory Rehevas. I was just like the rest of the girls in school and I hated it. So, when I started back painting, what I intended to be a serene landscape piece ended up a hot mess.

On my bedroom floor the next morning, I researched for the math project and came up with a plan on my own. Minute by minute, the amount of papers increased as I pushed myself for hours until the room shrunk. I scooped up all my work and relocated myself to the screened-in porch. It was a hot day but thankfully tempered by a steady breeze flowing through the screen. Most of all, it was refreshing.

I spread out the textbook and paperwork on the floor and reorganized my steps. I kept at my drawings, then moved to other things only when my fingers started to ache. My mama and grandma both took turns checking on me by bringing snacks. Still, I worked hard.

It was almost two in the afternoon when I stood up to stretch. The sketches and notes scattered all over the floor. I covered much ground but huffed at the amount of work left to do. At least I would be done, though. I was sure of that.

"Sorry about last night."

I turned, and there Greg was. Sitting on the steps at the screen door and from the way he was propped on them, I guessed he'd been sitting there for a while.

Greg continued. "I sort of had a rough day. I didn't mean to take it out on you."

"Thanks," I replied. "thanks for the apology."

"So… do you always talk to yourself?"

"Only when I'm trying to work out a problem."

"Your idea sounds cool… can you tell me more about it?" Greg stood up and faced me. The screen door felt like an ocean between us. I was still on edge, thanks to his surprise visit. But I was fortunate that I wasn't experiencing anything like what I felt the night before.

"Yes," I finally said. "Come in."

Walking over to my work, he joined me on the front porch. I reorganized my papers, preparing to explain my progress when he sat down on the floor across from my spot. The light breeze stole his scent and ran it clear across my face. I melted, then inhaled the sweet, sweaty smell of him as my heart beat heavy against my chest. Quickly shaking the effects of him off, I retook my spot. Before beginning, I inconspicuously pinched my wrist. His complete turnaround from last night was still unbelievable, and the fact that he was on my porch was mind-boggling.

"I thought it would be a good idea to buy a house. Based on the occupation and typical salary, how much the house would cost and how long it would take to pay it off. Maybe an emergency fund…" As I chatted about the project, Greg sat and listened. Even though I was seeking his buy-in as I talked, he never interrupted. He gave me his undivided attention until I was quiet long enough for him to clear his throat.

"Sorry, I talk a lot when I'm nervous,"

"You're nervous?" he asked. I didn't respond. "It's alright, I think it's a good idea. I mean, I think we have to figure a lot of stuff out first. Where do you want to live? How much land? Will we have kids? How many?"

"We?" I asked.

"You're not the only one doing this project, are you? What's that in your sketchbook?"

I showed him the drawing of my house and how I envisioned it. He must have been more interested in my drawings than our project. Greg was full of questions. But I didn't care. It was the first time he and I had an actual conversation since we met. For a short time, it seemed like we were friends. I relished it.

That day, we spent four hours on my front porch talking about the house and how we were going to blow their minds on the project. After a while, his dad called out to him and, just like that, he was gone. He reassured me before leaving he would help with the project, and I should keep doing what I was doing. I had no doubt that he would after our time together.

Gregory didn't wait long to go back to treating me like crap. The next day, he was back to not speaking. It shocked me at how easily he turned himself on and off like that. Still, I continued working on my part of the project; I was determined not to let him impede my grade point average. When Mama asked about Greg's role, I assured her he was doing his part. Even though I didn't know if he was doing a thing.

The day of the project, my palms were sweaty and my stomach was turning flips. So far, that prick was nowhere to be found. All I had was a bunch of paperwork with drawings, equations, and graphs on it. It was more like a blueprint. I was so embarrassed, I thought about calling home sick. I was certain Grandma wouldn't have picked me up until after the presentation, though. At that moment, there was no one in the world I hated more than Gregory Rehevas.

One by one, students stood up and presented their work. Many were good, but a few of them really impressed me. Almost everyone had slideshows. All I had was a report and equations I wasn't sure made any sense to anyone but the teacher. I wanted the Earth to open and swallow me. Yeah. Grandma was going to kill me, I thought.

I remember walking to the front of the class, fighting back tears as I mutely cursed Greg. When I reached the front of the classroom, I opened my mouth to introduce the topic when he came rushing in, out of breath.

"Sorry I'm late, Nhoell. I needed help getting the model here."

"The model?"

He threw his bookbag down and disappeared from the classroom, then returned, pulling a five-foot cart. A black sheet covered something huge underneath it, and I thought my curiosity would drive me berserk. I peered my head around the teacher blocking my view and stood on my tiptoes while extending my neck. His dad helped push the cart to the front of the class, then left. Gregory ran over and stood next to me, then faced the class, still trying to catch his breath. When he nudged me to start, a tickle ran through my body. I turned back and began our presentation.

Towards the end of my delivery, Gregory finally removed the sheet, showing a modeled house. My mouth hung open and the flutter from my chest ran deep into my fingertips, turning into drumbeats. Our classmates nearly jumped out of their seats to see the lifelike model. My legs were unable to move even as Gregory explained how he constructed it. He'd paid attention to every detail I'd given him and replicated my sketch into this miniature archetype. I was in total bliss. Of course, he added a few things of his own. He didn't just build my house; he included himself in it as well. Things I never mentioned, he added, like a garage and fireplace. But what I loved the most is that he said, "we" and "our" during the presentation.

After that, Greg wasn't so standoffish. We still didn't talk at school or at home, but every now and then, he would smile at me then go about his way. I was fine with us not being as close as that Saturday, but it felt good to know it was possible. By the time the science fair came two months later, Gregory and I reconfigured the house and added electricity and a sprinkler system. We won first place in the school science fair.

Chapter 11

Two days passed since Jake lashed out. Or maybe three? The hours blurred into one another after he left, thanks to the pain meds that knocked me on my ass. During those few days when I was conscious, my mind didn't trail far from Gregory. Either I dreamt of rubbing my fingers over his contact name or I'd become obsessed with it. And the way he looked at me in the coffee shop. Even though my body remembered how he made it feel, my memories didn't forget my last image of him. His last words. His sorry expression.

The few times I got out of the bed had been to eat or drink. I dwelled on blaming Gregory for the situation I was in during those stints. Examining how my life detoured since then. How I lost the scholarship, the baby and him all in the same day.

After what was likely the second or third day of icing my wrist, the pain and swelling subsided. I still took the medication to keep from thinking about him. But even in sleep, he consumed my dreams when the shadows weren't. I knew it was risky. Not only that. Just seeing him that one time had me distracted from our plan. Forgetting he existed was the best option. Because even with the ten years of despising him, I still loved every bit of Gregory Rehevas. That was dangerous.

Finally calling Carla on that third day, she answered on the first ring. It took ten minutes of me repeating I was okay before she was reassured. I heard her with clients and tried rushing her off the phone. She wasn't haven't it.

"So, what's the intel with you and that dark god-like man? Honestly, I've never seen you so… well… dazed,"

"Nothing," my face flushed. "just a guy I dated in high school." I whispered, moving from my bedroom to the bathroom. I turned on the faucet, placed the seat down on the toilet and sat.

"Really? So, you promise to marry just some guy you used to date? I think not. Nhoell, what's really the deal between you two? I saw the way he looked at you. And when you ran out of that coffee shop, you should've seen the look in his eyes. That man seems like he isn't done with whatever you two had going on."

My head fell in my hands as I unconsciously shook it.

"What we had going on is in the past. What we had, Carla has nothing to do with the now. And right now, I'd rather not talk about him."

"Don't you see it? This man still loves you. I bet my life that your old boyfriend will help us with that fucking… fucking. Shit, I ran out of names to call him."

I lifted my head so fast. If only she could see the dirty look I shot at her comment. She'd honestly lost her mind. To think telling Greg about Jake was ludicrous. If running from him put me in the hospital, I imagined running from him with Gregory's help would put me in the grave. I didn't want to risk it. Most of all, I didn't want to risk my heart.

"Let me tell you this once, and only once." I sat rigid on the toilet, spaced out as if she was in front of me. "There is no way in hell I will ever let that man back into my life. What happened between us hurt more than anything Jake as ever put me through. So, he can't do a thing for me." I took a small breath before speaking again. "Okay?"

The phone was quiet. I looked at it to make sure she was still there.

"Okay. But I'll tell you this. Right now, your feelings toward him do not matter. Your life does. He and I can help you save it."

"Carla-"

"-no. You've said yours now let me say mine. I looked up your Mr. Rehevas. Hell, I didn't have to do much but press the damn enter button. I thought I had the wrong person. Your ole beau? He's a highly acclaimed architect, Nhoell. I mean, the places he's designed are just phenomenal. Where he's been, world leaders he's met,"

My hand clutched my chest as I listened to Carla talk about Gregory with admiration.

She continued, "I couldn't believe it. I don't know if I believe in coincidence or fate. But, I do believe you were meant to bump into him that day. I don't know what happened between you two. Hopefully, you can tell me in your own time. Right now, there is a man out there that I believe would do what he can. Just like me."

"Thank you, Carla. For everything you did."

"Yeah, yeah. I want you to be extra careful, okay? Those assholes wouldn't let me into your place, so I can't check on you until they go back in hiding. Jake is a rich, spoiled brat, but he isn't stupid. Just think about what I said."

With that, she was gone and back to work. I sat there, glaring at the marble wall. Replaying all she said. Contemplating the idea over in my head. Constructing viable plans. Every time the thought of asking him crossed my mind though, I recoiled and grew angry all over again. But Carla was right. My feelings had nothing to do with it. It was only about helping us get out of the shit hole I created. But it was difficult to think of him that way. Not when everything that transpired in school seemed like a lie. Nothing but a reality I conjured up myself. I still wasn't so sure I could trust Gregory. So, my and Carla's plan to create a decoy would have to work.

#

I strained my eyes then widened them to see the reports in my lap. Even with the interior car light on, I still struggled. My mind fought the exhaustion from either too much sleep or too little. Nora's urgent phone call at one o'clock in the morning had me riding with Jimmy to the Vaughn's family mansion. Requiring me to drop off documents for Jake in the middle of the night as retaliation crossed my mind. Plus, the fact that he didn't call me himself. But I was too tired to care or become angry.

In the backseat, I made the changes as best I could with the bumps and turns Jimmy made. He didn't seem happy about having to drive in the middle of the night. Still, he didn't turn down my phone call. It took nearly the entire drive over for me to finish the reports. I was exhausted and I could barely see anything. I mumbled vile things against his entire family and the reports.

We drove almost a half mile up the driveway before arriving at the gate of the mansion. Once we pulled up, I stepped out of the car, pulling my jacket tighter as I raced to the front door. My knock didn't take long to get answered. Eleanor, their head housekeeper, let me in. With the stack of papers in my hand, I followed her into the main hall.

"It's good to see you again." She greeted me with caution.

I didn't blame her. It was after midnight.

"You too, Ms. Eleanor. I'm truly sorry it's so late but I have to get these to Jake."

"Come this way. I'll bring you."

After leaving the main hall, she walked me further into the home, showing me areas I hadn't seen before. I struggled to keep up.

"So, have you worked here long? Sorry if I'm stepping out of line. I'm just curious."

"Yes. I worked here all my life. My mother did too. I raised Mari," she spun around. I stopped instantly before bumping into her. "not those other two. I took care of the late Mr. Vaughn, too."

"I see. So, you know them well?" I checked our surroundings. "Jake? What was he like? Growing up? Did anything happen to him?" She cocked her head to the side, her brows wrinkling, then softening again. Eleanor turned on her heels and kept it moving. I followed suit and immediately regretted asking.

"Mari was her father's favorite. She looks like her mama, so he loved her more."

We made another turn.

"You can't force a man to do what he don't want to."

After climbing down a set of stairs, we finally ended at a large oak door. I realized I didn't know how to get back out. If they wanted to, they could kill me and no one would ever know. That thought alone gave me goosebumps.

Eleanor opened it, revealing a circular office and hundreds of books lining the shelves from the ceiling to the floor. Next to the door sat a large desk. Behind it hung a long, black, velvet curtain draped to the floor. I moved closer to the velvet curtain and pulled it back. What should have been a view of the night sky turned out to be a wall of ash gray bricks. It was that one image that turned the entire room into a beautiful prison.

"Where are we?" I sat the reports on Jake's desk then turned back to Eleanor who had closed the door and stood watching.

"The mistress? She called you here." Eleanor's tone changed to a harsh, urgent whisper.

"Yes. Do you know why? I'm sure it has nothing to do with those." I nodded at the reports.

"It's not my place to tell you what needs to be told. Not my place to tell this family what I know, either. Not if it will cause more harm than good."

"What do you mean?" I walked closer, urgency and anticipation in my throat. "Tell me."

"When I saw you a few months back, I knew who you were. I didn't know why you were here. With him. I still don't. It isn't like him to behave without thinking. Having you here is dangerous."

"Dangerous? Me? Eleanor, what are you talking about? Go back for a minute, what do you mean you knew who I was? Who am I? What can't you tell me?" By then, my hands had made their way on Eleanor's arms without me realizing. The woman who knew so much was too afraid to tell me even a little. Or maybe it was an obligation. The answers to the questions I asked myself for the past few months was standing right in front of me.

"Please, Eleanor. I need your help."

"I know. Mari. Talk to her. She can help you."

Footsteps approaching startled both of us. Her eyes raised in alarm and mine did too. Eleanor shoved me to the curtain and I struggled with her to keep from pushing me in.

"What are you doing?" I whispered harshly. Panic struck me as she shushed me with sharp eyes that reminded me of my grandma.

"He doesn't know you're here. I will come back for you."

"No," I whispered again, but she was moving away fast to Jake's desk when the door opened.

"Eleanor, do you have business in here?" Jake's voice echoed throughout the room.

"No, Master Jake. Taking out the trash. One of the maids left it. My apologies." Her feet shuffled away and a few others stepped into the room. The door closed moments later. My heart raced fast as I kept my eyes closed shut, relieved he hadn't found me.

"Now, as I was saying. My name should never have come up in the same sentence as yours. There is a reason I have you in place. There is a reason you are paid such a profit to do your job. But you've made a grave mistake, Mr. Vinitto."

What? My eyes shot open and my head inched over until I could see the men. Jake stood in front of Vince Vinitto, the leader of the local gang that had been vandalizing small business around the city. Vince sat on his knees in front of Jake with two large, armed men at his left and right.

"I don't need the FBI on my case. When that happens, I lose connections. Do you understand?"

"Yes, Mr. Vaughn. Like I told you earlier, it won't happen again, sir."

"I'm sure."

He nodded his head, then reached out his hand. The guard handed Jake the gun and just like that, the back of Vince Vinitto's head was open and his body was falling limp on its side. My hands shook, and I bit down on my lip to keep from screaming. Tears raced down my face as I screamed internally for someone to get me out. With my eyes closed, I saw a replay of Vince's head exploding and his body falling. I reopened my eyes only to see his lifeless body still lying there. I turned away. Steps closed in on my directions, echoing with each movement.

"Call the cleaners. Tell them they are needed immediately and make sure you," He stopped. My heart raced faster as I pictured him swinging the curtains back and finding me. "just let them know to stay on call. I'll need them for another job." His steps faded, and the door opened and closed. I didn't know how long I stayed hidden or what happened in between. But when Eleanor finally came back, the body was gone.

Chapter 12

Since third grade, I spent each summer at an art camp. So, when I returned home after eighth grade summer, Grandma and Mama seemed to be at each other's necks more than usual. Which led me to believe that something happened while I was away. One thing they seemed to agree on was that they both wanted what was best for me. Picking out hoochiefied clothes for school was not part of that plan, my grandma said. We knew for certain I needed a new wardrobe. Because in a matter of months, I outgrew all my old ones.

There were only a few memorable events during my high school years that changed the course of my life. Losing Althea, riding with Gregory and his dad after an incident. Then, there was the first time we had sex.

The first day of school, I met up with Althea in front of M.T. Walker high, home of the lions. It took twenty minutes for all the incoming freshman and sophomore students to be seated in the auditorium. Finally getting everyone quiet enough to speak, our principal, Mr. Watkins, walked onto the stage and wished everyone a good year.

I leaned forward and stretched my neck in both directions. Then I turned slightly in my seat, bumping into Althea, while glancing over my shoulder. I hadn't seen Greg since I'd been home. According to her, he grew up. I didn't know what she meant by 'grew up,' but seeing how her eyes bulged out when I asked about him, it must have been a good thing.

"Nhoell Sandbrook…"

With wide eyes, Althea beamed at me and clapped excitedly as she hopped up and down in her seat. Principal Watkins stood, searching the crowd.

"Nono, what you doing? Get up there!" She shoved me to my feet.

As I made my way across the aisle and to the stage, the applause amplified and my stomach grew queasy from the roaring screams. I squeezed my fingers together and smiled, not sure what to do next. When I stood next to the principal and looked into the crowd, I thought of Greg's reaction. Was he clapping and screaming for me too?

"Nhoell, we are glad to have someone like you in our school, someone else that will make history. We look forward to the next four years." Principal Watkins motioned for me to stay put. "Another student entering today who will make history at M.T. Walker. Please welcome… Gregory Rehevas!"

The noise from the students screaming matched the heavy drumming in my chest as I stood warily waiting for Gregory. Then I saw him. Not some cute pimple-faced boy, but a good-looking guy that made my body feel like convulsing with each breath. He had been working out. A lot. Grandma Cordelia would've gone crazy had she seen the way I lusted over him. I wouldn't have blamed her though. Gregory's dark skin glowed golden. I was sure of it.

In his football jersey, he jogged down the aisle of students patting him on the back and screaming at the top of their lungs. His jersey clung to his defined arms and the way his jeans hugged his hips sent thunder crashing between my legs. Althea was right, Gregory had grown.

He climbed onto the stage, flashing that beautiful, genuine smile of his. The one he gave me during our project together. Then walked the rest of the way to Principal Watkins, shook his hand, then faced the crowd. The heat rolled off his body and pushed against me, or it was my own body that grew hot. Either way, being so close to him did wonderful things to me. Most of them were things I didn't understand.

"… Nhoell? Gregory? Thanks for choosing to represent our school.

Go Lions!"

The crowd roared and jumped up and down, making the stage shake. I didn't see Althea, but I knew she was out there screaming like Gregory and I were performing. The happiness surged through me as the creases in my face grew wider. I'd never experienced anything like it. Letting my trembling fingers go, I waved to the crowd and blushed from another uproar. I glanced up to see how Gregory responded to them screaming for us. But when I saw his furrowed brows, his teeth slightly biting his lips, and a half snarl directed towards me, the smile disappeared from my face in an instant. That single act numbed my senses and the drumming from my body. The crowd ceased. The tips of my fingers tickled and my legs wobbled from the tingling vibrations shooting through them. Before I knew it, I was leaning to fall when Gregory grabbed my hand and lifted it to the crowd. He roared with them, then took another look at me and smirked before yelling again. Swooning from his save and the realization that he wanted me. The spot in the center of my being intensified tenfold.

When I rode with Gregory and his dad, it was after winter break. We didn't grow any closer after that first day, but at least he spoke when we passed each other. That first week of school was a blur, but I stayed out for a few weeks after breaking my arm. Mama said I'd fallen through the door leading downstairs to my studio. It was the door that wouldn't stay closed, no matter how hard someone shut it. Grandma always told her that someone would get hurt one day.

Althea moved back to Memphis with her aunt around that same week. My best friend, gone so fast and so suddenly, seemed to take the pep out of me for a while. That and staying out of school. By the second week of hanging around at home, I painted as much as I could. Mama and Grandma checked on me, which seemed like every minute of the hour. Most of the time, I sat in my window and watched Gregory go in and out of the house. Each time, he looked my way. By the third week, my energy was so chaotic, I was ready to leave and go anywhere. TV, internet, my phone. None of it occupied my time. Not even my art.

Sunday of the fourth week, I told them I was going back to school. I came with a letter explaining why it was necessary for me to return and how it would benefit them. I argued my case and didn't take no for an answer. That night, they both argued in hushed whispers. I remembered it perfectly because I stayed up all night wondering if I'd done something wrong. So, the next morning I was dragging when I spotted my mama talking to Greg's parents at their door. I quickly threw on the rest of my clothes and ran downstairs, my book bag beating at my back. She was just walking through the door when I made it to the bottom. Out of breath.

"What was that about?" I stated, trying to play it cool.

"What?"

"You talking to Gregory's dad."

"Look how you say his name?" She laughed out. Mama teasing me about a boy wasn't normal. I didn't know what gotten into her but it was never my place to ask.

I headed out the door and said, "Not funny. I don't say his name any kind of way."

"Oh wait, Nhoell, you're going to ride with Gregory and his dad until your cast comes off."

I spun around in disbelief. "You're joking, right?"

She smiled and walked away, shaking her head as if something was funny. It had to be a prank.

"Oh my God, why is everybody making a big deal out of a cast?" I yelled out, then immediately covered my mouth. But she didn't scold me for raising my voice. She didn't turn around or slow her pace.

"Be safe, Nhoell." Her voice broke off.

It was the nerves that made my legs wobble as I crossed the street. I greeted Mr. Rehevas and thanked him, then turned and finally faced Greg. He was so beautiful. When he opened his mouth to speak, my insides melted away. Hearing his voice seemed to make the worries in my life disappear. Almost like my art. For weeks, all we did was stare at each other through windows. Each time, I wished I was standing near him instead of being blocked by a barrier. So from the moment I approached their car that morning, subtle vibrations laced my chest and didn't ease up for the next couple of weeks. Since that day, Greg and I became closer than I could've imagined. Our friendship became the light of my life and I was content with simply being near him. Thinking of how Althea would've responded sent a smile across my face, then a sudden sadness. With that, I made a mental note to call her.

There wasn't a thing that Gregory and I didn't do together. We both made excellent grades, and we continued to bring recognition to our school. Believe it or not, high school was great. At home was a different story. Some of the mystery behind Greg's mood unraveled as we spent more time together. He didn't say that his dad hit them, only that abuse came in many forms. Mr. Rehevas controlled every aspect of Gregory's and his mom's life. He didn't want to speak much about it when we were together, and I didn't push it. I knew it was the main reason he played football. So I tried to make it a habit of mentioning he can do what he wanted when he graduated on random occasions.

In my house, both my mama and grandma still seemed at odds. They didn't stay in the same room for more than a minute. Dinners were quiet and mama even stopped test-tasting food. It wasn't until tenth grade when Greg I and began dating. His parents didn't find out until two weeks later when they questioned him about spending so much time with me. Being labeled a distraction, his dad banned him from seeing me. Two weeks later, it surprised me to learn that Gregory stood up to him over that decision and won. With the condition that his training came first. I didn't find out until later that he stopped attending practice and sat out the last game just for his dad to agree.

As much as I thought Mama would blow up about the whole thing, she didn't. "You have to grow up one day, just remember your priorities," was all she said. Grandma, on the other hand, threw a fit, then gave us the silent treatment for a week. After that, anytime I wanted to go out, there was an issue. If I wanted company in my studio, there was an issue. For a while, it seemed never-ending.

It wasn't until the end of senior year that Greg and I had sex. Beforehand, he and I made a mutual decision to wait. It was enough to just be around each other. That alone was intense. Two weeks before graduation had sealed the deal. Greg stood in the middle of his room, naked. His body was so contoured with deep shadows and angles in just the right spots. He was free of scars and his face was shaved neatly. I was hot all over with what felt like electrical currents flowing through my veins. My eyes trailed down his chest until I reached the hairs at his abdomen. I had to stop there because as I sat on the edge of his bed in my bra, I couldn't help the sensation in my fingers. I was scared, but the feeling in my heart and in the pit of my stomach overpowered everything else. I wanted him like I'd wanted nothing else.

Greg climbed above me and I laid back, his warm skin against mine. Our tongues danced to the rhythm of our hearts as he maneuvered between my legs. I released soft moans into his mouth when he pushed against me, touching my throbbing spot. Easing himself gradually into my opening, I let out another moan, while still dancing to his tune. The pressure grew heavier with each slow thrust and it stung, making me wince. I broke our kiss and buried my nails into Gregory's back as he stroked me. He sighed into my ear, burying his head in my neck. One more thrust and it felt like he'd reached the depths of my soul. Gregory remained pinned against my body and I contemplated telling him not to move.

He whispered, "You okay?"

Swallowing, I said, "Yes. Keep going."

He stroked me slowly for a long time, and each time it was better, more pleasing, more heated. The more Gregory worked his hips, the more in sync our bodies became. I yelped and panted with each thrust. Feeling the need to feel more of him. Arching my spine and gyrating. Sweat droplets fell onto my breasts as he went deeper, then groaned, then deeper again. Once I opened my eyes to watch the ecstasy on his face, I exploded. Arching my back and losing myself in the billions of stars floating around, clouding my vision, bringing me to tears.

But Greg kept at it. This time he wrapped my legs around his waist and sucked and squeezed hungrily on my breasts. That overpowering sensation swallowed me again and again until my body had gone limp and he released too. Underneath Gregory's body, he laid on me, exhausted. Beads of sweat rolled off him onto me. I rubbed and massaged his back as he placed gentle kisses on my neck, making me shiver from the sudden coolness.

"I don't think I can move." He said, breathlessly.

"I don't want you to move."

"I love you, Nhoell. I can't wait to marry you?"

"Is this your way of proposing, Gregory?" I replied playfully.

He smiled, then finally pulled out of me. Even him slipping out felt good, but I was empty without him there.

"Fuck!"

Hearing him alarmed, I jumped up. How much blood had been spilled? What if his parents came home. I needed to get up and wash, and so did he.

"Is there a lot?"

Rolling from my spot, it was part of the condom on the bed, in my blood, that silenced me. My hand went to my face, covering my gaping mouth.

"Nhoell, calm down. We can fix this."

"Fix? How can we fix this! The condom broke, Greg." My fingers shook frantically as my hand rubbed over my head and face.

"What is the chance of you getting pregnant?"

"You're asking me that question? Do you really want to know?"

"God, how could I be so stupid!"

Greg paced the floor, and I too got stuck in my own head. About what my mom and grandma would think. About school. I was so lost that I didn't hear him calling after me. He kneeled in front of me and grabbed my hands.

"You know I'm going to marry you, right? I wasn't just saying that."

I smiled. I shouldn't have as scared as I was, but he brought a smile to my face anyway.

"Whatever happens, I got your back. I will take care of you no matter what. You hear me?"

I nodded my head as tears clouded my eyes. I knew he was telling the truth. There was no doubt in my mind. But things didn't happen that way. My cycle came on two weeks later and all was well. Until my final physical arrived three weeks before I was to leave for college. It was then when I learned of my pregnancy and it was then when I lost it.

Chapter 13

It was only a little after eight. I paced the bedroom floor for eighteen minutes with the small phone in my hand. Sweat trickled down my forehead even though the digital thermostat read sixty-eight degrees. I had planned everything by the minute, and my call to Jake ended fifteen minutes before. Right at the time. That left me with three hours until my next call at eleven. Since I didn't account for nearly twenty minutes of freezing up, that left me two hours forty-two minutes until my next call. Inhaling a deep breath, I turned the surround system at max volume before locking myself in my walk-in closet. I wondered if anyone would hear the music and complain about it being too early for it. Before my mind waged war, I pressed the call button. Gregory answered on the second ring and my chest pounded at the iron cage that shielded it. Before I spoke, he called out my name, already knowing it was me.

"We... can we meet?" I blurted. "In an hour."

He agreed in an instant, then I told him the location and ended the call. Letting out a long breath, I waited in the closet a few more moments.

I hardly escaped unnoticed the previous night. After Eleanor returned two hours later and pulled me from behind the curtain, I stood still in shock. All I remember was feet shuffling from at least three people. The entire time, no one spoke a single word, and I never looked to see who had done the cleaning. But the chemicals they used burned my nostrils, and it's a smell that will forever be embedded in my head.

Eleanor apologized insistently as she directed me between halls, doors, stairs, and more halls before I finally noticed the chill in the air. Everything was a blur as she led me outside and to the car where Jimmy waited. They exchanged words and my next memory had been waking up in my bed to Jake's call. His only question, "What time did you drop off the reports." I replied with the truth, then added, "the housekeeper said you had company, so I left them. Did you get them?" His silence alone left me unnerved. That ended our conversation. My next thought was of Jake putting a bullet through my and Carla's head if he really knew the truth. After seeing him carelessly kill a man, I had to use any means necessary to keep Carla and myself from being his next victims. If that meant involving the man that nearly destroyed me, then I was ready to choke it up. But before I asked Gregory for help I wanted, no, I needed an explanation for his actions ten years ago.

#

Forty minutes later, I sat inside a little corner restaurant not far from the hotel. For once, I didn't sit by the window. I hid myself as far back as I could go. So many emotions coursed through my mind and body, it was difficult to concentrate on how I truly felt. I worried most about leaving my phone at the loft and missing a call from Holly or Nora. Or worse, Jake. Because the morning rush hour had people in and out of the door, I feared someone would recognize me first.

With my purse in hand and running shoes on, I stood at the front door viewing the peephole at Jimmy for twenty minutes before he finally left into the room across the hall. As soon as the coast was clear, I bolted to the stairwell and sprinted two floors down. My heart beat so hard and so rapidly, my ears palpitated along with it. Though the thought of being caught by Jake hovered over, the anger building up in me matched that tenfold. All I thought about as I made my way to the small restaurant was what I would say to Gregory. What would be his excuse for leaving me? Why didn't he contact me? Questions that had been unanswered for ten years all came rushing back to me. Each one made me angrier. But the fact that he could lend a hand or two stuck with me as well.

Ten minutes had gone by as I sat waiting with my coffee, my finger taping the table. From my view, a man and woman sat separately and two other people were leaving. I checked the time again. I wasn't late, and it hadn't been a complete hour since we spoke. But my thoughts were going wild as I kept asking myself what I was doing there. Deciding to take my chance with Carla, I stood.

"Leaving already?" His voice again, so enthralling my own voice caught in my throat. Again! "Let's sit."

Without saying a word, I sat. The sun had done his skin wonders by turning it a bit darker. His eyes still had the same glow from when I bumped into him at the coffee shop. His hair was cut low like in high school, and now he had a full beard trimmed, too.

"It's good to see you, Nhoell. I'm glad you called. I didn't think you would."

"Why is that?"

Even though my mind swarmed with heated thoughts from our past, I kicked myself for thinking about it and feeling that way.

"Haven't seen you in a long time. And from how you ran off, I didn't think I would ever again."

"Oh,"

"You've been good? What's been up with you?"

"I've been okay," I started. "I'm sorry. I'm just," I took a deep breath.

"Nhoell, are you okay?"

"Yeah, I needed to ask you something. But I wanted to talk to you first."

"Okay. What's up? Talk to me." He leaned in a little.

I avoided his gaze, cautious to look into his eyes and feel my chest explode into a thousand more pieces. After waiting so long, I realized I feared his answer.

"You've grown more beautiful, Nhoell. He's a lucky man."

"Yeah," I whispered again.

"What's he like?"

His question brought my mind out of the bubble we'd been floating in since he spoke.

"He... well, he's successful. He has his own business."

"Sounds good. So, what's he like?"

I cocked my head to the side. But he wasn't at all fazed by the twisted expression I gave him. Gregory clearly knew how I felt about his questions, but the blank look said he didn't give a damn. That irritated the hell out of me and the fire lit in me all over again at his audacity.

"He's strong. Powerful." Vince Vinitto's body flashed in my head. I closed my eyes.

"But that's not important to you."

"How would you know? You've been gone, what, ten years?"

Though it was slight, I could tell by the look on his face that comment took him by surprise.

"He leaned back a bit. "You're right, I haven't seen you in a while. I wouldn't know that."

I scoffed then we were both silent for what felt like forever but was only seconds before he started back up.

"You love him?" He asked.

"Are you serious? Is that any of your business, Greg?" I snapped.

"I honestly want to know if you love him."

Gregory moved the conversation too fast for my liking. At the same time, the more he spoke, the more it seemed like he had ulterior motives. And the harder it became for me to ask what I wanted to. All over again, I felt like the smitten high schoolgirl who couldn't tell her left from right. The one that loved everything about Gregory.

He leaned forward, and the space between us thickened. When I sucked in a deep breath, the scent of his cologne melted my insides.

"I want to know if he makes your heart beat through your chest with so much intensity you're overwhelmed.

"Stop it! How can you sit here and talk like everything is okay? Like we can just go back to how it used to be. I have not seen you since that day, Greg. You left me. You didn't stand up for us, so don't sit here-"

"-Wait, wait, Nhoell." He sat up straight in his seat. "What do you mean I left you? I didn't leave you," he replied instantly.

"Who was the one that went off to school and who was unconscious in the hospital?" I gritted, then turned my head away from him and swallowed a sob. Fighting to keep from wiping my eyes. When I turned back to him, Gregory faced me with pain etched in his face. I realized I wasn't ready. I wasn't prepared to face him or even ask for his help.

The door to the entrance slammed open and startled me. The tunnel vision I seemed to get around Greg vanished and I glanced around the small shop. Had the crowd gotten smaller? I wondered if anyone heard our conversation. What were the odds that the other patrons knew Jake? Knew me? How much time had gone by? I had it in my head that I missed his call. Not thinking about Gregory or the questions I wanted answered, I snatched up my purse and rose from my seat.

"I can't do this. Not yet, I'm sorry."

Stepping to leave, Gregory gently grabbed my wrist and I cried out. He pulled his hand away as if my touch burned him. Sure enough, the other customers heard us and were looking our way. Gregory stared hard at my bandaged wrist under my long sleeve, then scanned up my body in till he reached my eyes. I let my hands drop to my side.

"Nhoell? What is this? Did he do this to you?" He rose from his chair. "Is this why you wanted to meet?"

"I'm sorry. I don't know what you were expecting."

"I wasn't expecting anything. Sit down, please. I want to help."

"Like you did ten years ago?"

"I'm sorry about what happened then. I was young."

"You can't blame something like that on youth."

"I've seen this look in your face before." He whispered.

"What?"

"Will you let me help you, please?"

"What did you say?" I raised my voice. His regretful expression staring down at me. Pitying me. "How could you possibly know what I'm going through?" I jabbed a finger at my chest.

"Just sit. I'll tell you."

Taking a beat, I slowly sat down then dabbed my eyes to make sure a single tear hadn't fallen. Gregory's eyes followed my wrist until it disappeared underneath the table.

"Ninth grade year..."

"Yeah."

"... something happened."

"Something like what?"

"Remember when you rode with my dad and me?" He adjusted himself in the chair for the third time, reminding me of the boy he used to be.

"Yeah, I had to wear a cast."

"You didn't fall and break your arm. Something happened to you. Somebody did something to you... and Althea." The lines in his face deepened.

"Althea? What are you talking about? I fell through that broken door at my house." I said, confident that I was right.

"Wait, I'm telling this wrong." He wiped his hands over his face, then clasped his hands together and inhaled deeply. I watched his shoulders rise and fall with each breath, his hands shivering.

"Gregory, what the hell are you talking about?"

The door slammed shut and the phone beeped from my purse. I jumped, Gregory immediately lifted his head and placed his hand on my shoulder. I turned back to him and saw that the nervous boy that had been trying to tell me something important was no longer there. Gregory's persona seemed to change right before my eyes. His instinct to protect me had replaced everything else.

"I'm right here, Nhoell. I won't let anything happen to you," he soothed. "The first day of school, after winter break. Remember?"

"I'm not sure, I guess. It was a long time ago." I glanced at the door again.

"What do you remember about that day?"

I thought for a moment. There wasn't anything clear coming to mind.

"Nhoell, you wore blue jeans and a pink blouse," he smiled. "my eyes lit up when I saw you that morning." For a moment his deep lines softened, then went cold again. "Was Althea at school?" he asked.

"What does this have to do with-"

"Was she?"

I thought back again, trying to remember the last time I spoke to Althea. But it was so long ago. Everything seemed fuzzy.

"No. I didn't hear from her the entire winter break."

"You went to her house after school. Something happened to you there. From what your mom told my parents... no one knows what happened."

Muddled by his story, I thought as hard as I could to remember anything from that day. The only thing that came to mind were days spent at home or in the studio. I couldn't recall when Althea left or the last time I saw her.

Gregory continued, "You were missing. Your mom and grandma called the police as soon as you didn't come home. To this day, I still don't see how they could get them involved so quickly. But we were all looking for you for hours. I called the team, your friends.

"It was late when I heard your voice. You yelled my name. You were running down the middle of the street. When I got to you... I saw the look in your eyes... in your face. I knew that something happened to you. There was blood and you smelled like alcohol and cigarettes. You kept screaming for Althea. That's all everyone could hear. Over and over again.

"The first few months after you came back to school were the worst. I was afraid to say the wrong thing or slip up and mention it. No one else knew that you didn't remember, so I never let anyone get close enough to ask. I was apprehensive something would trigger it."

I sat silent with my face cringing in disbelief. Horrified that I remembered none of it. As hard as I tried to conjure up a memory, nothing came to me. What he said sounded like something from a movie. I wanted to call him a liar, but he had no reason to lie. I remembered Althea leaving for Tennessee, but that was all. I never spoke to her after that. Why? Did I ever try to call her? Write to her? Did she try calling me?

"That's what I remember, Nhoell. Please, let me help you."

I got up, and so did he.

"Nhoell, please!"

The room spun as I grabbed up my purse again and walked to the exit in a swift motion with Gregory fast on my heels.

"Nhoell, please!" He pleaded this time so I stopped at the door.

"I wanted to talk to you about what happened ten years ago. And ask for your help. He is a powerful man in this city, and he has eyes everywhere," I whispered. "Please don't follow me."

"Don't leave. I can help you. I can get you away from him. I promise."

I thought about his proposal for a moment. But I knew Jake would always find me. I wanted to believe Gregory. Believe that just like that, he can get us out of the city. Still, I harbored anger towards him. And now, I had a new worry—unknown trauma.

"I never stopped loving you, Gregory. Even after you left. But I can't be with you again. I will call you." I walked out the door, leaving him standing alone.

Chapter 14

After sneaking back into the hotel, I waited nearly forty minutes for Jimmy to leave before running back into the condo. Twenty-one minutes before my scheduled call with Jake and no missed calls on my cell. A bunch of alerts for upcoming events and task were the only notifications. Everything went according to plan.

I thought over Gregory's story another hour before deciding to confront my mama. I hadn't spoken to her in a month and felt guilty about calling her to get answers and not calling at all. Those random occasions when she called, I didn't speak up about what I was going through. I gave mama the same information about Jake that I gave her during the time he cast his bait. The less they knew about each other the safer she was.

When Mama picked up the phone, I mistook her tired voice for just waking. She wasn't sick, but the hard work she put in over the years weighed on her like bricks.

"How are you? Did I catch you at a bad time?" I stood at the living room window.

"I'm fine. Just doing some paperwork. I'm happy to hear from you. How are you up there?"

"I'm okay. You shouldn't worry about me though."

"Ah, I'm still your mama, I'll always worry. I miss you."

"I miss you too." I held back tears as I pressed my forehead against the cool glass. "Mama? I have to ask you something. Can you be honest with me?"

She blurted, "I knew it had to be something. Is that man around you?"

"No."

"That's too bad because I was gonna give him a piece of my mind. Still haven't brought you back to see me, and I still haven't seen this man. So much for respect." She mumbled under her breath.

"Mama?"

"I'm here. What you need to ask me? It's always good to hear from you, no matter what."

"I ran into him." The line when silent, then I waited a beat before speaking again.

"He mentioned something that I need you to ask you about."

"I've been waiting for this day to come. I just knew it was going to bite us in the butt one day. When Mama was alive, she was a strong woman. You know that. So much happened that we kept from you. But you were just a child, Nhoell. I knew Gregory was a good boy. Back then, it seemed like the right thing to do."

"Ma?"

"Yes, baby?"

"What happened in ninth grade?" there was a long uncanny silence. "Mama?"

"I'm here." Her voice trembled into the phone, and I placed my cell to my chest. Hearing her cry made me feel so unsteady. When I put the phone back to my ear, she was apologizing.

"It's okay. I just need to know what happened. I can't remember anything about that day."

Silence again.

"I don't know." She whispered stronger than her apologies.

"What do you mean?" I lifted myself away from the window and faced the living room.

"Nhoell, you forgot. It only took a week for you to suppress your memory. You woke up one morning and didn't remember how you broke your arm. We thought you were lying, trying to act like nothing happened. But after two days, we knew you were telling the truth. You didn't remember, so we decided to go along with it."

The room spun, and I eased onto the couch, holding my head in my hand. Something happened and no one, not even me, knew what transpired. How many things had I suppressed? What had I experienced throughout my life and blocked from my mind? My eyes and head throbbed, but I tried relaxing my face to ease the tension.

"What about Althea? What happened to her?"

"You kept screaming her name," Mama spoke like she wasn't talking to me, but replaying that memory instead. Not stopping to answer my questions. "Althea. Screaming and crying at the top of your lungs, calling for her. Your face was bruised, and there was blood on your mouth... and your clothes. Your arm had been broken, too. I cried. I cried so hard because your screams were terrifying and you were alive. I thought I lost you. What monster would put his hands on a little girl? We thought someone took you." She sniffled.

"His? A man?"

"The police found Althea unconscious in her bedroom. She had been beaten and... raped. God knows for how long. I was so scared."

My heart sank into my chest. Feeling like it retreated further into its cage. Althea, beaten? Raped? Who? The shadowy figure from my nightmares flashed in my head along with the hot smell of musk and alcohol. I shook it off and clutched my shirt as if I could reach my heart.

"Did he..."

"He didn't touch you. You said that, but spoke nothing else of it. We don't know what he did to you. After Althea recovered and left, you... just forgot. You were back to being you. It concerned us. And I wanted to take you to see someone, but Mama thought bringing it back up would make it worse."

"No," I breathed.

"You were so ready to get back to school," she continued.

"Grandma didn't want me to. I remember that."

"I knew you needed to go back. Get back to doing normal things. I told Gregory and his parents that you couldn't remember anything that happened. I knew he would be there for you. I always paid attention to you two. That next day, you went to school, I didn't go to work. I sat out in front of that school until it was over to make sure you came back home. I did that for a few days, and you always had the biggest smile on your face."

"Mama?"

"You and Gregory were the best of friends and you were happy. He made you so happy, and I loved him for it. For loving you."

She was silent again and the tears that streamed down my face dropped into my lap. I thought that about Gregory too. So why did things happen the way they did? The lump in my throat didn't allow me to speak as strongly as I wanted.

"What happened to Althea? Did she ever call me?"

"She wrote you, called you, and missed you so much. We didn't want you to remember what happened, Nhoell. That's why we never told you. Once we finally told her you didn't remember, then she stopped calling."

As heavy as my chest felt, I didn't know if I was angry or more hurt by the revelation. I didn't know if I could be angry with them for making those decisions. I couldn't say I would've done those things differently.

"Did you throw those letters away?"

She was silent again. Then, "Where should I send them?"

I gave her Carla's home address.

"Nhoell, I'm sorry. As parents, sometimes we do things because we think it's the best thing at the time."

"I know, Mama. I know."

The small phone vibrated against my hip. I pulled it from my pocket and checked the text. It was Carla checking on me.

"Mama? One more thing. How did you get the police to respond the way you did?"

After a few seconds, I looked at my phone screen, making sure I hadn't muted the call.

"I called a friend that worked on your father's case back in Virginia."

Chapter 15

The last thing that occupied my mind was planning for the wedding. It seemed like every other day and week Nora had meetings and appearances to keep up, too. Holly had upcoming events to plan but wasn't willing to do the footwork herself. So, my phone dinged with one reminder after another to either do something or prepare for it. That was the minor issue, though. I didn't get a wink of sleep the night before. One nightmare after the other crashed into my dreams like a tsunami and I woke up drenched and heaving each time. Vince Vinitto, the shadowy figure that I tried to turn into a lucid dream. Then there was Jake Vaughn and his motives. When I was awake, Greg and my mama's conversation consumed me. And every time I thought of what Eleanor said to me, I thought of Vince and the smell of cleaning supplies. No matter where I turned, there was something or someone hunting me.

The surround system rang, and I left the closet and grabbed my cell from the bed. I dismissed the call after seeing Holly's name and walked back to the closet. My phone rang again, and again. Each time I ignored the call. The grouchy, bitchy mood I was in didn't have time for Holly screaming demands at me. The vibration in my breast tickled my stomach. I reached my hand into my bra and pulled out the Nokia phone, putting it to my ear.

"Yes?"

"Morning, Nhoell."

My heart clamored into my chest. I closed the room door and headed to the bathroom and turned on the faucet.

"Good morning."

"I know you said you would call. I didn't want to wait any longer. Is now a good time to talk?"

I thought of my mama's revelation so much in the past eighteen hours, what she said about Gregory still lay fresh in my mind. I took a deep breath and erased the feelings that already rose to my chest. Gregory Rehevas was only a means to an end. That's all.

"Yes," I replied.

"I need to see you. Is this morning okay?"

"No. Yesterday was already pushing it. I can't just… I can't go off on my own."

"I figured as much."

"How so?"

"I only need an hour of your time. I understand your situation."

I exhaled slowly, then faced the ceiling. After a moment, I shook my head. There was no way of getting away from Nora and Holly. Even if I was to get away from them, that still didn't fix the Jimmy and Lee problem.

"I don't think I can. I'll be with his family today. I can't get out of that."

"That's fine. I'll send you the address anyway. If you do find the time, I'll be there." He said.

"You can't wait?"

"I will wait."

I took an exasperated breath. "Greg?"

"Yes, Nhoell?"

I held my breath before I let the words escape in a hushed tone. "Thank you."

"Be careful today."

I bowed my head and prayed as the water somehow eased the anxiety that built up. I thanked God for allowing me to cross paths with Gregory again. Because I felt a warmth in my chest I hadn't felt in a long time. It truly felt like my soul had returned to me. Most importantly, enlisting his help increased my and Carla's chance of survival. Having her in the crossfire of whatever Jake wanted from me was not on my list. Once she and I were free to live our lives, looking ahead and not back, Gregory and I were parting ways.

#

I walked into the florist shop downtown where we were meeting. The scent of fresh lavender overpowered many other aromatic smells in the room. Holly had been calling me almost nonstop since leaving the house. When I finally answered her call, she chewed me out. By then, I was approaching the table set up for clients like the Vaughns. Her face turned red as she tightened her lips and slammed the phone down. I was fifteen minutes early. It surprised me to see Marilyn again when usually she wasn't around. Since that night at the Gala, it hadn't gotten past me that I was seeing more of her.

"Good morning, Nora. Hi, Marilyn."

She gave a nod and whispered a reply. I looked at Holly who stared at me with a lopsided snarl. "Holly." I nodded my head to her. Although I was still apprehensive that Jake would hear about those unanswered calls, my patience had dwindled with Holly. It had become even more difficult to deal with her stepping on me.

"Morning, Nhoell. You look nice today. I told Mother and Holly that I spoke with you already," Marilyn said with a soft smile.

One look from Holly, though, and her smile retreated. I could only imagine what they were like to her behind closed doors. That reminded me of Eleanor's conversation two nights ago.

"Thanks, Marilyn." Her smile almost returned, and again, I saw something oddly familiar in her, but couldn't put my finger on it. We had definitely crossed paths before. Either in college or some art show. She seemed interested enough in it for it to be likely.

"Thank you, Nhoell, for joining us," Nora replied, almost genuine. "I'm glad you're doing well."

For a second, I cut my eyes at Nora. She had to know Jake put his hands on me. I thought of his phone call that night before it happened.

And the fact that Nora clearly set me up to witness Vince Vinitto's murder. If all my speculations were indeed true, and Nora had her hands in everything, why would they do it? Why would she?

I smiled at her. "Yes, of course."

"How dare you act like nothing is wrong?!" Holly yelled out.

"I'm sorry?"

"You ignored all my calls!"

"Holly, you're really causing a scene," I leaned in and whispered, directing my eyes at a few women near the dandelions staring at us. "Besides, I didn't ignore your calls, I just couldn't answer at the time."

"I don't care! When I call, you need to answer. Instead, you were able to pick up for her. And when did you two start talking?" Holly sneered at Marilyn and Nora let out a loud hacking cough. She put her hand on Holly's shoulder, who shoved her away. I reached for Nora, concerned.

"My goodness, Holly! Nora, are you okay?"

She still coughed as though her lungs were fighting to get from her throat. I motioned for the woman behind the desk to bring water. It was Holly's turn to look confused.

"Holly, I really think you should calm down, Jake would not like this behavior representing him." I held my hand out for the water as I rubbed Nora's back, easing her coughing fit.

Holly jumped from her chair and stormed off. I looked at Nora, then at Marilyn.

"I think I should check on her. To see how she's doing." I stood to leave, and Nora gently pulled me back down, the color returning to her clammy face.

"She'll be okay. I don't want any delay."

"Yes, ma'am."

A glance at Marilyn told me she was suspicious. Eleanor still led me to believe that Marilyn wasn't like the others. 'She was her father's favorite', right?

My phone vibrated in my purse, which meant it was my private line. Seconds later, my cell phone rang, and it was Jake. Sure enough, he was at work, probably in a meeting or doing something just as important I imagined.

"Is that Jake, Nhoell? Tell him I said, good morning,"

I nodded to Nora, then answered. His voice blared through the phone like a freight train. Reflexively, I pulled the phone away from my ear. My chest seemed to cave in as a nauseous feeling reached my stomach. I'd gone too far. The volume of Jake's voice told me that. I'd fucked up. There hadn't been a single time where he used such a tone with me. Jake didn't need to raise his voice to me. Not to get a message across.

God! I cursed myself for being so goddamn reckless. Holly must've told an outrageous lie. A few missed calls shouldn't have tipped him over the edge so much. Not Jake. Not to the point of listening to curses and name calling in clear and precise words. Along with what he would do to me when we were home. Nora grabbed the phone.

"Jake? Sweetie?" she said gently.

Almost immediately, he hushed. "Why are you using such language to talk to her? The entire establishment can hear you. I accept your apology. Now, Nhoell has been sweet since she arrived. Call Holly back and tell her to get to this table this instance. I am tired of waiting for her to pull herself together." He spoke again.

"Yes, Nhoell, Marilyn and I are waiting for her," she moved the phone away from her ear, looked at the screen then turned to me. "well look at that, he hung up."

She handed me back my phone and started speaking about the plans for the day like I didn't have fifty million reminders. I was stuck on how easily she controlled Jake. Make him stop, listen, and hopefully get on Holly about her exaggerations. So easily.

Interrupting my thoughts was the sound of Holly's chair scraping the floor. She flopped down and glared at me then to Nora. Her face softened when she looked at her mother.

"Mommy, I want to apologize for my outburst and making you wait." She looked at me. I could see her jaw tighten. "Nhoell, please forgive me for my behavior. I'm sorry."

If only someone knew how good that made me feel on the inside. To hear Holly apologize was enough to make the rest of my day go by.

"Thank you," I said casually.

Chapter 16

It was around 11:30 when Nora grew tired and left. My concern for her when I first arrived was selfishly motivated. That turned around when she dragged slower than usual and looked famish. Still, she didn't say a word about it to either of us. After coughing up a storm again and barely recovering, Holly convinced her to leave the rest to her. Surprisingly, I hated that she left. Once she did, we ended up behind schedule with the two other appointments because of Holly's indecisiveness. Which meant I spent more time with her than I wanted. We completed them, though. Mostly in silence.

Walking out of the jewelry boutique onto the busy sidewalk, I sent Jake a text then called Lee, who pulled up a minute later. He jumped out and opened the door for me, but Holly stepped ahead, too. We were short a car or two. I looked at Marilyn, who didn't seem to care. As if we were complaining, Holly offered to take the car and suggested Marilyn and I catch a ride.

"Sorry, Miss. I have to stay with her." Lee spoke.

My jaw dropped, then closed just as fast. I never heard him say a single word. Not one.

"No, you can take me to my appointment and she can wait here." Holly ordered.

"Not my job."

Holly stormed away from the car and pulled out her cell phone. The three of us watched as she stood in the middle of the sidewalk with her cellphone to her ear. People moving about their day had to go around her.

"Jake. Please tell Nhoell's driver to take me to my appointment. No, mommy wasn't well, so she left early. She was tired. No, just coughing. Yes. It's right down the street and she isn't by herself. Well, Marilyn's here, but… okay. I love you." She put the phone into her purse and called over Marilyn, who went to her without hesitation. She went to Holly, apologizing to the people that had to keep detouring around them. Holly spoke in hushed whispers before they made their way back to us. Marilyn pulled out her cellphone.

"It's settled. You will take me down the street then come back for them." Holly brushed past Lee and jumped in the car, closing the door behind her. Lee stared at the door, then to me and pulled out his cell. The car window rolled down.

"You can call him, but he said he was going back into an important meeting. So," She rolled the window back up.

"I'll be back in ten minutes. Please, don't go anywhere." Lee ran around the car and jumped in. Seconds later, Marilyn and I watched the car pull into traffic.

She and I both stood on the busy sidewalk, closer to the curb, out of the way of other pedestrians. Across the street was a coffee shop that reminded me of Gregory. It was already after two o'clock. Would he still be waiting? Would I ever get another moment like this? But I knew that Marilyn Vaughn was standing next to me looking ahead in no direction, just like me. That, I was sure, was a rare chance.

"Why did you lie?" I asked, not raising my voice over the blaring vehicles that passed.

"Should I have told the truth?"

"Thanks."

"Why didn't you pick up?"

I fidgeted with my fingers at my side and thought of a response other than blurting out what I wanted.

"I take it Holly is becoming overbearing."

I whispered, "It could be worse."

"Yeah. It could. I'm sorry you're going through this."

"Why does your brother want to marry me?"

Marilyn turned to me and stared me in the eyes. She cocked her head to the side.

"I don't know. That's what I'm trying to find out."

"What?"

"My brother. Why is he marrying you, of all people?" She eyed me up and down, but it didn't seem to be any jealousy or envy in her eyes. Only curiosity. "What is he up to? You've been around him long enough to learn a few things. Jake does nothing unless it benefits him. For him to marry you there must be something he's gaining."

"So, I guess we are both after the same thing?"

"I guess."

"Can you help me get away from him?"

She smiled, but it didn't reach her eyes. That expression answered my question.

Marilyn turned her focus back across the street. "Have you already tried running from him? If so, then you know that there is no getting away. Not from Jake. I've tried enough times to know," She looked back at me. "If you want to get away from Jake, you need to know what he wants. Without that information, there is no fair fight. I don't have all the information either. That's the only reason he always won against me."

"What do you mean?"

"I'm not their favorite person. I didn't know about this engagement until a few weeks ago, for one. That alone tells you what? I wanted to see how he acted around you."

"And?"

Marilyn turned her body completely towards me, and her brows wrinkled together.

"I have never seen him act this way to anyone. Not to this extent. And marriage? I saw what I needed at the cake tasting."

My face flushed, and I turned away from her. My breast vibrated, sending shivers down my spine. Gregory. I glanced at the time on my phone. Ten minutes had already passed. I glared down the road to see if Lee was in sight. When a jeep pulled in front of us and rolled down the window.

"Com'on." Marilyn opened the door to the jeep.

"To where."

"Holly lied. She didn't call Jake." She jumped in and slid to the other side, making room for me. I slid in after her.

"What? What if he finds out?"

"He'll be pissed at Holly for doing it and at the driver for believing it. And me, well just because."

"And me, for nothing."

"It shouldn't be a problem. You'll be at the hotel by the time he finds out. If he finds out."

"Wait. I was, I was meeting with Carla. For about an hour."

"I can't leave you, Nhoell. I'm sorry."

#

My heart drummed in my chest so much the vibrations rippled through my body. The closer we came to the location, the more it turned into a steady hum than beating drums. As much as it had been happening, I still wasn't used to the sudden feeling. My stomach wasn't any better; the roller coaster I was on took deep drops. No matter what, I had to remember that I didn't ask for Gregory's help to rekindle our past.

We pulled up across the street from a parking lot with a stoned, square building behind it. Marilyn and I got out of the car and entered the restaurant that sat across the road to the building I was going to. I understood why she wouldn't leave me. Jake would blame her. From our conversation, she was no stranger to his rage. Thankfully, she agreed to wait across the street until "Carla" and I finished. At first, I was hesitant, but I saw no reason not to trust her. That didn't mean tell her about my escape plan.

Only two cars occupied the lot of the building I walked to. Once I entered the foyer with an information desk at one end and a single door in the opposite, Gregory stood from a bench that sat across from the entrance. He wore dark jeans that insinuated his thighs and a fitted gray button-down rolled at the forearm. I was suddenly warm against the breeze in the air.

"I'm glad you came." He approached and wrapped his arms around me but didn't stay long. Oh god, my body hummed when he released me, "How are you?

"Um, I'm okay. Sorry to keep you." I internally shook my head to focus.

"It's fine. I would've waited all day. Besides, I felt you coming. Let's head in. I have something to show you."

I blushed before following him, all the while thinking of just how difficult focusing was going to be.

"What is this place anyway? Why isn't anyone here?" I asked curiously.

"It's their day off."

He grabbed my hand and led me through the only other door in the foyer. My eyes trailed directly to the ceiling in awe once we entered. A museum. We were in a museum. From the outside, the building looked like a three-story concrete rectangle. No walls and only one door. On the inside, the large room was in the shape of a pyramid. It amazed me at how beautiful the large room had been, and I didn't stop staring until the lights dimmed. That directed my attention to glass cases surrounding the walls of the room. There was one glass case in the center of the room that seemed to call to me. I took two steps, but Greg pulled me back.

"We'll save that one for last."

He led me to the left towards the first enclosed case. His hand around my waist felt good and let off heat underneath his touch. I pulled away from him. I had to stay focus. Being around Gregory made me lose sight of reality. When that happened, mistakes were too easy to make. We couldn't afford a single one.

Inside the first case was a model of a house. The architecture was so beautiful and the designs were very intricate. The detail in the model was so mesmerizing that it almost looked real. I wanted to take it apart piece by piece and dissect it. I was astounded, and Gregory saw it on my face because his smile broadened. I walked around the model several times looking at all angles.

"I can't believe this. The detail. The pa-" I stood up straight and looked at Gregory standing back, watching me.

"The passion." He finished my sentence.

"This is your work? All of this?"

"In this room? Yes."

"It's beautiful."

I went back to looking at the model, then moved to the next, which was just as beautiful. Interior and exterior. Each time I passed one, it held a different feel to it. Like different people created each of them. Gregory had designed, built and constructed all the homes and commercial buildings and each time he opened his mind to the possibility of something different. I was beyond impressed with his skills and what he had accomplished. I was proud of him for building his dream.

"You're amazing, Gregory. Is this your museum? I bet you did this, too."

He smiled at me. "I have these museums all around the country and some in other countries. I figure I could gain clients this way rather than showing slides and proposals. I built all the models using the same material I would for the house. I have a substantial business, so I use these museums to showcase and promote my work. It's beneficial for clients who aren't sure what they are looking for and field trips for anyone interested. My work isn't the only work I promote, though. Let's look at the last one."

We were back where we started. Greg hit another switch, and the lights went off. He had a skylight in the center of the ceiling, and the rays from the sun lit up the model in the middle of the floor.

"You are truly remarkable!" I exclaimed. "I didn't expect this."

"Close your eyes."

Reluctantly, I did what he asked. He put his hands on my arms, and we walked. The heat from his body warmed my back as he guided me.

My chest thumped, and I was sure his had done the same. He stopped moving.

"You ready?"

I nodded my head.

"Alright, open them."

Once I opened my eyes, they'd gone wide in surprise. The model he showed me was a replica of the one from 7th grade. It was more beautiful than the original with added space and significant landscape changes. Adding another house on the land, a walk-through garden, a river flowing down the property and turning into a waterfall, and what looked like a guesthouse near the home. Gregory had blown me away with this one. The style was traditional but was just as unique as his other work. I read the description. The only model given a description. *Home, remodeled, 2013.*

"I'm always thinking about you, Nhoell. About us."

I wasn't facing him, so he couldn't see the tears rolling down my cheeks. I wanted to jump in his arms right then and there and go home. Put my feet in the river, relax in the gardens, I wanted to explore the land in the model. My mind held me back, though.

"The other home is for your mom."

I turned to him, surprised that he even thought about her. He was just as surprised to see my tears. He used his thumbs to rub them away.

"I have something else for you."

I pulled away while fighting myself to stay put. To not jump back into his arms. He took hold of my hand and led the way towards the back of the room that led to another door.

"Will this be more of your work?"

"It's actually more of someone else's work."

When he turned on the switch, it lit up a long, oval, arched hallway. The symbols casing the walls in black over the burgundy had me speechless. They reminded me of the symbols from the gala. His talents were one of a kind, and I wondered what his best work looked like. The thought of decorating the places he'd designed and how it would fit so well with his work made my fingers itch. I knew Greg and I would make perfect business partners.

Once we reached the end of the hallway, he opened the door to a beautiful multi-colored gallery with paintings and drawings hanging on the walls. I recognized none of the work until we walked into the first area, painted in maroon. This time I was beyond speechless. My paintings; paintings I created in middle school hung around the room. How? How did he get my paintings under the same roof as his work and why were they so magnificently framed, adorning such a beautiful space? I couldn't answer the questions myself, not at all. Calmly, I made my way around each of the sections.

He filled the entire space with framed work of mine from middle school through college, and some even after college. I took a closer look at how he arranged each piece. Not by time period, but by the emotion my work incited in me when I made it. He'd taken care to tell a story with my paintings. My heart hummed at him, knowing the meaning behind them. Knowing their intention. When I approached one of the last areas, I nearly lost my breath at the sight of my work from Carla's gallery opening. He was the second buyer? I looked at him after taking in my surroundings.

"Do you display my work in all your galleries?"

"Many of my galleries. I chose a few and sent them out of the country. My clients love your work."

"Your clients?"

"Yes," he took a step closer. "work you sold for so little, I bought back and sold it with what I built."

"You bought and sold my work? Why?"

"I wanted you to be a part of me and what I was doing for so long. You helped me become the person I am. I wanted to make sure I was able to share it with you."

"I can't believe it."

I glanced back at my art as it took me through an ocean of childhood memories.

"You should. You were always this big optimist. Believe it or not, Nhoell, you are a very wealthy woman. Just as I am a very wealthy man. Ten percent of what I make goes to you."

"Ten percent?" I laughed, but he wasn't laughing with me. He was serious. "You sold my work for ten percent?"

"Yes. Every one of my clients has a painting created by you hanging in their home or office. Nhoell, I have never met a woman like you. Even after college. There has never been another person that made me feel the way you did. Once you're safe, I intend to build that home for us. The guesthouse outside is for you. To do anything you want with it, even get away from the children."

"Children?" My heart raced dramatically.

"I hope you remember us planning that, too." He pulled me closer to him.

"I can't."

I let out a low whisper and turned my head away to keep from seeing the disappointment in his eyes, then pushed myself from his grasp. "I told you, Greg. I can't do this again. This," I pointed to the paintings and drawings on display. "I'm so confused as to why you would do this after everything that happened. After," I took another deep breath and balled my fist to keep my fingers from trembling. Talk about building a home together, getting married. Children! It was all moving too fast. He was moving too fast when I didn't want to move forward with him. Or maybe I did want it.

"Nhoell, I don't know what you remember that day. But I remember watching you get hit by a car. And I remember staying in that hospital room day and night praying you woke up."

"Then why did you leave?" I inhaled a sob. "When I woke up you were not there. My baby was not there. I went through that on my own."

"I'm truly sorry. I am. And I can't imagine what you went through. I wished every day that I was right there with you."

I let out a chuckle that said, 'are you serious.' If Gregory wanted to be with me, he wouldn't have left. I shook my head.

"I'm sorry, Greg. I have to leave," I slowly moved further away, directing my gaze to the floor. Afraid of looking him in the eyes and seeing the hurt in them. "I can't do this again."

"Nhoell, wait."

"I can't."

I hurried off in the direction I'd come, pulling my phone out to call for Marilyn. Instead, a new text from Carla scrolled across my phone changing my plans.

Package delivered.

Chapter 17

"Where have you been? I've been waiting for an hour."

"Carla, I got here as fast as I could. Besides, I took an Uber." I walked up the few stairs that led from the entrance to the second floor and took a seat on her cream-colored sectional. From where I sat, the open space allowed me a clear visual of the shoebox-size package sitting at her dining table.

"What's really going on? Why are they there 24/7 now?" she asked suspiciously, stepping into the living room.

"Ever since the cake tasting, he seems on edge. This time I was with Marilyn." I replied, pondering her questions more.

"This is new."

"No, this is complicated."

"I have been so tempted to open this damn box. It's been calling my name since they delivered it."

Carla grabbed the box from the dining table and walked it back to the living room. She handed me a knife, then sat next to me on the couch.

"Well, what are you waiting for? Open the damn thing."

"I'm anxious, but I'm scared, too."

"It's okay to feel that way. But whatever it is, I'm right here for you."

I used the knife and cut open the box. Inside it was a shoebox that I pulled out and set on the table. Lifting the top, my fingers trembled slightly. It was unbelievable at how many faded envelopes were inside. They were worn and most appeared unopened. But Gregory's name written on the top of the first letter hit at my heart. I shuffled through more envelopes as I read his name and Althea's.

"She didn't mention a thing about Greg writing to me, what the hell," I whispered as I traced my fingers over one envelope. "my heart felt like a thousand explosions in my chest every time I was around him." I looked at Carla and clutched my shirt. "he tried to stay away from me when we were young because the same thing happened to him."

I poured the contents of the box onto the table. My heart swelled at the number of letters with Gregory's name on it. I never knew he tried to reach out and suddenly felt guilty and angry. Before we began reading, I recanted the last few days to Carla, minus Vince Vinitto's death. She squinted her eyes and stared off for a moment after telling her about Eleanor. And with what Marilyn said earlier that day, we both agreed that there must've been something Jake wanted.

"You ready to read?" I interrupted her thoughts. "I'm looking for a letter from Althea that might mention something about ninth grade." I opened the first one, and she picked up another and did the same.

After an hour and going through nearly half of the letters, Carla brought us each a glass of wine. I cried, I laughed, I smiled and cried again as I read them. Gregory's letters spoke to me in a way he never did. He believed I didn't want him. That I hated him for what happened. The hurt and rejection in his words turned my stomach into knots. The loneliness he felt came off those pages too. Most of all, the way he wrote still showed me the dedication and love that kept him pushing. He talked about school and the different people he'd met. And he always ended the letter expressing his love. He put his heart into them, and I was even more confused than before about why he left.

Gregory never stopped loving me, and he had written it repeatedly. In one of his letters, he promised to marry me no matter what. He promised he would become successful so he would take care of our family. I cried, because he was ten years too late. What should have been said after losing our baby, wasn't. Instead, I was left to face everything on my own. Reading his letter also made me angry at my mama and grandma. Had I seen those letters ten years ago, things may have been different. I may have gotten the chance to hear him say those words rather than writing them. I clinched the letter to my chest and let my tears fall.

"You okay?"

"He loved me. He loved me so much?"

"He still does, Nhoell. He never stopped loving you from what I've read. Open your heart. You have to."

She was wrong. I didn't have to open myself up. Even though my body felt complete and my heart beat for him, letting him in again was like preparing for open heart surgery without anesthesia. It was bound to end very painfully.

"I don't. There is only one thing I must do that involves him. It doesn't concern my heart."

We kept reading. By the time we got underneath most of Gregory's letters, Althea's letters surfaced. The envelopes were dingy, and her handwriting covered it. She had written just as many letters as Gregory, if not more. Like Gregory, Althea believed I didn't want her in my life. Especially after she didn't hear from me. She always asked how things were. If Greg and I were together yet. Even though I wasn't writing her back, she remained optimistic about our friendship. As I read on, I imagined the facial expressions and gestures she used to make.

"Nhoell?"

Carla snapped me out of my trance. She was holding what was probably ten sheets of paper. "I think this may be something." She handed me the letters and I flipped through them.

"It's about fifteen pages here." I exclaimed.

"I know. The first sentence told me it was for your eyes only."

I read the sentence, *This will be my last letter*. My arms turned to jelly as I began reading through the letter. By the time I finished, I was in tears and still at square one. Althea felt guilty for everything that went on that day. She wrote that mama told her I'd forgotten the events, but it was for the best because I wouldn't look at her the same. For years, her mom's boyfriend had abused her. During winter break, her mom disappeared. She never told anyone about the abuse until I got mixed up. Still, even she didn't know what happened. She didn't even remember what he did to her that day. The tears she cried when writing the letter left visible stains. I put it down and grabbed hold of Carla.

"What happened to me, Carla? What happened? It's all too much."

"One day, Nhoell. One day you'll find out. But you need to listen to me. Right now, there is a man out there that will do anything and everything it takes to protect you. This isn't just some man. This man is your other half. You have already started to change since you saw him that day. You wouldn't be here if you weren't."

Carla was right. One day I would find out what happened. She held me for a while longer before we broke our embrace and cleaned. In those five minutes, we put away the letters and I pulled myself together. What Gregory wrote had only intensified my want. Still, I couldn't shake the feeling of what loving him had cost me in the past. Clearly he tried to contact me. But what happened that day was something I couldn't forget. That was enough to push me away. But it wasn't enough for me to refuse his help when needed. A knock interrupted the battle in my head. I looked to Carla, who shrugged her shoulders before going to the door.

"May I help you?" Carla asked.

"I'm here to pick up Mrs. Vaughn." It was Lee.

"Can you tell me how in the hell you got through the community gates because I didn't authorize any visitors."

I could sense Carla's attitude was about to present itself like a Jack in the Box. It didn't surprise me that Jake pulled strings to get his driver through. And I wasn't surprised that he'd found out where I was. If Carla hadn't realized by now, she wasn't as safe as she thought she was, I hoped she did soon. Her home was her safe ground, her sanctuary. The security for her community was a prison lockdown. That was the reason she chose it. Jake's people getting through without a hitch didn't sit well with her, and it reverberated in her voice as she yelled at Lee.

"I'm not able to provide that information, Miss," Lee responded.

"Well, I suggest your ass step away from my goddamn door before you meet my pistol, then the police. In that order!"

Lee looked at her, stone-faced, but a devilish smirked peered across his face. He could see me now, standing nearby.

"Unfortunately, I am unable to leave without what I came for."

"She is not a damn package, she is a fucking person. Now get your ass off my steps. If she wants to leave, she can. But your ass will remove yourself from my property before I shove my gun in your throat!"

"Carla! You don't have to do that. Sir, can you please wait in the car? I will be right behind you."

"Thank you, Mrs. Vaughn."

He faced Carla again, gave her a sly smirk. "You have a good night, Miss." He turned and walk away, and Carla slammed the door behind him.

Chapter 18

I made it to the loft, not knowing if the night would be a bad one. Even though Holly left Marilyn and I hanging, it was her words against ours. Still, after Marilyn dropped me off, and I checked in with Jake, I caught an Uber to Carla's without Lee, who was still driving around the city looking for me. That was definitely out of the question.

Jake was sprawled out on the sectional when I entered. To see him laid out on the couch like a drunk made me a bit suspicious. The last time he stayed over, he injured my wrist.

Upstairs, I washed hastily, not wanting Gregory's scent to linger any more than it had. Stepping from the shower, the frigid air struck me. I wrapped my arms around my body and reached for my towel that was no longer hanging. Shivering, I walked out of the bathroom. Jake sat on the edge of the bed holding my towel. I halted. I'd fucked up enough to know Jake could possibly use the belt on me again. That he was going to tell me to hold up the wall and don't move. And when the pain becomes too bearable, I will fall and he would be satisfied that I disobeyed him. The night wouldn't end well.

"Nhoell?"

I blinked my eyes one long time and was back with Jake and not in my head.

"Yes."

His voice mellow and drawn. "Come here, woman."

I walked over and stood in front of him bare-ass naked with my hands still holding my waist. Jake picked up the towel and dried me off. His hands caressed my body in sensual strokes, making sure every part of me was dry. His eyes went from my breasts to my hips. My bruises from past weeks were barely visible, but more recent ones darkened.

"You make all of this more difficult," He whispered, then grabbed my waist and pulled me closer to him, his mouth inches away from my shaved spot. Instead, he used his fingers to play with my clit and I moaned. He was a terrible man, a murderer. A man I wanted nothing to do with. But how could I say no to such a man without facing the consequence for my actions? I nearly fell when he inserted his fingers, but he caught me in midair.

"Don't move." He demanded.

I wanted to lie down and spread my legs any way I could. I wanted Gregory to… no, it wasn't Gregory. But I wanted it to be. I wanted him to spread my lips and use his fingers to rub my bud that had been aching all day.

My moans grew louder as his fingers moved faster. With each stroke, I became audibly wetter. The sound made my nipples tighten, and I squeezed them harder, gyrating against him until I climaxed. That night, Jake made love to me as he'd done before the engagement. He caressed and massaged my body as if he cherished it. But he would not cherish the body I gave him. He would keep trampling on it until he got what he wanted. I was sure of that.

Chapter 19

Pungent musk burned my nose. My stomach and throat burned from the taste of bile. My arm. I couldn't feel it anymore. The room was dark, but the sun was shining brightly outside. A soft whimper on the other side of the room made me raise my head. I strained my eyes wider, but only darkness appeared. Footsteps echoed from the other side, and I whipped my head in its direction and struggled to see. But my stomach turned in knots and the bile rose again. I didn't know why my chest seized up and down as the steps drew closer. Unwillingly, my head bowed between my legs and I tried forcing myself to look back up. To see. But the force holding me down was stronger than me.

A long, slow squeak sounded, heavy steps followed. The floorboard creaked afterward, and my breathing stilled while the musky, burning smell of alcohol and smoke thickened in the air. The heavy steps came closer. But not to me. I was relieved. My chest constricted as the sound of springs squeaked in my ears like fingernails to a chalkboard. I couldn't breathe. I tried forcing my head up, but my mind fought against me. I gasped, opening my mouth wide, trying to breathe. I couldn't. I couldn't.

\#

I wasn't surprised to find myself alone in bed the next morning. Jake sated himself and left. It had been a long time since he touched me the way he did last night. Even that wasn't enough to rid myself of the memories that flooded my head every time I looked at him.

When I went downstairs, the surprised look on my face could have fooled someone into believing I had forgiven Jake. The amount of canvas and dozens of bags from my favorite art stores covered the living room floor. Like a kid, I hurried to the closest bag and rummaged through it. Abruptly, I stopped, stood and moved away from what I found most dear to me. I hissed, then returned upstairs to get ready.

Nora greeted me with open arms and smiles as soon as I walked in the door for the PWNY luncheon. It was clear her health came after her social responsibilities. Still, she looked better than she had the day before. Moody Holly was still moody, snobbish Holly. I glanced around the room for Marilyn, but she was nowhere in sight. I hoped I didn't get her in trouble.

During the luncheon, I laughed while we ate and talked amongst the other women on the board and committee. All while receiving evil glances from Holly but not caring the least little bit. Gregory and I texted most of the morning too. I'd given bits of information about Jake, then later apologized for running off. He responded with a simple, *It's okay*. That text ached my heart a little but I tried to pay it no mind. After a while, I asked if he had a plan. I was reading another text when Holly intervened.

"Who are you texting that is so important?"

"Holly, not today," Nora snapped back.

"Nora, it's okay." I cleared my throat. "I haven't been in frequent contact with my mom. It's getting down to the last few weeks until the wedding. So, she and I are catching up." I turned back to Nora. "My mom has never met Jake, and she's looking forward to me settling down and having kids. That's all she seems to talk about."

"Really now? Well, I look forward to meeting her." Holly replied sarcastically. I opened my mouth to speak, but Nora beat me to it.

"Holly! Now you shut your mouth. One more word out of you and I swear!"

Nora's voice echoed, and I froze up just like Holly. The entire room went quiet. Not once had I ever heard her so much as raise her voice. And here she was, ready to bite Holly's head off. The flabbergasted look plastered on Holly's face probably mirrored mine. She bowed her head and apologized to us all. Not a peep was heard from her the rest of the luncheon.

#

Around three, I saw them to their driver and Jimmy drove me to meet with Carla. Even though Jake hadn't said a word about me going off on my own, I knew he didn't forget.

In the restaurant, I looked around for her. With my phone in hand, I sent a quick text and was led to our table. As usual, Jimmy sat at the bar nearby. Nearly thirty minutes later and dozens of unanswered phone calls, Carla came rushing in with her purse hanging loosely in her hand. I was relieved that my initial thought about Jake killing her wasn't true.

Her eyes shot daggers at every breathing soul that looked her way. Something wasn't right. Few things made Carla mad; work, men and work. She flopped in the seat and threw her purse in the chair next to her. Speechless, I waited for the fire that covered her to die down.

"Carla? What's going on?"

She lifted her head then rubbed her temples. Grabbing a server walking past our table, she ordered two shots. After taking a deep breath, she finally spoke.

"An inspector came to the gallery today. They said I was in violation of some code and fined me. Ten thousand fucking dollars! If I don't pay the fine and fix the violation, they will shut my business down."

The server returned and sat both shots down in front of Carla. She drank one. I ordered a glass of wine. She gulped the other, then took another deep breath. It stunned me to even hear of a code violation she didn't know about. Carla researched and studied ordinances when she first set her mind on what she wanted.

"What kind of code?" I questioned, suspicious of the entire ordeal.

"That's the crazy part! I've never even heard of this code. And the guy was rude— "

"— Oh no, Carla. You didn't cuss him out, did you?"

"He had some nerve walking into my place, telling me there was a complaint and that I'm in violation! That's bullshit!"

I placed my hand on her arm, giving it a gentle squeeze. The server brought over my wine and another shot for Carla without having her ask. I thanked him.

"That isn't the worst of it. On my way here, I get fucking pulled over, Nhoell. Pulled over! They said I was speeding. I don't speed. You know I don't speed." She put her hands back in her face and let out a long sigh. "I've never even had a damn ticket before." She scrambled through her purse and pulled out the ticket. "But they gave me a ticket when I wasn't speeding. How could they lie like that?"

"Why were you driving?"

"I couldn't catch a Lyft, Uber or damn taxi. Which is weird as hell."

As much as I didn't want to say it, it sounded like Jake was beginning his assault on Carla. With a few placed phone calls, he had her scrambling. Yeah. Jake didn't forget. He hits you where it hurts.

"Carla? I'm sorry this is happening to you. I'm really sorry."

"Did you call the inspector? And the cops, too?" She asked in sudden surprise. I smiled, shaking my head. That was the Carla I knew. "Don't worry about it. I will have this code thing looked into and find out what's really going on," she added, grabbing her purse and looking through it.

"Carla, just pay it off. If you need help, I'll find a way to help. I don't want you to make enemies over this."

"To hell with that! I'll take care of me," She called over the server again and ordered. I opted out. "now about Gregory— "

I shook my head and nodded toward Jimmy sitting at the bar. She looked over and rolled her eyes. "Have you spoken to him since yesterday?" she whispered.

"Yeah," I used my finger to trace the rim of my wine glass as I zoned out. "but only through text."

"Well, make sure you are careful with meeting him. Jake probably has his guys all over you."

I stopped playing with the rim and narrowed my eyes. Carla's words gave me chills.

"Are you okay?" I asked.

She hesitated before answering. "Nothing I should worry you about. I can take care of myself." She leaned back in her seat.

"I'm sure you can Carla, but— "

Carla held her hand up and gave me a reassuring smile. I forced myself to smile back. With all I had going on myself, I could see she didn't want to overburden me. It was just like her, always trying to protect me, even when the one needing protection looked at her in the mirror. I wasn't certain she understood the considerable amount of shit we were in. For that reason, I told her about Vince Vinitto.

"I heard of him. Only from the news though. I think the FBI is seeking him out according to CNN. Why do you ask?" Carla replied.

I leaned into her as close as I could without appearing suspicious. I took a quick glance over at Jimmy, who sat facing the bar.

"Jake killed him."

"What? Are you serious?"

"Yes, Carla. I was hiding in the curtains when they came into his study. He shot him, in the head."

"Oh, my god. We need to call the police."

"No!" I grabbed hold of her arm. "From what happened today, you know we can't. There is no telling which of them is working for him. Besides, I hope that Gregory can help with what he can."

"Are you sure he didn't see you? If he had, Nhoell, there is no way Jake will go down without a fight."

"I know. I know."

#

It was around 5 o'clock when we went our separate ways. Riding in the back seat as Jimmy maneuvered through traffic, I thought about Carla's last words. *He's watching you, hold off on seeing Greg.* She had me reviewing everything that happened since she flipped out on Holly at the cake tasting. Just like what Marilyn said about not having all the information, I found myself with more questions than answers. But the fact that Carla had me questioning things made me uneasy. Just a couple of days ago, she was very much for Gregory. Encouraging me to see him and to trust him. Now there she was, advising caution as I'd never seen before. So careful that what she said sounded more like a warning. A warning from my best friend, my sister. Right before me, I could see her walls breaking down. Her barriers filling with cracks. Carla was hiding something. And that "something" had to do with Jake. Whatever happened in the last day or two had opened her eyes to his world. In his world, Jake breaks down all barriers and makes the owner of those barriers succumb. She was his next target. And I couldn't allow that to happen.

After seeing Gregory in that coffee shop, I was a bit courageous. More courageous than I'd been in a long time. He gave me hope, which I hadn't had in months. He made me forget what was happening at home and turned me into the brave girl I became when we were together. The loving, reassuring way he spoke to me gave me a glimpse of his mental strength. His physical strength was apparent. But seeing Gregory's power and resilience from his accomplishments gave me my own. Though the possibility of getting caught with him weighed on me, in his presence, I lost all sense of reality. Even Jake became temporarily non-existent. So much so, that checking in after lunch with Carla slipped my mind. I was in complete euphoria. That's what Gregory did to me. That's what he'd always done to me.

Chapter 20

Back at home, the bedroom on the first floor had become my art studio. Again. My heart shuttered, and my fingers itched after walking back into the loft and seeing the canvases and bags where I'd left them. My pounding head didn't let up after leaving Carla. And the worry in my chest was tenfold. So, I decided to set up shop.

It took an hour to move everything and get set up. But the upbeat music playing over the surround sound system throughout the condo sped up time. I sat down after pouring myself a glass of wine. At first, the canvas stared at me as I stared at it, unmoving. My life, my situation. Jake's reasoning for wanting to marry me. Vince Vinitto's dead body slumped over. Carla. Keeping her from facing any more danger than she already had. Marilyn. And Gregory. What I loved about him, missed about him. How different and forward he'd become. How willing he was to help. I struggled at first with my bandaged wrist. But once my fingers coiled over the paintbrush, it's natural feel sent shivers down my spine. My heart tickled at the realization of what I was experiencing. Once I commanded the Bluetooth system to play a song, I got to work. In no time, my canvas was coming to life. So, I worked, then went through a quarter of a bottle, then worked some more.

I didn't look at the time; When I worked, there was no such thing; there was nothing but space. My space. There was no early or late. And there was never an on-time.

I engrossed myself in seas of blue and suns of gold. During those lost hours, I created a masterpiece. I looked at it and saw so many things, so many ideas, images, emotions — hate, love, regret, fear, loneliness. There wasn't one thing I could single out because what sat in front of me was more than just one thing. How people would look at it and how they would view, judge and recreate with their own mind and eyes told me that this was a masterpiece.

With a wine glass in my hand, I grinned from ear to ear as I stared at the canvas. A mix of classical and R&B instrumentals played through the house. Then, an Usher song took center stage. I moved to the rhythm, enjoying the violin solo, then the beat dropping. A warm sensation washed over me and I felt every bone in my body hum with in enjoyment. I stood up, stretched and made my way to the kitchen with the wine bottle and glass in tow. Still moving my hips to the rhythm and spinning in circles. My smile broadened at the realization. How long had it been since I last felt such a sense of accomplishment? Since I danced like a silly child in my underwear, drinking wine and painting? I didn't remember, but at that moment, I didn't care. Not even what I couldn't remember happening years ago. All I cared about was that moment. A moment of being myself. Being Nhoell Sandbrook from Atlanta, Georgia. But most importantly, it was me that brought me this happiness and it was through my art.

Before, I couldn't tell you who Nhoell Sandbrook was because I'd lost myself in Jake for what seemed like years. But that night, I found her. The woman that had been screaming for freedom and for release. That night, I released her on that canvas and found myself all over again. Yes, I was a proud woman.

In the kitchen, I set the wine bottle on the island and the glasses in the sink. My phone flashing green next to the sink stopped me before I turned back around. I stared at it, hesitant to grab it. I looked at the clock on the microwave. It was already 11:27. I had been painting for six hours. Where had the time gone? The six hours the clock said I'd been working felt more like one hour. I reached for the phone, and the sudden ringing jolted me. I relaxed when it showed Carla's name, then answered the phone, forgetting the loud music playing. I went to the panel on the wall and stopped the music.

"Carla? Hey—"

"Nhoell!? Thank god!" Carla's rattled tone knocked me to sobriety.
"What's wrong? Are you okay?"

"I should ask you that. We've been calling you!"

"We?"

"Where is your phone? Is everything okay? Are you hurt?"

"No, I'm okay, I'm fine. I've been painting. And Carla, I feel amazing. It's been so long since—"

"Have you heard from Jake?"

Something was not right. Carla asking for Jake. Carla warning me.

"Why are you asking—"

"Have you!" She screamed.

"No, I've been painting. Carla, you're scaring me what's going on? What aren't you telling me?"

"I'm sorry, I'm just worried."

I dragged the phone away from my ear and pressed a few buttons. My throat closed. Any air circulation I had was gone. I stumbled back, almost falling, but the island caught me. Jake had indeed called. From the office and his cell phone, adding the final count to thirteen. His office made nine calls. Marilyn, along with Carla had also called. I couldn't breathe. Yes, his guys were in the building and could confirm I was home the whole time. Jimmy, who could confirm he dropped me off and the bellboy, also on Jake's payroll.

"Nhoell?"

I said, my voice breaking. "I missed his call," My chest was tight, and already, tears were flooding my eyes. Thoughts of how the night would end swarmed in my mind and I couldn't think of any way out of it other than running. He wouldn't care I had been painting. It wasn't more important than being at his beck and call. I screwed up. I screwed up and got distracted.

"Nhoell, everything will be okay. I'm coming to get you," She yelled through the phone.

"No! He'll think I'm running. I will talk to him. I'll explain."

"Yes, please do." Jake's deep, steady voice encased me.

Promptly, I turned around to meet his deep gray eyes. They were as cold as the night he beat me with the belt. Detached and dark. All I could do was whisper his name. Carla called out to me, but I couldn't respond. Jake meandered to me and gently pulled the phone from my grasp and hung it up. My legs quivered, and I opened my mouth to speak but didn't.

"You didn't answer the phone?"

"I'm sorry, Jake. I didn't pick up because I was in the guest bedroom... my phone was out here." I stuttered. Already, the wine was back to running its course, and the bile turned in my stomach. Jake lifted his hand, and I flinched. Instead, he cupped my face and massaged my cheek with his thumb. His hands soft and warm against my face.

"You've been drinking, too," he added.

"Yes, I came to put the bottle away when I saw you called, I'm sorry."

"And you called that bitch instead." He gruffed, sending shutters through my chest and bile to my throat. I swallowed it back down. Jake stroked the side of my face again. How could I answer without him thinking I was lying? Changing my story would put me at higher risk. Feeling a slight grip on my face pulled me from my thoughts. Jake yanked me closer, causing my body to fall into his. I sucked in a deep breath and held it as I held the whimper coming from me, too. I just knew he was going to hit me.

"Did you hear me?"

"Yes," I answered. "Carla called me before I saw that you'd called. She said everyone had been trying to call me."

"Everyone? And?"

I hesitated. He lifted my head closer to him. Into eyes so beautiful, it was unsettling. There wasn't a hint of anger over his face, and that frightened me more.

"She asked me if you'd called," For a moment Jake glanced away and as if thinking. But within seconds, he was back to staring me down. "That's when I saw all the calls, that's when you came in."

I waited, breathing faintly.

"Have you forgotten our deal?"

"No, Jake. I haven't said a thing to anyone." My voice shaking, barely noticeable. In an instant, his other hand grabbed the back of my hair, and he pulled me in for a kiss. Wincing from his grip, I took it in as my life depended on it.

I let him lead the kiss, and I followed suit. It would've been forced if I hadn't given in. Jake nipped my bottom lip as we ravaged each other's mouth. Ignoring the sting, I kept pace. Then he bit me. I whimpered, the sounds muffled by our kiss, but I kept going. The next bite was so painful I screamed out and pulled away, then checked for blood. There wasn't any. I covered my mouth and stared at Jake, mystified and breathless.

"What's going on with you?" he asked.

"Nothing—"

He slammed his fist into the marble countertop. "You've been going off on your own, not checking in, spending more time with that bitch! Why would I call her? Do you think I need her to find you?! Do you honestly think I don't know where you are every second of the day? And now, you don't pick up your fucking phone!" With the back of his hand, he smacked me across the face. I clenched my teeth but didn't lift my hand to cover. My chest rose rapidly and my body tensed, getting ready for the next blow. If I could withstand tonight, I would be okay. I told myself. The next day will be a new day.

"Do I need to remind you where you are? Who I am? Huh?" He raised his hand again but didn't swing. Instead, he let out a low laugh.

"No. You don't. I know who you are."

He slapped me again. I bit my tongue, then a metallic taste filled my mouth. I swallowed hard.

"Then, who are you?"

My lips quivered. "… I am yours."

After the high of being on top of the world just minutes ago, I was already losing that momentum. The control I gained eased from my body into Jake's. Once again, I wasn't Nhoell Sandbrook. He took every ounce of power I gained. Ironic, I thought, how Gregory gave me strength and Jake took it. So effortlessly he knocked me down after I worked so hard to get up. Without difficulty, this man, this human being that bled like me and breathed like me had placed his foot on my throat again.

Jake moved over to stand in front of me and pushed closer, pinning my back against the island. His large hand moved to the side of my face again, rubbing the spot he'd hit. He trailed his hand around the back of my neck and caressed it, then stroked to my throat then collarbone. With his free hand, he grabbed hold of my hips and dug his fingers into my skin.

"All of you,"

Jake kissed the side of my face, and tenderly bit down then grabbed between my legs. "It's all mine."

My chest rose against him, and he pushed me further into the island. My breathing shallow and heart beating faster. He squeezed between my legs harder as the kisses on my face became rougher. Barely able to breathe, I pushed back against him, but his body pressed harder against me. I squeezed my eyes tight as his bites trailed heavier to my neck. When his grip became tighter between my legs, I finally screamed out, letting go of the island. I grabbed Jake's wrist and pushed against him and scratched at his hands. But the stinging and burning only increased by the second, and his grip only grew tighter.

"This is mine, Nhoell! You're mine! Everything that belongs to you, that was given to you, will belong to me."

Before I could cry out again, he moved his hand from the back of my neck and clasped his long fingers around my throat and squeezed. Letting go of his wrist, I used both of my hands to claw at him strangling me. My body convulsed, trying the get from underneath him and breathe air. I dug my nails into his skin but I still couldn't catch a single breath. My throat burned as the tears rolled down my face and my head grew heavy.

"That phone shouldn't leave your sight," he whispered grotesquely in my ear. "Next time I call, you better be on the other end. Do you hear me? You've been off lately. Don't forget what I can do to you," His grip tightened between my legs and around my throat. I couldn't focus on a single pain as I loosely clawed at his arms. He was about to kill me, I could feel it. My eyes cloudy, my head heavy. I thought of Greg. How could he help me get away from this man? The man who was set on destroying me.

"Whatever Carla has going on, I suggest you not get involved. I'm not done with you until you've taken my name."

That was the last thing I heard before blacking out.

Chapter 21

Carla called my name softly as she rubbed her fingers through my scalp. When I opened my eyes to see her face above me, she smiled as she mouthed a, hey.

"How are you feeling?"

I nodded my head, relieved to see her.

"You're hard-headed," I whispered, then winced from the soreness it caused. I swallowed, trying to clear my throat to speak more clearly. Even that hurt. Carla got up and fled toward the bathroom. She came back with a small glass of water and put the straw in my mouth.

"That's why I went to check on you. Because I'm hard-headed," she averted her eyes.

"How did you get in? What if he comes back and you're here?" I stammered hoarsely. I swallowed again to ease the soreness. It didn't help.

"Nhoell, you're in the hospital."

"What?" I sat up, causing pain in my back, between my thighs and up my arms from the IVs. I looked down at them as Carla eased me back down. I finally paid attention to the beeping monitor over my head.

"It's okay. You're okay."

"How did I get here?"

"Nhoell, stop talking. Your trachea is under stress after…" Carla bit down and turned her head away. The tears she tried hiding fell onto my gown and my stomach churned. "That fucking bastard. That piece of shit. I could just strangle him and see how he likes it."

"Carla? I'll be okay. Just wait."

"How long, Nhoell? How long will you wait?" She sat back down on the edge of the bed. "How long will it be til he squeezes just a little too long and kills you?" Her eyes filled with tears.

"I'm not alone in this anymore,"

"You were never alone. I've been here. When I saw you on that bed. What he did to you. I thought you were dead. I thought you were fucking dead. I could've done something to get you out long before now. I could have."

"Stop, Carla. Please. You did what you could."

"But I didn't do what I should have. You didn't have to go through this."

I lifted myself from the bed and held onto her, sobbing with her. The guilt she felt shouldn't have been hers to bear, but mine for getting her into a fucked-up situation.

#

Even though I couldn't feel much of anything, Dr. Winston suggested I stay for a day or two until the swelling subsided. Sitting in the hospital for 48 hours wasn't pleasant to hear, even if it meant being away from Jake. The last time I checked myself into a hospital, Jake pulled strings and had his men get me out. He wasn't lying when he said the hospital was his. That night, he'd done enough damage to send me right back to the emergency room. Instead, he hired a doctor to come to the condo instead.

One thing was for certain, I wasn't leaving the hospital even if I wanted to. Carla set up camp on the recliner a few feet away from me. After our emotional breakdown, we wiped away each other's tears and just laid there. After a while, she left to make a phone call and had been less tense since she returned. The television was on, and she was transfixed on the news anchor reporting the number of small businesses getting burglarized, burned down and some just closing because of gang-related activity. I watched her as she stared with her hands clasped together as if praying.

"Carla? You okay?"

"I'm fine." She turned back to the television and stared a bit longer before turning back to me. "How do you feel? Good, I hope. I'm sure they gave you a nice dose of the good shit."

"I'm okay. I'm worried Jake found the phone. I know he'll be here."

She dug through her purse, then pulled out the Nokia phone and smiled.

"Thank goodness. Where was it?"

"In your purse. And I don't think Jake will come so soon."

"What makes you say that?"

"Just a thought. It was too easy to get you here. Your watchdogs weren't blocking the door for once. But don't worry. You'll be safe soon. He won't get to you here."

"He's gotten to me any other time."

"Well, this time is different. Here. Call your guy." She handed me the phone.

It had been two days since I'd seen Gregory, and I couldn't stop thinking about when our next encounter would be. Maybe the pain relief opened my thoughts, but Gregory occupied it more than usual. Our last conversation, our "date," his touch, his smell. Everything he'd done for me over the years. I knew I wasn't marrying Jake after Gregory showed me that building. Because I was sure he wasn't leaving the city without me. Even if we didn't end up together. As much faith as I had in Gregory, I knew Jake would never let him have me, either.

Carla stepped forward and leaned over me. Her loose blouse tickled my face, and the scent of her perfume reminded me it was still her. She planted a kiss on my head, then sauntered away. Before I could protest, Carla held her hand up, gave a slight nod, then proceeded out. I stared at the phone. I could've scrolled through my contacts to speed-dial him, but instead, I pressed every single digit in his number. Gregory answered in a low, hushed tone.

"Are you okay?"

His voice unsteady and the slight whistle coming through the phone let me know he was on the move. Just hearing his heavy breaths made my heart skip a beat.

"I'm in the hospital," I whispered.

"I know," His anger shot through the phone. "Did you call the police?"

"How did you know?"

"He isn't the only one with eyes on you, Nhoell. Did you call the police?" He asked again.

"I'm okay. A few scratches."

I lied. But telling him that was better than telling him the gruesome truth about how Jake degraded me. How he scarred my womanhood.

"Did I catch you at a bad time?"

"No, just a meeting. What happened?"

"I started painting again, Greg," I laid back in the bed and smiled at the thought of the piece I'd just finished. "It's been so long since I picked up a paintbrush."

Still silent on the other end. His breathing slowed, and the whistling stopped.

I continued. "But seeing you helped a lot. It's like you came back into my life at the right time. Then you offered your help, not knowing who you were up against."

"Nhoell."

"I didn't answer my phone last night. I lost track of time painting."

"It's my fault. I should've—"

"—how can it be your fault?" the line grew silent for a few seconds. "I'm okay Greg, I'm telling you I'm okay," I caught my voice shaking. "I think he may be on to us."

The door opened and a doctor came in with Carla fast on his heels. Once he looked up from the clipboard and smiled at me, my stomach soured. Dr. Jegsty, the only doctor who treated me every time I ended up in the hospital after a beating. I yanked the phone from my ear, stuffed it quickly underneath my leg , then sat up. He walked over to me at his usual fast pace.

"Mrs. Vaughn? How are you feeling?" He asked, his brows furrowing and face softening.

Dr. Jegsty was probably in his mid-fifties, but his hair showed no signs of graying. He was tall and slender with a clean-cut beard. But his entire presence made me uncomfortable. When he talked, his hands always fidgeted with something in his pocket. I didn't think there was ever anything inside, but if his hands weren't writing on the clipboard, that's where they were. Apart from his blatant lack of interest to help whenever I'd ended up in his care, the obvious fact that he was on Jake's payroll and my life was always in their hands made me close my mouth whenever he appeared.

"I... I'm okay."

My voice shook from the reality check before me. Jake was around, even when he wasn't.

"Of course, she's okay. She's been seen and treated by her doctor," Carla exclaimed with authority, moving to the opposite side of the bed to face Dr. Jegsty.

"I understand that. Since I know Mrs. Vaughn's history, it's best if I check for any abnormalities."

"Abnormalities? Every time she came to this shitty hospital, there were abnormalities!"

"Carla, please," I replied, barely able to speak above them.

"What makes you think today would be any different? As I said, she has been treated by Dr. Winston."

As if on cue, the silver-haired Dr. Winston that treated me earlier walked in. He looked as calm as he did when I first arrived. Only this time, he looked better. He strolled over and stood at the foot of my bed and smiled.

"How are you, Nhoell?"

The concern was genuine. He waited for my response and for some reason, I couldn't take my eyes off him. Even in those circumstances, I felt more relaxed with him patiently standing there waiting for me. That's when I realized Dr. Winston was indeed a man of his profession. Helping people, saving their lives, making them smile when there wasn't a thing to smile about and providing a sense of trust. He embodied a quality that many people didn't. It was his kindness that made me feel comfortable and unafraid. I let my lips part and spoke.

"I wasn't okay, but now I am. Thank you, Dr. Winston."

"I'm glad."

"Doctor," I turned back to Dr. Jegsty. "they have admitted me under your care countless times. I did not receive proper care any of those instances. Even going as far as discharging me mere hours after admittance, most times, under unthinkable conditions. You do not protect me as your patient. I'm sorry, but you are no longer my doctor."

When the phone in my hand became sweaty, I fumbled with it until I was sure it hung up. I had already lied to Greg about my condition; having him hear just the opposite could cause more harm than good.

"You cannot make that call. They appointed your primary doctor, and until your husband says otherwise, I will continue to provide treatment." Dr. Jegsty stood sternly, but it was Dr. Winston who took one step forward.

"Dr. Jegsty, I'm afraid you have me confused. Only a few days ago, they appointed me the overseer of this hospital. Due to... well, a few complaints. The hospital's questionable treatments, the rise in deaths during operation, and a few disputes with law enforcement.

"You have failed over and again to follow proper protocol when dealing with your patients and your staff. A prime example is Ms. Sandbrook, whose been here more than half a dozen times in a the last few months. Each time, you failed to follow protocol in a situation like hers. Mr. Jegsty, you should be fired."

"How dare you!"

Watching from the bed, they surrounded me in all three directions. Carla's phone rang, making things more awkward. She ignored the call.

"I will have your job for this. This is still my hospital!" He tossed the file on the bed and stormed out of the room. I watched the door, waiting for it to open again. Waiting to see Lee or Jimmy because I knew they were coming. If Jake didn't know I was in the hospital, he was about to find out. Carla's phone rang again. Mouthing "Sorry," she was out the door as fast as Dr. Jegsty. I didn't know what to do next. On top of that, the only person that could help me was Carla. And it was at the price of her business.

"Ms. Sandbrook?" Dr. Winston spoke up softly.

"Thank you, Dr. Winston." I kept my head down and fondled with my fingers. My time alone was limited, and I still hadn't spoken to Greg for more than a minute. Jake was on his way, and things were getting worse.

"He'll send someone. He'll take me again."

Chapter 22

Carla was back fifteen minutes later. A nervous smile replaced the troubled one she wore when she got the call. She walked past my bed to the lounger with her phone still clutched in her hands. Nothing usually startled, scared, or even made her nervous. But the woman that sat before me was a nervous wreck. She stared off more than twice and kept her eyes averted to the TV, not taking a single glance in my direction. Her mind wasn't in the room, and for the first time today, it wasn't on me. Her fingers worked fast across her phone screen. Carla had her own life, her own problems, and probably things to deal with. The number of phone calls she stepped outside to make confirmed it. But here she was, in the hospital, putting her problems on hold to deal with mine. The unrecognizable look on her face tugged at the pit of my stomach.

"Carla?"

"Hey," A weary smile tugged at her lips.

"I'm sorry," I said as clearly as I could. "You have so much going on, and yet, you're here."

She finally gave me an honest smile as she stood and came closer to me.

"There is nowhere else I need to be."

I took in the scent of her perfume again. I needed her. She was the only person in my life that kept me above water when I was too weak to swim. At every step and every turn I made since meeting her, she stood by my side. I loved her more, knowing she was willing to stand by my side against Jake. And because I loved her, it ached my heart I was still pulling her down with me. I trusted that Greg could help me, but there was still a part of me that didn't believe it possible. Not after what I witnessed.

"You should be taking care of yourself. Your business."

"That, I do well. But right now, someone needs to take care of you. I'm okay, and so is my business."

"Is it? Is your business okay? I've seen you. These past few hours, these past few days. Carla, I'm not okay, and neither are you. Talk to me. What's happening?"

She paused as if trying to search for the right words. Then exhaled and took her seat back on the lounger. Her head hung low and her hands clutched her phone.

"Carla? Talk to me."

"I'm sorry," She shook her head. "I'm sorry, Nhoell."

"What's going on?"

"Jake. He's been following me."

"Jake?" I said, confused at mistaking her fear for guilt.

"Not Jake, but he has people following me." She took a deep breath. "I'm not stupid. I figured it out after the cake tasting. Those goddamn idiots. I've been taught a few things." She lowered her head, almost as if she was more disappointed at herself than at the people following her.

"We knew that. You are the closest thing to me. Of course you'd be followed."

That, I knew very well from the random threats Jake sent my way to remind me of how easily he could take her out.

"And, I met with Gregory, Nhoell. I met him to talk about you. I didn't think... I figured Jake's guys would probably think it was just a date or some random person I was meeting."

My eyes stretched wide and my stomach felt like it caved in as everything connected like a jigsaw puzzle. Her behavior over the past couple of days, the guilt-ridden look she had been given me. Her warning. I knew there was something wrong. But I never would've imagined that. It put me on an even higher alert because if there was a possibility that Jake followed Carla's dates, I was screwed.

"Did they say anything? Or do anything?"

"No, they didn't say anything. But the fact that you know me and I'm seen with him while they're following me. That isn't good, at all. I'm sure that could start some shit. I mean major shit."

When she lowered her head, I hated it. I hated to see her so afraid that she had to walk on seashells around me. It was all because of Jake. But I wasn't going to let her get consumed in his world. I couldn't.

"How could they know what you were meeting him for?"

"I know that, but—"

"—but nothing. Don't blame yourself."

"It's not a coincidence you're in here." She blurted.

"I know. It's his way of showing me what he can do to me. Don't feel guilty about it. The fault is Jake's, not yours."

#

Another excruciating hour passed, and Jake still hadn't sent anyone to collect me. I struggled to keep my lids open while the pain medication from the IVs provided much needed relief. It didn't provide mental relief, though. Each time the door opened to my room, my blood pressure spiked. Finding out about Carla's lunch meeting didn't help ease my worries either. Neither did her continued silence and the light circles that formed around her eyes. She'd gone in and out of the room, taking one phone call after another. But still sat with her hands clasped in her lap and back rigid, like she was waiting for something. As much as I wanted her to stay and keep me company, I saw the weariness in her eyes. Once she dozed off, I'd finally sent her home to rest. I dozed off a short while later.

Later turned into two hours when the slamming of the door woke me. I sat up, my eyes cloudy from sleep and the pain meds no longer protecting me. That agony disappeared as fast as it had come when I saw Jimmy charging towards me. His face twisted in a grimace and teeth seething. His stride across the room forced the air to reach me before he did. Every part of the room blurred around me and the thought of having a bad dream crossed my mind because Jimmy had never looked at me with intent to kill. When he reached me and grabbed my arm, yanking me up to him, my thought of dreaming vanished. His face was inches from mine, his breath warm and nose flaring. His teeth clenched tight, as was his fist.

No doctor, police or lover could save me from Jake. Not with all of them at his disposal. I was his, and no one else in the world could tell him otherwise.

"Did you think he wouldn't be able to get to you? I won't pay for your mistake. Com'on." He yanked me from the hospital bed and my feet hit the floor and quaked beneath me. I was falling when Jimmy's grip on my arm caught me. It snapped like it was snatched from its socket and I screamed out in pain.

"Jimmy, Please!" I shrieked.

"Who the hell is Jimmy! Com'on, let's go!"

"No!"

My vision grayed, and the hospital room faded into a distant haze. A twin-size bed with a pink bunny comforter replaced the hospital bed. I looked at Jimmy, my arm still in his grip, but it wasn't Jimmy that stared back at me. A broad, dark figure, smelling of cigarettes and alcohol loomed above. My chest and throat burned like hot liquid oozing down my esophagus into my lungs. Then the room tremored and a gush of wind surrounded me, sending goosebumps down my body. When I opened my eyes, an officer stood in the doorway with his gun drawn at the dark figure. He yelled, but I couldn't hear his voice. My chest rumbled harder, burning hotter. I realized it was me screaming that caused the burning in my throat and rumble in my chest. I commanded myself to stop, but like my dreams, I had no control of myself.

A sharp pain shot through my head, and a thick, seeded fear hit me. A monster. My vision grayed again, then the cold hard floor was suddenly against my face. Jimmy's combat boots walked away from me and Doctor Winston appeared. My chest still burning as I watched him pull a needle from his pocket. It disappeared from my peripheral and almost immediately, my chest loosened, my body felt lighter and darkness consumed me.

Chapter 23

I followed the harmony of his voice through the darkness. I followed the harmony of all their voices. The road warmed underneath my feet and the trees appeared along the sides. Flashing lights ahead, my arms pumped faster. He spoke to me. His voice stood out from the rest, and his face came into view. I ran harder, breathing better. I was tired, but I was almost there. He called my name again. Greg, I whispered back to him. My face warmed, and the pain evaporated, taking the weariness with it. He'd disappeared. Then the roads and the trees vanished with him. My eyes fluttered open and Greg stood, leaning over me. His eyes glazed from tears he must've wiped away. He was with me. In the hospital or in my dreams. Either way, my heart warmed at the sight of him. I never thought I'd be owned by a man and begging another to save me. My mama taught me many things. One of them was not making myself into an object to be kept. Throughout college, I remembered and took heed to her words. But I loved this man, and I needed his help. Kept or not.

"You're here."

Gregory put his strong, warm hand on the side of my head and stroked my brow. I turned into his hand, feeling more of his soft warmth. He tenderly squeezed me and placed a long kiss on my forehead, sending tingling sensations through my veins. When he lifted his head, tears already filled my eyes, trailing my cheeks. He wiped them away.

"I'm here."

"Greg?"

"Yeah?"

"Don't leave."

"I won't."

#

"Fourteen hours?" I exclaimed, sounding better than the day before. Warm throat compressions and no stress from yelling for fourteen hours made a difference. Gregory sat at the bottom of the bed in ash gray jeans and a black t-shirt, his black boots propped on a chair.

"For the majority of fourteen hours. I took a thirty-minute lunch. I didn't want you to wake up alone. Not after they told me what happened." Facing the room door, he clenched his jaw then rubbed his hands together. "I should've been here."

"Greg?" he looked at me. "Thank you for being here now. If you'd been here, things might have been worse."

"Maybe, but he wouldn't have had the chance to enter that room." There was a brief silence between us.

"What's going to happen now? He knows I've been talking to you."

"He doesn't know. If he did, we'd be face to face by now."

"They're watching Carla. He knows, if he doesn't, he will soon," Gregory stared at me, then lowered his head. "She told me."

"I should have told you myself, Nhoell. When I came here on business, I didn't expect to find you. After meeting with Carla and finding out about him, I knew if I told you, you wouldn't want my help."

"Telling me you'd met up with her wouldn't have changed anything. It was about him finding out before we could get away," I hesitated. "When that guy came last night, the look in his eyes."

His head tilted and brows furrowed, Gregory asked, "What did he say?"

"I don't remember," I rested my head back and exhaled. "I

remember little of anything after he came in. But they'll be back. He won't stop until I'm back. The things I've seen... the people he knows."

"When they come, they won't be able to get through those doors. I have a few friends too, Nhoell. And I know exactly who I'm dealing with," He touched my leg hidden underneath the light white blanket while goosebumps ran up my arm. "I've arranged for you to stay here. There will be officers outside at all times, and they'll move you to another location at every shift change."

"What? I can't stay here," I replied in alarm. "He's coming. He'll come back. Those officers are probably his. They've never helped me in all the times I asked! Take me now. Why can't you take me now?" My heart rate spiked on the monitor.

"Because it wouldn't be safe," he reasoned, easing closer to me on the bed then grabbing my hand.

"I'm not safe now! Neither is Carla! If you take me now, Carla will fly home and be safe, too."

"Listen, Nhoell, I can get us out of here now. Right now. But he would be on us before we reach the airport. Even if we manage to get you somewhere safe, he'd look for you." He cupped my face and rubbed his thumb across my cheek. "I don't want you looking over your shoulder wondering if he's watching. Or afraid to live. If I take you now without finishing, that's how it'll be."

"Finish what? I can help, just don't leave me out of the plan. Don't leave me here."

He wiped away the tears that escaped my eyes.

"I've seen the things he's done to this city... to the people. He isn't working alone, and he has allies everywhere... enemies too." Greg surprised me by climbing to the top of the bed next to me. When he laid down and pulled me into his chest, I melted. He rested his chin on my head as I inhaled his scent deeply. My heart skipped a beat, and the monitor spiked. I wondered if he knew. Knew that I was still head over heels for him.

"I need to make sure he goes down for everything he's done. I can't have you in the middle of it when that happens. I need you safe,

Nhoell. So much time between us. You don't know the things I've done or the type of man I am. I have my demons too," He nestled his face in my head again. "You've been through so much. Protecting your friend, yourself. You survived. You've been so strong to hold on this long... but I'm here now and Baby, I need you to trust me. Just trust me."

I nodded, wrapping my arms around him, feeling his fullness near me. His words sent vibrations rippling through me. The confidence Gregory excreted, the truth in his words, had my heart crashing into my chest. He squeezed me tighter. I knew he'd felt it too.

"Only three days?" I asked, still muffled in his chest.

"Yes, that's all I need."

Greg leaned in, kissed my lips, stirring up the intense feelings rushing through me. Heat rose from my body. From the faint smile that cut across his lips, he felt every wave I emitted. It felt like a lifetime since his lips touched mine. But the drumming of my heart took me back through a series of our childhood kisses. I returned his kiss and fell deeper into whatever fantasyland he had taken me to. His hand tightened around my waist, and my heart pounded, my fingers and toes tickled, and if I weren't numb, I was sure I would've felt throbbing in my panties. Greg pulled away but kept his hand around my waist. At that moment, I didn't care what had transpired in the past between us. The man that lay next to me was far from the boy that broke my heart. I lost so much the day I learned I was pregnant. I was sure I gained most of that back when I bumped into Gregory.

Chapter 24

I didn't sleep comfortably through the first night after Gregory left. Every little movement from behind the closed doors startled me. Every muffled voice that rang through the doors and walls made me stare at them until my eyes stung. Three times, I called the nurse. She was one of three nurses allowed entry to my room, courtesy of Dr. Winston. The nurse, Andrea, pronounced Un-dreEE-ah, always answered, walking into my room with a smile plastered on her face. Rather than retreating after realizing, yet again, that I didn't need a thing, she would sit and talk with me for ten minutes or so. I listened to her talk about her husband, her two little boys, and singing. She sat in the chair and told me about the acting classes she took and how it became unaffordable after having her boys. Still, she spoke with bright eyes and energy so strong, my worries went away when she was with me. The soft, melodic voice she spoke in put me at ease all hours of the night. Ultimately, I would drift off and wake up on the opposite side of the hospital to another nurse rolling in the loud metal cart.

Around three o'clock, Carla finally stopped by. She'd called four times that morning to check on me and each time promised to stop by once she finished with business. My eyes lit up like fireworks when she walked through the door. Her hair was nicely done and make-up flawless. The hip-hugging jeans and low-collar blouse merged into one as she gracefully crossed the room. Her Bluetooth blinked a steady blue light against her ear and I beamed at her stunning presence, then thanked God. Carla reached out, giving me a tight squeeze and a light kiss on the forehead. She stood back to look at me, then gave me another hug.

"Feeling any better?" She sat on the edge of my bed, placing her purse on the foot. Maneuvering her feet, she kicked off her shoes and pulled her legs up to get comfortable.

"I could be better. But I'm okay. They said I'm healing well. You look good, Carla."

"So do you."

I gave her a blank stare. I hadn't washed apart from the routine of changing the bandages. My hair was a mess, and I was sure the bags under my eyes were darkening from lack of sleep.

"Don't do that to yourself. You look a whole lot better than you did yesterday."

"That's true," I shifted the conversation. "So, how are things at work?"

"Pretty good. I told you it wouldn't be a problem. My brother is in town. He's been looking into a few things for me. Now he's coming to clean it up."

"Wait, what? You actually called?" I whispered.

She whispered, "Yeah."

"Well, I'm glad. I hope they'll drop the fine. How long will he be in town?"

"I'm not sure yet. Probably however long it takes. They rarely hear from me, so when I requested a favor, well let's just say he was here in under an hour."

I chuckled, feeling an extra few pounds of worry leave my shoulder.

"How did you find the room, anyway?"

"I went to your old room, freaked out when I didn't see you," She lowered her head. "I thought he came and took you. After calling around a few times, they showed me where you were." A mischievous smile crept across her lips as she looked at me. "Evidently there's a guest list to see your ass. I take it Mr. Rehevas took care of that?" She pulled at my toes, tickling me.

I blushed, then bowed my head. "I guess so,"

"I wonder what he does to pull strings like that. I doubt he's just an architect," she mused. "I saw at least five officers standing in the halls when I came up here. Looking all sexy and manly and shit." She rubbed all over her body in exaggeration with her head held back as she kissed the air. I burst into tears laughing as she went on and on, eventually laughing with me.

"I love you, Nhoell." I stopped laughing and looked at her serious tight features. "I am truly grateful... so grateful you are my friend. We'll get through this just like everything else. Do you hear me? Don't just sit there like a platypus."

I burst into laughter, covering my mouth to keep mucus from coming out my nose.

"And now you want to blow snot on me? After I just seriously poured my heart out to you."

We both laughed until we could no longer take it. After a while, she left to pick up something to eat, then ate dinner in bed with me. I used her computer to do some much-needed research of my own. My business, which indeed had been soaring, but the work showcased in recent months differed from my own. I cringed at the amazing reviews that weren't for me, then moved on to search countless public record databases. My aim? The Vaughn family. Jake's father, Andrew Vaughn, started Vaughn Inc. while still in college and his grandfather had been a real estate broker. Around that same time, Andrew married Nora Fairwell. Nora came from a prominent black family that held major ties in the church. Magazines and newspapers from different parts of the country and a few from other parts of the world described them as angels of God. Over eighty years, they donated billions of dollars to families in need, sent children of color to college, and reduced the homelessness in the districts their churches resided. Nora's great grandmother founded the Prestigious Women of New York, a group dedicated to working alongside the churches the family owned. Then in the early nineties, a few bad investments left both the Fairwell's and Jake's grandfather bankrupt. After trying to dig deeper into those bad investments and having no luck, I left it at that. The last article I read pertained to Andrew Vaughn's premature death and all he had accomplished over his years. Everything that came after was redundancies, and none of it was useful. But if I knew anything, it was that the real scandals wouldn't be on the internet.

#

The next day I found myself in the radiology area. Dr. Winston granted me permission to move around the room. So I sat on the windowsill above the small bed-like couch. Even with the few books, magazines and iPod that Andrea loaned me. I sat there for an hour staring out the window at the cars speeding by and people moving about. No sooner than I began to relax, a commotion from the hall stole my attention. I looked at the door, keeping my place on the windowsill. I strained to listen, but the multiple voices made it difficult to hear the people involved. Truly, Jimmy or Lee's voice was the only two I was listening for. The commotion grew louder, and I stood from the window, all the while keeping my eyes on the door. I jumped back from a loud bang that shook the wall. One quick scan around the room showed only a window that wouldn't allow me to escape alive, and no other door in the room gave me a way out. I squeezed my eyes shut, took multiple deep breaths and counted to ten. One more day. That was all I needed. Reopening my eyes, I stood as tall as my legs would allow me, balled my fist and took one last deep breath. I exhaled just as the door flew open. For a moment I saw no one, but then two cops moved quickly into my room with their backs facing me and guns drawn. At the other end of the guns was Jake, walking toward them, pushing them back as if he marched with an army. My eyes widened and I moved back a few steps, nearly falling onto the bed. Seeing his heavy frame enter the room, I tried to remember to breathe. Jake was smart. Yeah, why not walk through the doors himself to make his presence known. In all honesty though, his presence threw me off balance.

Out of all people, Jake was the last person I expected to come. He never had to. Now that we were face to face, the police were no longer an issue to him. His confidant demeanor turned my stomach. As they yelled for him to step back and leave the room, he trained his eyes on me. In one intense look, he made it seem as if we were the only two in the room. The darkness that came with him showed nothing but my death at his hands. I couldn't go back. Though my legs felt weak, I stood tall. He may have gained entrance, I thought, but I trusted Gregory to protect me. Past him, two other officers held their guns drawn at his back. All I had to do was stand my ground.

Jake's mouth moved, but I heard nothing other than the police yelling. He spoke again, almost in a whisper. Then I heard it.

"Nhoell, it's time to leave." His voice was steady, even with the amount of danger that surrounded him.

I shook my head then flash of surprise crossed his face but disappeared just as quickly.

"Nhoell—"

The officers' yelling drowned out the rest of his words again. He took another step forward, and the officers instantly followed by moving a step toward him. Seeing them make that move, I took another steady breath, then straightened my spine and raised my head. I had to trust in Gregory.

"No, Jake." My voice carried through the room when I finally spoke, quieting everyone. "I'm not going back with you. I'm done. Please, just leave."

"Nhoell, I don't think you understand."

"Jake, I understand well. I don't know what you want. But I will not leave this room, and I will not marry you. You can keep what you took from me. Just leave and no one will get hurt."

"You are right about one thing, No one needs to get hurt. Not even Ryan."

"Mr. Vaughn, she's expressed to you she will not leave. Please step back, sir!" one officer said.

Ryan? I didn't know a Ryan and Jake knew that. His lips curved in a wicked grin at my confusion. His unexpected retreat drew in even more suspicion. Ryan. Who was Ryan? Jake took another step back, and the police slowly followed.

"That's right, Mr. Vaughn. Slowly," the same officer said.

I stood, still staring Jake down, watching him leave. Was he really retreating? I could almost feel the relief in my heart. Just one more day, I told myself. That's all I needed. Ryan! Jake stopped mid-step and smirked.

"No," I whispered to myself. Not Ryan. All because I enjoyed his wife's company, my devoted nurse. "No." I shook my head in disbelief, feeling all my emotions in the pit of my stomach.

"I'm sorry, did you say something, Nhoell?" Jake asked.

"Keep moving, Mr. Vaughn!" the officer ordered.

"Once I leave this room, it's over, and you know it."

I knew it. I wish I didn't. All I imagined was the same gruesome death as Vince Vinitto.

"Mr. Vaughn, that's enough making threats."

"These are no threats, Nhoell. I will let you have the honor of explaining." Jake turned and walked away.

"Wait!" My heart raced and my head pulsed. I stopped asking myself 'how I get in this deep' a long time ago. Finally, an opportunity to walk away presented itself, but my only thoughts were on the bloodshed of a husband. A father. On my hands. Andrea was a beautiful, kind and just an all-around great woman. She was great to me. What would she think of me? I couldn't face her, to tell her that her husband died because of me, because I wanted to leave Jake.

"I'll get my things."

"Ms. Sandbrook?" one officer called out. "We understand what he is doing. If there is someone he's threatening, we can help you and them. But we cannot allow you to leave this room."

"For the record, I'm not threatening anyone. Officers, she has decided. You wouldn't want to hold her against her will, would you?" Jake stated plainly.

"Now, that's enough! Back up or we're going to apprehend you!"

another officer yelled out.

"Please go ahead, and that'll be another lawsuit against you. I've committed no crime. Officer, Gentry, is it? Wouldn't happen to be James Gentry?"

The officer's face distorted and his muscles flexed underneath his uniform.

"Now, she has asked to leave. Allow her to do so." Jake's rose with each word.

"Please," I spoke again. "Officers, I have agreed to leave. I checked myself in, and I am under no obligation to stay. No one needs to get hurt."

"I'm sorry, we can't allow you to leave."

"Yes you can!"

"Ms. Sand—"

I yelled out, "Enough," my voice trembling, struggling to hold it together.

By this time, my ears were ringing, the muscles in my face ached, and I could see the two officers behind Jake staring at me, pleading with me. My eyes welled with tears as I stared at them head down. I glanced between three of them and saw wedding rings on two of their fingers. Did they have children too? My chest ached as I squeezed my eyes. It became clear to me that the reputation of the company was not a worry. How far would Jake go to keep me? I was terrified of that answer.

"I'm leaving," I walked to the other side of the bed and gathered my things. "If you do not mind, I need to get dressed, unless you care to watch."

"Ms. Sandbrook—"

"Please, I want to leave. Send in the nurse." I stared at Jake's accomplished smile, then reached up and undid the top of the nightgown. Before turning my back to him, I gave him the angriest glare I could muster. I didn't care about the consequences; I knew what they were. I also knew that I couldn't let innocent people die. As the gown dropped, I heard the door shut behind me. I finally sat on the bed and let out a long breath. I wouldn't cry. Not now, not anymore. A few moments later, the door opened again.

"Nhoell? What's going on? Why are you leaving?" Andrea rushed to me.

"I have to." I kept dressing, gathering the few items I had.

"You don't have to go with him."

"Call your husband, Andrea. Call him now."

"Ryan? Why?" she questioned.

"Just check on him, please." I put on my shoes, then opened the drawer next to the bed. I grabbed my phone and dialed out Gregory's number. The call didn't go through. I was sure being in the radiology area had nothing to do with it. I stuck it in one of the pockets in my purse. Andrea was already listening to the voicemail of her husband's number.

"He's not picking up. Nhoell, what's going on?"

"Andrea, you have such a beautiful spirit. You made my stay here comfortable and safe. I befriended you and that was my mistake." I picked up my purse and gave her a hug.

"Keep checking on Ryan. Stay safe."

Chapter 25

The car ride back to the condo was quiet. Except for a phone call he made telling the person on the other end to release him. I assumed *him* was Ryan. I sat as close to the door as possible, remaining firm. At the hospital, the officers followed us from the room to the waiting car like watchdogs. Two of them pulled me to the side, pleaded with me to stay, and tried to get information on the other person involved. My only concern, though, was Ryan, Andrea, and their kids.

Walking back into the condo, I braced for a blow to the head as I walked ahead of him. But it didn't come. Standing at the edge of the living room facing the cityscape, I dreaded the memories that surfaced. Even the clean smell that housekeeping left behind daily annoyed me. From behind, Jake came up and pressed his body against mine, moving his hands around my waist.

"Welcome home, Nhoell. You almost got away from me." He massaged my hips as he leaned down my neck and spoke. I stood still, listening, staring out at the dark sky. "But what I find most interesting are the things I must do now, to get to you. It should never be that difficult, sweetheart."

He wrapped his arms around my stomach, yanking me closer, pressing me deeper into his body. I shuddered from the trail of kisses he laid on my neck and turned away once he reached my face. Jake spun me around and I braced myself for the first hit. Instead, he grabbed the back of my neck and pulled me in for a hard, angry kiss. I didn't return it, not this time. Not after feeling Greg's lips on mine. Feeling my reluctance, Jake pulled away.

"Nhoell, you belong to me. Understand? Luckily, I've found another use for you." He kissed me again. "I'm not done with you yet. Not yet, sweetheart." He smirked, then brushed a finger smoothly down my lips, then walked away from me. "My mother will be here later to check on you, seeing as they weren't allowed entrance to the hospital. You will be my wife, Nhoell. One way or another."

"Why? Why do you want to marry me? Why are you doing this?" He stopped and turned around slightly.

"You don't know? As brilliant as you are, I thought you would have figured that out already. I actually enjoy you, Nhoell. I wouldn't be the first to make such a mistake. But at least I understand now. Also, I would never let a key witness get away." The door slammed shut.

I watched the hall for a few more moments. In disbelief that he knew I witnessed the killing. Still, he hadn't said or done a single thing about it. And to believe that tearing me down was enjoyable was disgusting. Pulling my gaze away from the door, I sat my purse on the living room table and dug for my phone. I pressed a few buttons and dialed Gregory's number. It didn't ring. I dialed his number again. Still no service. Standing in a rush, I took three long strides to the window and dialed again. Nothing. I tried Carla, my mom, even Nora. None of my calls went through. I raced to the bedroom, feeling a tinge of pain between my legs. Ignoring it, I grabbed my laptop from under the nightstand. While it booted up, I changed into sweatpants, tennis shoes, and a loose tank top. After waiting restlessly for the computer to load, I checked for a connection. As I suspected, no internet. Running back downstairs, I grabbed my purse and headed for the door. An armed man in all black cargo pants, fitted shirt, and combat boots stood blocking my path. He stood like a combatant tank with his holsters, clips, and knife on his waist. Yeah, he was nothing like Jimmy or Lee. He wouldn't be easy to dodge.

"Is there a problem?" he growled.

"No. I'm going for a walk."

"Orders are clear; you're not to leave the premises."

"You can't keep me here."

"I'm not incompetent like the last two idiots that fucked up."

"What amount of money would possess you people to go along with this?" I gritted.

"It's not about the money," he chuckled. "Get back inside and close the door. Let's make this easy on all of us." I slammed the door.

Jake had blocked all access to the outside world, caging me in. Yeah, the Dwayne Johnson size man was nothing like Lee or Jimmy.

#

An hour went by, and just as Jake promised, Nora, Holly, and Marilyn walked through the door. With her nose flared and raised to the ceiling, Nora walked through the hall into the living room. Beads of sweat graced her forehead and the coloring in her once bronze complexion paled. Nora stood over me with her hands clasped in front of her as I sat on the couch looking up. She looked at me with that no-nonsense attitude all moms had. Behind her stood Holly with a disapproving glare and Marilyn approaching. She sat on the couch opposite me with pity written all over her face as the other two remained standing. I placed the glass of juice I'd been holding on the table, then stood up to face Nora. All the respect my mama taught me to show my elders, I withdrew.

"Do you know what you put my son through? All he has done to get you out of that hospital?"

Her tired voice made me almost feel sorry for her.

"I needed to be in the hospital after what your son did to me," I said.

"You look fine to me!" Holly yelled out.

"Trust me, I'm better than the condition he left me in,"

"Enough!" Nora snapped and stared daggers at me. "It's you that makes him like this. And what he has planned, I have no idea anymore. You'll find out that this has nothing to do with you. You're just in the way."

"In the way of what? If you want something, how about asking for it first?" I retorted.

"I knew getting engaged to you would be a mistake. But the satisfaction you will finally bring him… I thank you for giving my son… his happiness." She gave me a sly smile before raising her chin higher and turning to walk away.

"Answer me, Nora!"

"Don't dare raise your voice to my mother!" Holly yelled back.

"Holly, I am exhausted from the sound of you. I have nothing else to lose, so I suggest you shut the hell up."

"Two days," Nora said. Holly grinned with her hand on her hips. "There will be a private ceremony in two days. Now, what were you saying about having nothing to lose? Does that include your life? The life of your friend? Have you forgotten how easy it is to take one?"

From the corner of my eye, Marilyn rose from the couch, startling me with her quick movement.

"Is there a problem, Marilyn?" Nora asked plainly.

"No," she whispered.

I stared down at Holly's smug face with my jaws clenched and fist balled, ready for battle. Marilyn looked ready as well. Her eyes bore deep into Nora and her chest rose steadily. It reminded me of the glare she'd given Jake the night of the gala.

"Good." Nora stated coolly.

"What about my mom? She's expecting to attend."

"Is she?" Holly hissed. "Even if that's true, when my mother says private, that is what she means."

"If you all honestly think that I will marry that man, you have another thing coming."

"I want you to remember one thing, Nhoell. It was my son that saved your life. Are you bold enough to ask me from who?"

She waited for me to respond. I didn't. Just like that, Nora and Holly left, as Marilyn strolled slowly behind, keeping a watchful eye on me until she was out of sight.

I fell back and sat almost statue-like on the couch with my hands clasped together. I took a few deep breaths, counted and allowed my shoulders to ease while I recalled the words that left Nora's mouth from the time she walked in until she left. It was clear that she was the one who'd sought me out. The one who had been pulling the strings. I grabbed the glass and walked it to the kitchen. My mind still consumed with the fact that Nora tried to have me killed. Not only that, there was something Jake was after, too. Like Marilyn said that day, he didn't just pull me from his mother's grasp because he cared. No, that wasn't it.

It was the stack of papers in the sink that pulled me from my thoughts. I stared at them for a moment, wondering why they were there. Picking them up from the sink, I slammed them back down on the island and rolled my eyes in disgust. Since I'd come back, I avoided the kitchen as much as I could. But standing in that same spot gave me an unpleasant vision from a few nights ago. I shivered, then took a step back and eyed the hidden trashcan compartment. Turning back to the reports, I grabbed them, opened the drawer and tossed them in. They stared back at me as I waited to close the drawer and get rid of them. But I couldn't. I couldn't break the feeling of needing to go through them. Because they were in the damn kitchen. I picked up the reports from the trash can and reviewed the first page. Then the second. In quick sporadic movements, I flipped through a few more pages, took them to the living room and laid them out. I'd gone through enough of Jake's reports to know what to look for. Surprisingly, there wasn't a single thing to change. Not in the first stack of papers Nora gave me. Or was it Holly that left them there? As I continued to comb through the documents, I got a sense of familiarity. I had already corrected the reports lying on the table. Not this version, but another. I recognized all the number sequences and patterns from months ago. And the next couple of pages were of another report I'd corrected before, as well. What I found to be especially odd were the dates. Although all the documents were correct, the dates differed from the versions given to me over the past few months. Many of the reports in my hands were from two to fifteen years ago. I couldn't fathom why Jake had me correcting financial reports. Especially when they were perfectly done.

Instead of stopping, I continued to run the calculations until finally leaning back against the couch some fifteen minutes later. All the work I did over the past few months was for nothing. Even so, the work that laid in front of me wasn't my own, but someone else's. I put the papers back in order and started from the beginning, looking for any inconsistencies from the documents given to me before. The only thing that stood out was the letters "MV" in the bottom corner of the page. I flipped through them again, looking at the first and last page of each document. Sure enough, "MV" was at the bottom pages of each report. There was no doubt it was Marilyn. I was sure of it.

Chapter 26

It was Marilyn that came back a couple of hours later and called out to me. I'd come downstairs to find her in the living room and the Dwayne Johnson-like guard at the entrance hall waiting. I looked around for Nora or Holly.

"Can you give us a minute?" Marilyn said to the guard.

"Not going to happen." He leaned against the wall, his arms crossed.

"Seriously, where can she go?"

"It isn't her I'm keeping an eye on right now."

Marilyn rolled her eyes, grabbed my hand, and my heart fluttered as she pulled me to the large window on the other side of the room. I looked back at the guard still holding his ground.

"I'm sorry," Marilyn spoke in a hushed tone. "For everything you're going through. That we have put you through. It is so much you don't understand. The reason he wants to marry you." She whispered.

"Why?" I stumbled over my words. "Did you find anything?"

"It's too much of a story to tell with him nearby. Jake, he's horrible, but Nora, she can be far worse. She'll realize I'm not where I'm supposed to be."

"Nora? Why do you call her-"

"She isn't my mother. My mother died giving birth to me," I could hear the anger in her voice as she spewed the words. "But Jake and Holly are my siblings. Nora killed my father. The story she painted to Jake and Holly about him is false," she spoke sadly. "Hearing her say that to you earlier, well, I can't let that happen."

"Marilyn? What does this have to do with me?" I said louder than intended. She placed her hand gently on my shoulder, calming me.

"Nothing, despite that, everything. I can only get bits and pieces of information. I'm not included in meetings like Holly. They resent me that much." She seemed to be in a daze for a moment, but then turned her attention back to me. My racing heart didn't let up.

"They believe you own some property. That is what Jake's after."

"Property? I've purchased nothing other than the property for my business. He has that already."

Her eyes softened, then she glanced into the lights out the window, brightening the night.

"I found out about that. I'm really sorry, Nhoell. There's more." Marilyn pulled her gaze from outside and back to me. The confusion in her own eyes caused a lump to rise in my throat. I swallowed it back down. "You are in my father's will. I overheard Nora say it herself."

"Wait, what?"

"Sorry, I did my own investigation on your family. I still can't figure out why. And Jake, he has been so out of it lately. I've never seen him like this. He knows someone is helping you besides your friend."

I blurted, "Carla has nothing to do with this"

"Times up." The guard shouted.

"Okay, just a minute," She yelled back. "Even so, things haven't been going his way, if you know what I mean." She looked at her phone screen and quickly put it back into her pocket. "It's been hard to make certain things happen. He thinks that's because of you. Whoever you have helping you must know what they're doing."

I looked away.

"Nhoell, I'm sorry for what my family has put you through. I wish I could do more."

She walked away, but I stopped her.

"It was you, wasn't it? Do you check the reports for Jake's company?"

"Had I known you were checking them, I would have swapped them a long time ago. It's been my job since high school." Marilyn walked away and left me standing there with my skin flushed.

"We're done." She yelled out.

She sashayed away, pulling her jacket close around her neck. The guard pulled himself from the wall and waited, his arms still folded. Marilyn approached, less than two feet from his enormous frame, she kneed him in the groin. In one seamless motion, she jammed a black object into his neck. Blue and white electrical currents flashed as his body stiffened and veins protruded from his neck and head. His raged filled face distorted as he groaned aloud, staring daggers at Marilyn. She didn't release the taser, but the guard wasn't going down. Inch by inch, his arm rose. Marilyn's eyes widened as she pushed harder.

"Go!" She yelled, her voice traveling through the small hall.

Without thinking, I ran past them to the front door but turned around just before opening it. The guard's hand was inches from Marilyn's neck and I shifted from one foot to the other. She yelled again for me to leave. Instead, I ran back to the living room and grabbed the stone art piece from above the fireplace. Rushing back to Marilyn and the guard felt like I was moving with the speed of light in me. I extended my arm back as far as I could and slammed the weighty stone against the guard's head. He made a loud grunt, then fell toward Marilyn.

Chapter 27

Marilyn jumped from the way of the falling guard and held her hand to her chest as she leaned against the wall. Beads of sweat trickled down the side of her face while she looked on, half believing what she'd done.

"Thanks,"

"No, thank you. Will you be okay... going back?" I asked, truly concerned.

"Don't worry about me. Just go. Now. And be safe, Nhoell."

"I will. Thank you, really."

I took off without hesitation out the front door, then to the stairwell. Taking two steps at a time, I made it three floors down before getting on the elevator. It was already close to eleven o'clock and people still filled the foyer and halls. The adrenalin coursed through my body as I put aside every fear I had of being caught.

I slipped into a side door marked employees only. Speed walking down a long hall, laughter and conversations echoed off the walls. Machinery and metal clanking against metal rang out too. Taking random turns, I hoped an exit showed up quick because the hair on the nape of my neck stood. The longer I stayed in the building, the more at risk I was.

I made a left turn, and the voices grew in the distance. Further down, an employee crossed the hall from right to left and was out of sight just as quick. When I reached the end, the smell of cigarette smoke stung the air, so I turned to the right, following the scent as it grew stronger. Making another turn, the exit sign stood just ahead, and

I trudged faster. Almost tasting the cool air in my lungs.

Once my hands touched the door, I pushed hard and the loud metal hitting the wall echoed through the halls and loading dock. A handful of employees faced me in silence. One man held his cigarette to his mouth mid-puff.

"Ma'am?" someone spoke up. "Are you okay? Do you need anything?"

"No,"

"You need to get out of here?" Another male voice asked.

I looked at each of them. Young and old, probably mothers and grandfathers. The last thing I wanted was someone's blood on my hands. Andrea and Ryan had come too close. For all I knew, they could end up dead just by helping.

"If they come this way, please, tell the truth." I walked to the stairs of the loading dock and descended.

"When you get to the street, make a left, then cross the street. If you cut through those three alleys, it'll get you away from here faster." A young woman said.

I recognized her. She was the woman that gave me a massage after a fight the night before. I remembered her being excited about the request, telling me I was lucky. That was before I undressed. I smiled at her and thanked them, then took off down the alleyway.

Following the directions the woman gave me, I zipped between people and dashed across streets. I ran through puddles of water that splashed on my shirt and face. I kept my arms pumping and my legs moving even though the pain between my thighs lashed at me.

I ended up on a strip with corner liquor stores, grocery stores, and fast-food joints lining the streets. I ran into the closest convenience store, out of breath, sweaty and jittery.

"Please," I wheezed. "Can I use your phone?" The wide-eyed woman behind the desk fumbled with a cordless phone, all while keeping an eye on me.

"You cool, sis?"

I nodded my head then she handed me the phone. Fingers shaking, I pressed the buttons to dial Gregory's number. He picked up after the third ring.

"It's me,"

"Are you okay? Where are you?"

"I'm at a convenience store a few blocks from the hotel."

"Get to Carla's house as quick as you can." He said in urgency.

"No, he'll know I'll go there. I can't keep dragging Carla into this."

"Listen to me. You're safer there than anywhere else right now. Get to her. I know you can do it, Nhoell. Please go and don't stop for anyone."

"Okay, Greg." I hung up and handed the woman back the phone.

"You okay? Sounds like you jumping ship. I did that once—best decision I ever made. By the way you looking, I take it this will be the best decision you ever made too."

"Ma'am, thank you so much."

"You welcome." I was halfway out of the convenience store as she was ending her sentence and a taxi was dropping off a passenger. Checking my surroundings first, I bolted to the taxi and jumped in and provided Carla's address. Resting my head on the seat, I kept my face from the window. My hands were still shaking, and my breathing worked its way back to normalcy. The driver's eyes darted in the rearview mirror from me to the road, then back to me.

"You alright back there? You want some music?" the older man said.

"I'm okay, thank you."

"As in, you alright or you don't want music?" He chuckled.

"Both."

"Look like a woman on the move. It's alright, I've met enough of 'em." He reached to his dashboard and flipped a switch. All the numbers and lights on his meter disappeared. "Don't need nobody trying to track you, so I got you. My daughter ran for a while until she finally ran back to me. Brought some trouble along, too, but I took care of that."

"Thank you."

It was all I could say. I sank further down and thought of Carla's words about having help and not seeing it. This time running from

Jake felt different. This time, people knew I was running.

#

The taxi driver pulled in front of Carla's gated community. Keeping my face turned away, he put in the code I'd given him and we were buzzed in. A few turns later, we arrived at her house when I asked him to wait for me to grab the fare. He declined. I thanked him and ran to the front porch and rang the doorbell. Instead of Carla opening the door, a dark-skinned man whose frame nearly filled the doorway met me. My stomach lunged, and I whirled to run.

"Nhoell? Get in here! Hurry." Carla standing next to the man, looked just like who he was. I dashed past them into the house. Once the door shut, I embraced her as she held onto me.

"You made it. He knew you would."

"Is he here?" I stammered.

"No, but I got a call earlier from him saying you were on your way. Other than that, nothing. Haven't heard from him since."

My shoulders slouched at the news and I bit at my bottom lip.

"Nhoell, he will be fine. Don't worry."

We walked up the stairs from the doorway and to the living room. Sitting at the dining room table, covered with papers and three computers was her brother. I gawked at him hunched over, speaking to himself as he moved from one computer to another.

"That's Chris. He knows squat shit about computers. He's the oldest."

"He's talking to himself?"

"No, he has a small earpiece in. You can't see it. My brother Eddy actually designed the coms he's using."

My eyes widened and I mouthed a 'wow, are you serious?'.

"Yep, I told you not to worry about me."

"I mean, it's nice. Dropping everything to come and help you." I nudged her in the side. Just then, another man walked into the dining room and stood over Chris. I did a double take and watched him while he pointed to something on the computer, then on the table. Chris spoke into the earpiece again.

"You didn't tell me two of them were in town. Your business, is it okay?"

"It'll be fine," She waved it off. "that's Eddy. He's the bastard lawyer I was telling you about. Seems to think he knows every damn law the world created." She shook her head and snarled. "You do not want to be in a debate with him, trust me." I snorted out a laugh and we both giggled. The brothers stopped their conversation and looked to me and Carla. I turned away. When they spoke in hushed whispers again, I turned back.

"Do they know?"

"Only what I want them to know."

I nodded my head.

"We need to talk. Marilyn helped me get away."

"How about we get you cleaned up, first? You're looking rough."

"I feel worse."

Carla led me to her bathroom where I showered and changed my bandages. I wanted to settle down in the tub, but I still felt uneasy. Greg wasn't with me and Jake, I had no clue. I put on a white t-shirt and a pair of Carla's sweatpants and my running shoes too. A cool shiver ran down my spine and I glanced at the window. The blue curtains flowed with the light breeze that reached my damped hair. I waited another moment in silence before closing and locking it.

I found Carla in the kitchen where three guns lie on the countertop. Next to it had been a few clips and ammo sticking out of a duffle bag. My mouth fell open. Carla shrugged her shoulders.

"It belongs to Chris. Military bastard. He doesn't come empty-handed. What's this about Marilyn?" I pulled out the barstool and lifted myself into the seat slowly.

"To start, she's not Nora's daughter and there seems to be some animosity. Just like Eleanor said. Marilyn says there is property left to me by his father and he's trying to marry me for it."

"What? His father?"

"Yeah, that's what I said. She thinks Nora killed him, too."

"Are you serious? Well, I wouldn't put it past that evil witch. But, this will. That's odd?"

"Exactly. I didn't have time to think about everything. As soon as I found out, I had to run."

Carla stared off in the distance, her finger lightly tapping her lip.

"What about your mom?"

"My mom? Seriously. How could she have anything to do with this? Or them?"

"I don't know. Just thinking of alternatives. It makes little sense that your name would be in the will unless your mom had something to do with him or the family, I guess. Did she see your name?" Carla asked curiously.

"No, she overheard them."

"Is he your dad?"

I twisted my face and shook my head at her nonsense.

"What? You said it yourself that you know next to nothing about your dad."

"I'm sure they would have known if he was. Right? Besides, I look nothing like them," I replied. "She's already ran a background check on me and my mom."

"Okay, forget all that, even if your name is in the will, he doesn't have to marry you to get it."

"I know. I thought about that. He knows about me being there when Vinitto was killed, too. He called me a key witness."

"You got to be fucking kidding me. Seriously?"

The room grew silent as we both sat pondering. From the other room, the brothers argue.

"How do you expect me to defend you! I can't help you break any laws, Chris," Eddy yelled.

"Is it really breaking the law if it's for a good cause? Besides, it'll get things cleaned up easier!"

Carla excused herself from the room. In an instant, the arguing ceased. The doorbell rang, and my heart leaped in my chest. *Greg.* My body felt so heavy. I toyed with my fingers as the footsteps of one brother shook the house. Waiting impatiently on the stool, I listened intently. Both muffled voices were male, for sure.

"Like I said, she's not here," Chris stated, his voice deepening every time he spoke. "I don't give a damn who sent you, brotha. Go back and tell your boss that whoever he's looking for is not here!" Carla appeared at my side and placed her arm around my shoulders. I met her eyes with a sure smile.

"They're assholes, Nhoell, but they can keep you safe. Besides, it sounds like we're dealing with idiots. If this is what Jake resorts to, then there really isn't much your boyfriend has to do."

A loud crash shook the house, startling us, and a single gunshot rang out. Eddy ran into the kitchen, grabbed a gun, and ran out just as fast, commanding us to stay put. I looked at Carla with worried eyes. She didn't seem fazed at all by the commotion surrounding us. Another shot let off and Eddy yelled out.

"Stay here." Carla pulled from me and grabbed the other gun.

"No! Don't go out there," I gripped her arm. "You'll get yourself killed."

"No, I won't. Anyone come back that isn't me or my brothers," she slid the last gun near me. "take their fucking head off."

My stomach clenched as Carla took off, disappearing out of sight. No sooner than she took off, her screams rang out as another bang echoed through the house. Before I could think of making a move, a soft creak from behind me jolted me from where I stood. I turned to face a hooded man wearing a ski mask. Sensing my oncoming scream, he held his fingers to his lips and walked slowly toward me. As if it was second nature to me, I immediately grabbed the last gun and pointed it at him. That made him stop mid-step.

"Get back." I hissed.

My knuckles tightened over the gun, and another crash shook the house. Carla. The hooded man lunged at me and I screamed out, dodged him and pulled the trigger simultaneously. Nothing happened.

He came at me again and I scrambled around the island, fumbling with the gun and getting the safety off, then squeezing the trigger. The noise rang through my ears, deafening me for a moment. Before I realized it, the hooded man fell over on the kitchen floor. I stared at his body as my hands shook uncontrollably. There was so much blood that I grew lightheaded. I closed my eyes and leaned against the counter.

"Nhoell! What was that?" Carla yelled out and my heart relaxed in my chest. I opened my eyes to a clean floor where the body laid. I avoided it as I crossed the kitchen to stand against the wall that separated Carla and I.

"Carla?" I yelled out.

"Are you okay?"

"Yo bitch!" a voice yelled out. "I'm gonna need you to get yo ass out here before more of ya people get hurt!"

Forcing myself to look back at the body on the floor. He wore fresh white and red basketball shoes and jeans hanging just below his waist. A colored rag, barely visible, hung from his jeans pocket.

"I'm fine."

"Just stay where you are!"

Noise from the kitchen directed me back to the body, but the hooded man was in my face, knocking the gun from my hand. He held his own gun to my head and my eyes followed the tattoo of a dragon on his wrist until his finger was at his lips. Again.

"Nhoell? What was that?"

He nodded his head to the hall leading to Carla's room, then he took a step back.

"Nhoell!" Carla yelled out again

"Carla? There's someone up here with me," I looked the hooded man in the eyes and dared him to shoot. I knew he wouldn't. He shook his head, almost as if disappointed in me.

"Chris! Get up there!" Carla yelled out. More gunshots fired downstairs, and I closed my eyes hard.

"Fuck! I can't!" Chris yelled back.

Still holding his gun to my head, the man pulled out a phone and put it to his ear.

"Light it up." He said in a monotone.

Seconds later, rapid gunfire rang out like fireworks. I dropped to my knees and covered my head as bullets pierced through the walls. The man grabbed me by the arm, pulled me through the kitchen as we stayed low. I screamed Carla's name at the thought of her body being rippled with bullets. The one thing I tried hard to keep from happening was happening right before me.

Before I knew it, we were in the bedroom, tears stinging my eyes as the gunfire finally stopped. Sirens rang out in the distance and I almost felt relief. That quickly disappeared when he lifted the gun and nodded to the open window. I shook my head. I had to believe he wouldn't pull the trigger. But he did. The bullet grazed my forearm, and I screamed out in pain, grabbing hold of my arm as the warm blood dripped to the floor. Turning back to him, he motioned me to the window with his gun this time. I took a step forward, panting softly and holding my arm.

"Please. Don't do this."

"Move. Now." His knuckles tightened around his gun and he pointed it to my other side. I moved to the open window, pushed back the curtains and braced myself to climb out. Just below, two more masked men stood waiting for me to drop down. I did, and the hooded man jumped down afterward. We dashed through the backyard, crossing through others as the sirens grew louder. My heart pounded in my ears as I followed them, keeping a close eye on the one behind me. The one that made the call to kill Carla. I choked on a sob and trekked harder through a wooded area. Ten minutes later, we were at a black SUV parked on the street. The two masked men stood off to the side as the hooded man pushed me to the idling vehicle. When he opened the door, I turned and faced him, his eyes dark and glistening in the moonlight. Again, he shook his head as if disappointed in me before turning away.

Seconds later, we were passing ambulances and police cars going in the opposite direction. It wasn't Jimmy, Lee or the Dwayne Johnson-like man driving. Two other men had taken their place. Although I could have guessed what happened to them, I didn't. Because the truth was, I didn't care. I wiped away the tears that trailed my face and held in the sobs before they could escape. It was the tears that burned behind my eyes that made me want to scream and the tightness in my throat that silenced me. My chest kept beating into my ears like drums and my hands suddenly shook uncontrollably. Each time Carla's beautiful smile crossed my mind, it was more difficult to hold back the magma that rose in me. What I initially thought was panic, was actually anger that rushed over my body. After all, I'd done to keep her safe. After everything I went through, in the end, it was for nothing. It was all because of one person.

When I saw the gown and pearl set lying on the seat next to me, my fingers stopped shaking and the tightness in my chest eased. There was still the slow simmer in my body when I grabbed the pearls, rubbing the cool beads between my fingers. I squeezed them tight, willing them to turn to dust from the fire raging in me. Instead, I let down the window a little, stared at them longer, then dropped them out. Turning slowly to the gown, I gently picked it up then let the window down completely.

Chapter 28

One guard led the way to the front entrance of the four-story building and the other followed close behind. We were out of the city but the streets were lively as people went about their night with laughs and energy so strong, I felt it breeze past me. It seemed I was the only one dressed down in sweats and a t-shirt. A flash of light lit the sky, a low thunder followed moments later and rumbled into my chest. I felt Carla's presence and knew what I had to do.

In the building, I followed the latest guard through a long corridor. After taking the elevator and turning down another hall, we were met with a heavyset man blocking the entrance. Lifting his hand to his mouth, he opened the door and stepped to the side for me to enter. In contrast to the dark corridor we'd come from, a yellow orange glow illuminated the establishment. Soft music played in the background, and the hum from the different conversations was a relief. The bar sat on the far-left wall, and straight ahead were at least a dozen tables and private booths occupied by a few people.

"The lady of the hour!"

The hair rose on the back of my neck and my lips curled into a snarl when I turned to face Jake's gleaming face.

"You're not wearing the dress. Nor the pearls." He stated.

"No," I looked him square in the eyes. "I'm not."

"I see," he chuckled. "Interesting. I hear there was a problem." He put out his arm, and I hesitantly looped mine in his.

"Problem? There was no problem at all."

"Oh, really? Your escape. You shooting one of my men. Your

friend... I heard they were taken care of nicely. I only wish I could have done it myself."

"As we both know you are very good at," He gripped the wound on my arm and I winced.

"Watch yourself."

Jake led me to a crystal clear ceiling-high waterfall encased in the wall. Five other tables occupied the private section of the restaurant, and I relaxed at the sight of four more patrons dining.

"Finally, my lovely future," Jake exclaimed.

Clearing the waterfall, I nearly stammered at the sight of Gregory rising to greet me. A bone-chilling coldness racked over my body as he stood and held out his hand. In my peripheral, Jake stood still, observing the interaction.

"Nhoell, meet my new business partner, Gregory Rehevas. It's taken a while to get him to sign on, but it looks like he's come around."

"It's nice to meet you. There's nothing he talks about more, and I can see why."

I flushed as the coolness in my body was replaced with a rush of warmth. I finally took Gregory's hand. He squeezed gently, then rubbed his finger along the back of it before letting go. My heart eased from his touch, but my pulse didn't slow like I needed it to.

"Now that we're all here, let's begin."

Jake took his seat across from Gregory, and I sat between them both, my back to the entrance. The readiness I felt seconds ago dissipated once I laid eyes on him. Working alongside Jake? It was the universe playing tricks on me. Or once again, it was Jake toying with me like a cat with a string.

"Right, Nhoell?" Jake asked, pulling me from my thoughts.

"Huh?"

The look he gave me in response to my lack of attention made me forget who was playing cat and who was playing string.

"Something wrong? You seem a little off."

"I'm okay, Jake."

"Good. We have a long night ahead of us. I'm glad the bullet wasn't a few inches to the right that would have been a problem."

His dark gray eyes dared me to open my mouth. Then the sudden thought of grabbing the fork and ramming it in his chest came to me.

"You see…" he spoke to Gregory again, who barely said a word. "There's a way for women to be handled."

I ground down on my teeth and felt the cold rise in me again.

"And how is that?" Gregory's deep voice pierced through all the coolness and eased me. Again, I was thankful he spoke. Because I needed to be level-headed, and thoughts of Carla kept resurfacing. And the sound of Jake kept boiling my blood like a furnace.

"If you don't rein them in from the beginning, you lose all control in the end. See, Nhoell here… in the beginning, she was a tough one. But once I broke down those barricades, the rest just fell into place."

Gregory chuckled.

"Something funny, Mr. Rehevas?"

"I think it's unusual you try to treat women like they're businesses to be managed. You can't manage a real woman, Mr. Vaughn," Gregory looked me in my eyes. "because those types of women are weapons in and of themselves. You'd end up getting yourself hurt if you're not careful."

Yes. Keep talking to me, I said to myself.

"Really? Speaking of business, I think now is the best time to discuss the terms and conditions in our agreement."

"I don't think you understand. I'm still not interested. My thoughts about your company, let alone your ethics, still haven't changed. Did you really think I would sign anything with you?" Gregory leaned forward and folded his hand on the table in front of him.

"No," Jake clasped his hands together too and slowly shook his head as if he pitied him. "I don't think you understand. For the life of me, I couldn't fathom why things had tilted since, well, meeting you."

"I have that type of effect on people. I assure you, it was a tilt destined to happen,"

"Sure, in my own time. You see, things here in this city tend to happen when I tell them to happen. People move when I tell them to move. Oh, but not you, Mr. Rehevas. You a good ole ethical boy. But you must learn quickly, or you will not survive this business."

"I've already survived. No threats against me will change what I decided. Men like you, are what poison the world. But I don't weaken under men like you. I've met worse. Now, this will be the last time I'll say it. I will not sign your contract."

Jake sat back in his chair as if what Gregory had said gave him the win he was looking for.

One of the security guards placed a legal-size envelope in the middle of the table and walked away. Jake laid his hand on top of it and pushed it to Gregory.

"Your contract, Mr. Rehevas. Containing my plans for the condominiums and your plans to design them. The compensation for your approval is far greater than I'd ever expected to pay." Jake pulled out a fancy black and gold pen from inside his suit jacket and laid it on the envelope. "But I have no complaints."

Gregory took a sip from his glass, then smoothly slid the envelope back.

"I see." Jake replied, then leaned back in his chair, almost as if assessing his next move. And it came. Quick. The sting in my face burned as I found myself staring at the polished floor. I let out a loud screech and used my hand to cover the hot sensation he'd left. The raging feeling I'd felt back in the SUV returned. My fingers trembled furiously as I squeezed my eyes tight to keep from losing my shit and getting us both killed. When I lifted my head, Gregory no longer sat across from me. He'd gotten to Jake so swiftly and had him pinned by the jacket. But I underestimated Jake. Standing behind him were two men. Behind Gregory were the four other men that had been dining. My eyes lit up in horror as I saw they outnumbered us. But he didn't let up. Gregory stared him down with hate-filled eyes. The sinister smile across Jake's lips made me recoil. He was toying with us, both Gregory and me.

"Don't you lay another hand on her."

"So, you have a soft spot for the ladies?" Jake said tauntingly.

"Don't you put your fucking hands on her."

"Or is it a soft spot for only this one? Release me, Mr. Rehevas, or your brains will paint a picture for her to look at later. You love her paintings, right?"

The guard that stood behind Jake pulled out a gun and held it to Gregory's head. My stomach plummeted at the image of Vince Vinitto's body slumping over.

"It's either that, or we can strike a deal,"

Gregory loosened his grip on Jake's jacket and slowly took a step back. Jake repositioned his clothes and took a seat back at the table and said, "Have a seat."

Hesitant at first, Gregory slowly took his seat, then looked at me. His eye blazed with fury as my insides burned to release the anger in me. When his eyes softened, a bit of me simmered down like water to a flame. I looked away in order to hold myself together because I already felt the guilt rising from the death sentence I sent him.

"You see? She knows who holds power here." Jake waved his finger, and the standing men in the room took their seats, and the guards stood back, not far off. "I was surprised that you two didn't come up in my initial investigation of you." He looked at Greg, who still watched me, his face expressionless. I wished our minds were connected like our hearts.

"Star football player in high school, all around star student. Saw a few papers about how you were making a mistake not playing in college." Jake turned his attention to me. "Oh, sweetheart. You, well, there was little to nothing about you, but I already had the information I needed."

"Why, were you looking into me?" I said in a whisper.

"You would've gone a long way had you not met him," he ignored me. "I'm guessing even after losing the child, they decided not to let you in." My heart sank, and I could feel the defeat in my chest, in my body. I turned away from him and away from Gregory.

"That's enough," Gregory yelled.

"It'll never be enough. I just couldn't figure out the connection between you, and that bitch. Just so happens, I had her followed the day after our first meeting. Suspected her to be your whore at first. But from the looks of it, there was something else. Your phone records didn't help until I took a second look and there was one constant number."

Jake looked at me and slowly reached across the table and grabbed the back of my neck. The hairs on my back stood at attention as my chest beat hard in my ears. I couldn't contain the shake in my hands as he forced me to look at him. My lips quivered, and I squeezed my fist until my nails dug deep into my flesh.

"It was you. In front of me the entire time. After checking all the times I couldn't get in touch with you and matching them with the times that Carla called, then called him, I knew it had to have been you.

"But I didn't figure that out until you were in the hospital. That's why I put you there," Jake whispered, then laughed again. "And you," he said to Greg. "I knew something wasn't right when you became interested in the project suddenly. You actually held me in meetings, for her. Did you really think you could take her from me?" Jake shoved me away.

"What do you want?" Gregory asked.

"From her? Not your concern. From you? It's lying right there in front of you," Jake responded. "And Nhoell? Like I said earlier, you've become more useful. Mr. Rehevas, the papers are there. What's it going to be?"

"You sick bastard," I gritted hard, tears flowing from my eyes, soaking into the tablecloth. "This entire time, you were setting me up. From the very beginning You took my business, you took my freedom. For what? Fucking property! You do this to me for something I have no control over? You put me in the hospital to test a fucking theory! How sick are you? How sick is your family for doing this to me?"

Jake reached out and hit me across the face. Before Gregory could make a move, the guard already had his gun drawn.

"Is that all you got?" I gritted. "my best friend is dead! I did everything you asked of me! I took your abuse for three fucking months and you kill my sister!"

As if possessed, my hands slung at Jake as I went flying across the table, attacking him with anything that I could get my hands on. I saw red as the smug look on his face kept appearing in my head, laughing at me. Laughing at Carla. The guard grabbed at me, but I continued my assault on any part of him he wasn't blocking. I screamed my rage into my fist, losing control of myself until a hard yank pulled me from the table.

"I'm going to kill you! All of you! Let me go!"

"Let her go!" Jake yelled out.

The guard released me and I charged at Jake with intent to kill. In one swing, his large hand grabbed my wrist, twisted my arm behind my back and pinned me to the table. Gregory stood, but the gun pointed at his head held him back. I screamed out in pain as Jake shoved my face harder into the table.

"You and my sister have become acquainted, I see. Well, I don't plan to marry you only for the property. I do enjoy you, Nhoell. That was the truth. Now," he pushed my arm further up and I screamed out again. "Take your fucking seat and control yourself. You need to save that fighting spirit for tonight." Jake released my arm and stood, towering over me. I stood face to face with him, tears staining my face, eyes blazing and out of breath. I took my seat.

"I want Nhoell. Give me her, and I'll give you what you want."

I looked at Gregory, still standing, the gun still pointed at him, his eyes trained on me. My eyes welled with tears as I shook my head. I couldn't let him

"Negotiations? You have no room for negotiations."

"Oh, but I do. You want my designs? She is my price."

"She has nothing to do with this."

"Then why is she here? To push my hand?"

"You're a smart man, Mr. Rehevas. From what I've gathered, I'm sure you'd do anything for her. So, let's not play games. The contract."

"As I said, my price is set. If you can't pay up, Mr. Vaughn, then there is no business here."

"I haven't had this much fun in a long time," Jake yelled out to no one in particular. He took one smooth stride from his chair to stand behind me. "You really do not understand your situation. Her situation."

He grabbed a handful of my hair and yanked my head back, forcing me to look at his face. I screamed out and instinctively reached and grabbed hold of him. I pleaded and begged him. All the while feeling the table hit against my torso. Gregory was fighting to get to me, and I could feel every ounce of power that came from the other side of the table.

"Jake, please!" I screamed.

"Mr. Rehevas, like I said before, she belongs to me! You are in no place to negotiate. I'll let her go once you've stopped fighting."

"Greg, please!" Almost immediately the table stopped moving and silence and heavy breathing replaced my screams. My chest rose fast as I took deep breaths to control my breathing. It was over. He was going to kill us. There was no way we were getting away without succumbing to his demands. That meant staying with him. That meant marrying him.

"She says his name, and he's tamed," Jake mocked.

He turned me around to face him and forced his tongue into my mouth as his hands seemed to squeeze the life out of me. I pushed Jake away, fighting against his kisses when he suddenly stopped and stared at me almost nose-to-nose.

"Don't even think about saying his name again. Wipe your face and take your seat, this isn't over." He left my side and took his seat back at the table. I raked my fingers through my itchy, burning scalp before taking my seat and bowing my head.

"No need to look so angry, I won't kill her. She's too valuable to me."

"This is how you treat people of value?" Gregory recoiled.

"Yes, when they find it difficult to understand their place. She seems to forget that."

"Seeing what you've done to her… what you did to her brought something out of me I'd put away years ago. I could kill you for touching her, but that would be far too gracious for you. Tonight, I'm leaving with her by my side, and if I have to kill you to do it, then so be it. I said I'd sign your contract for Nhoell…" the sound of ripping paper made me lift my head. Gregory held a piece of the envelope in either hand.

"You refused my offer, and now I'm not signing a thing. I'm not here to play games with you, Mr. Vaughn. Anything having to do with Nhoell is no game."

Jake's face twisted in a grimace.

"Mr. Rehevas, whether or not you know it, you will sign this contract. Torn or not. And it would have to be over my dead body for her to walk out of here with you."

Although they both spoke in even tones, their voices resonated around me like a cocoon. So easily when Jake spoke, I felt the need to cover myself and look away. But it was when Gregory spoke that always seemed to open me up.

"Enough with the bullshit. You and I both know that even if I sign those papers, it would be worthless. Seeing as you have no rights to your company."

I turned my head to Jake's skewed and distorted beet-red face.

"I don't know what you heard about me, Mr. Vaughn, but I presume it was what I wanted you to hear. You don't know where I come from or who I know. It doesn't surprise me that you would underestimate me. So, ask yourself. How was I able to make your world tilt?"

"Do you know who I am?"

"I do. The first and only son of Andrew Vaughn, but not the successor. According to my source, your older sister is actually the heir to your father's company and estate. What I couldn't figure out is how that little knowledge slipped through the cracks. You hate her for it, too. Don't you?" Gregory taunted.

"This is my company! I built it! Leaving it to her would have been detrimental."

"So, you stole it? Sort of like all the businesses around the city. You need space for your condominiums, am I right? So, grand larceny, arson, a handful of capital crimes if we include hospital records from East Region Medical Center and the interference you had in past elections… and did you think no one would learn that you're the one behind this street gang? That one, I missed. But not my friend. He does his job well."

"Oh, yes, he does. Well then, I'm sure you know I can't be touched. This is my city! And when there's something I need..." Jake turned slowly back to me. Gregory followed suit. "Well, let's just say I'll do what's needed to get it."

"If you cannot produce a legally binding contract under your name, Nhoell or no Nhoell, there is no business. Seeing as the rightful successor to the company has no knowledge of such, I will not agree to be part of your schemes."

"That is very unfortunate." Jake clasped his hand on the table and seemed to think for a moment. "That is the wrong choice, Mr. Rehevas! Not only will she not be leaving here with you, but neither will you."

Jake nodded his head and almost immediately, two men appeared from behind Jake and drew their guns. My heart lurched forward, and before I knew it, I'd screamed out.

"Jake, no!" I held his gaze and chose my words carefully. "Please don't do this. Anything. Anything you want from me you can have. I won't fight you. Please, don't kill him. You have me." He held my gaze.

"Nhoell, sweetheart, this is inevitable."

"Jake, I'm begging you!" Tears clouded my eyes as I slowly shook my head. He nodded behind me, and out of nowhere, someone pulled me up by the arm.

"Wait," Gregory held his hand up. "You are a very stubborn man and full of surprises too. I didn't expect that response. As much pain as you put her through, you won't kill her or let her die... she means something to you. In that case, Mr. Vaughn, FBI is on the other side of that door waiting for me to give the word. Let her go. Did you think I wouldn't come prepared?"

"You're lying. I know a bluff when I see one."

Jake waved his hand again, and the guard pinned my arms down and picked me up. I convulsed and jolted and screamed at the top of my lungs for Gregory. Apologizing to him and crying out I love you. The guns that the two guards aimed at him were the last image I wanted to see. It was the one burning into my memory.

The blurry vision from my tears kept me from seeing Jake's swift move to me. He stood in my face, blocking my view of Gregory while the guard held me to his chest at least two feet off the ground.

"You still haven't learned, Nhoell."

"And I never will. I will fight you to the death, Jake."

"As long as you're my wife first."

"If you would've asked me to sign over the property your father left me, I would have. Just to get away from you."

"That would be no fun." He smiled and touched my face. "I'll see you at home, wife." Before Jake could make another move, Greg had come across the table, tackling him to the floor. Both guards aimed their guns, but neither one of them pulled the trigger. I reared my head back as hard as I could, hitting the man in the face. He released me and I fell to the floor in time to see Jake's entourage crossing tables to get to Gregory. I ran to him as well.

"Get her out of here!" Jake yelled. Three men grabbed hold of Gregory and landed consecutive blows to his back. Large arms grabbed me by the waist, pulling me away as I jerked and scratched at the back of his head. He squeezed harder, taken the breath right out of me.

"FBI! Get down! Put your guns down now! On the ground!" My heart lunged in my chest as I fought harder to get away from the man and back into the room. I hit at his arm to grant me air and my body weakened. I couldn't let out so much as a whimper. Fear struck me as the memory of Jake strangling me resurfaced. The guard's forearm jerked against my rib cage as he ran down the stairs two to three steps at a time. Two flights of stairs above him, FBI yelled at us to stop, their feet knocking hard on the stairs like a stampede. Outside, my body shivered from the sudden rush of air as the pouring rain crashed onto me like freezing bullets. Seconds later, I fell onto the cool leather seat and I held onto my throat, gasping for breath as the SUV sped into traffic.

Chapter 29

The tires screeched and I slid across the seat. Horns from other cars blared as the engine roared. When the car steadied long enough, I lifted my head. The impact from another vehicle ramming us from behind threw me against the back of the driver's seat. It was the black SUV that followed us once we pulled away from the restaurant.

"Fuck!" The guy driving yelled out.

"Hit this next turn, we need to get rid of them." The other guard blurted.

Once we made the turn and were steady enough, I put on my seatbelt and held on tight. They rammed us from behind again, causing the driver to lose control a little before maneuvering back into the lane. I thanked God there was traffic ahead, but my hopes blew away when the driver made a sharp turn down an alley. The other vehicle followed behind us easily, picking up speed. We smashed through bags of trash lining the walls and other objects that flew over the SUV. Up ahead at the end of the ally, other cars zoomed past in both directions. I looked at the driver in fear, knowing he was going to go for it. As soon as we swerved into the middle of the road, I screamed at headlights blinding me and horns blaring. Two cars crashed into each other and stopped the vehicle chasing us in the process. They quickly disappeared as we sped down the road and I let out a long breath. After nearly five minutes of silence, I spoke up.

"Where, where am I going?"

"Don't worry. You're safe with us," one man replied.

"No, tell me now. Where are we going? The FBI is after you, why don't you just let me go. Just pull over and let me out."

I looked between both of them and neither one said a word. Sitting back against the seat, I crossed my arm over my chest. The night was dark from the clouds blocking the moon. Ahead, there was minimal light apart from the flickering lights in the distance that let me know civilization was still near. Before my brain could talk me out of the illogical thing that came to mind, I quietly unhooked my seatbelt then took a deep breath. I lunged at the driver, wrapping my arms around his neck and pulling hard towards the back seat. The SUV swerved as the driver clawed at my hands. The other guard reached for the wheel, but we were already turning. I released my arm and slid to the far side behind the passenger seat on the floor. The impact of the crashing SUV crushed my body into the back seat, dizzying me. For a moment I lay still. My body felt so heavy and broken on the floor, I struggled to breathe. Gently pulling myself from the floor and back onto the seat, I patted myself down and winced after touching my rib cage. The SUV hissed as smoke and steam floated above while both men lay unmoving.

Slowly, I tugged at the door handle. Fucking child lock. Inching over to the other door where the window was broken, I reached out to open it from the outside. Taking more effort than I thought, I rammed it open with my body, sending a sharp pain along my side. The first step down led me into a large puddle of water in high grass. The running engine of a vehicle approached from the road and sudden alarm filled my chest when heavy footsteps approached fast. I lifted to my wobbly legs to run into a sprint, but three steps later I was on my knees in the water again. I crawled, scrambling to get up, but my body moved slower than my brain. Strong arms wrapped around my waist and I screamed out in pain. Still, I fought with the energy left in me.

It was when a single shot went off that my screams grew louder. He covered my mouth and muffled my cry for help as I clawed at him. The overbearing man cursed me to stop fighting, but I refused to let up. When we reached the car, I gave one last attempt to break free and bit his hand. When he screamed out in pain, another man appeared from behind and opened the door to the sedan. The other guy jumped in and sped off.

I sat against the door, panting harshly from my scratched throat and shivering from my drenched clothes. Every time I took a breath, a stabbing pain ignited in my side. I was sure it came from fractured ribs.

"Sorry for manhandling you, Nhoell," The black man next to me said after a while. "You didn't have to bite my hand. That was uncalled for."

"What? What did you say?"

"It was uncalled for. You know, biting me." His eyes were soft and he looked uncannily familiar. Even the way he spoke gave me a sense of familiarity.

"Who are you?"

"Wallace. Nice to meet you." He extended his hand, but I didn't take it. "I'm with the extraction team. You're safe."

"What?"

"I said you are safe. He's not gonna be coming after you again."

#

I walked up the stairs of a small plane large enough to fit five passengers plus the two pilots. It was impeccably clean and I was relieved to get the chance to lie down. The pain had become unbearable and my body was nearing its end. Limping to the seat nearest the cockpit, a body lay folded and barely covered behind it. I cursed out and covered my mouth, moving away from the corpse. On his collar had been a golden pin in the shape of wings. I stepped back when another man peered his head from the pilot's seat. Momentarily forgetting the pain I was in, I jumped back about five feet. It couldn't have been the FBI.

"Nhoell," the pilot called out. Or the man pretending to be the pilot.

"Don't worry, he's not dead, he'll be out for some time though. I gave him a concoction I picked up in Zambia."

I looked to the floor where the body lay, then back to the pilot. I took another step backward.

"You're safe here, Nhoell. He can't get to you."

I was already standing at the entrance, ready to take my chances with Wallace rather than the man whose body nearly took up the entire cockpit.

"I said you're safe now."

"There is a dead man on the plane. FBI wouldn't highjack a plane."

"Whoa, there, not dead, just out cold. And we're not the FBI. We're better." He laughed out.

My heart fluttered at his familiarity as well.

"You met my brother, right? And Wallace."

"Your brother?" I looked at him, confused by his question. He turned his head away again and cleared his throat.

"He'll be in. Let me get back to the pit. I promise, everything's okay now."

"Greg?" I whispered.

"Oh, the brotha is good." He disappeared.

I moved further into the plane and sat down; away from the body. Greg was alive and Jake had been arrested. He'd done what he promised and got me away from Jake. But it was at the cost of Carla. Finally, I let my tears fall when weighty steps shook the plane. I turned, hoping to see Greg, then did a double take when I saw Chris. I followed him with wide eyes and a gaped mouth as he strolled toward me. It was difficult trying to come up with how he was alive. I was just as speechless when Wallace entered the plane right after him. Before I knew it, Chris was kneeling in front of me.

"Hey. Are you okay? I heard about what happened with the crash," he said gently. I looked at Wallace again.

"Carla?" I asked in a hushed whisper, afraid of his next words.

"She's okay."

I let out a choked sob and tears immediately filled my eyes.

"Thank God. I thought she was dead. I thought you all were dead.

She did this?"

"She may've had a hand or two in it. My sister loves you. The bond you two have is stronger than our bond combined. I saw that today. She wanted you out of there. We all would've gone through hell and back to make it happen."

"Thank you. To all of you."

Carla and I did have a bond. So easily I was willing to cut that off to keep her safe. At that moment, I thought of what could have happened had I told her sooner, rather than taking it all on myself.

"It's no problem at all. You're family." He smiled at me, and I returned it.

When his eyes trailed over me, I finally looked at myself. My sweat pants were muddy, my shirt was barely dry and dirty, but still exposing the dark rounds of my breast. Instinctively, I used my arms to cover myself. When he looked at the wrapped gun wound, I realized that Chris hadn't been looking at my body. Instead, he'd been looking at what was left of me after leaving Jake.

Chapter 30

Chris, Malcolm, Wallace and I stepped out of the Wrangler. The gentle breeze carried the scent of the ocean right past me, and a light fog bathed the large two-story villa in a haze. The chirps and whistles from the birds filled the quiet morning with songs and instant relaxation. It was the beautiful mossy oak surrounding the house that stopped my breath. Beaufort, South Carolina had been our final destination. After landing in Ohio, driving to Virginia, then taking another plane, we drove to Beaufort and arrived at the secluded Dunn Estate, the family's safe house. From what I learned about the brothers, a safe house was much needed. No matter where we were, they stayed close. Especially Wallace, the youngest brother. He was a mechanic with what the other brothers called "temporary hobbies." Once he became proficient enough in something, he would move to the next thing. He was a jack of all trades and a master too.

When I could change clothes on the plane, I got a better look at the condition I was in. Pilot Malcolm also Doctor Malcom helped re-bandage my wrist and arm and cleaned up my busted lip. As for my ribs, they were fractured, but he bathed them in a green paste he pulled from his backpack. Rare medicine he travels high and wide to get, he says. I was in awe of each brother and their seemingly interesting lives. I thanked Carla for calling them and thinking ahead with the clothes she sent. She took into consideration my still-healing body and old scars Jake left on me. The loose-fitting stretch pants and thin long-sleeve shirt were perfect for me and the location.

I followed Chris onto the porch where he rang the doorbell. Wallace and Malcolm stepped up behind us.

"I called this fool. I know he's in there, probably glued to the screen." Wallace huffed irritably.

"Now, now, Wally Walls, don't chafe your ass. You know he's messing with you," Malcolm replied teasingly.

A loud grunt let out behind me. I turned to see Malcolm bent over with his head nearly between his legs. I looked at Wallace, who shrugged his shoulders.

"Com'on, y'all, show some manners." Chris fussed.

Next to the door, a space the size of a light switch cover disappeared into the wall. A digital keypad appeared in its place and lit up. Chris punched in a few numbers, and the keypad disappeared back into the wall. A loud movement sounded from inside the door then he turned the knob, and we were in.

"Do we need to do that each time we come in?"

"Not if it's disabled. Hermit doesn't get out much, so he usually gets everything in advance and just locks himself in."

"Hermit?"

"Kyle."

Chris motioned me through the front door and the homey feeling from the living room welcomed me. There was a matching sofa and couch set and a lazy boy reclined back, facing the flat screen. Dozens of photos lined the walls and mantle above the fireplace.

"Nhoell?" Malcolm called out. "You need rest, try to get as much as you can. And don't go working out those ribs too much. I'll leave the medicine for you and a few more things. Car said don't worry about a thing and to call her once you're up."

"You spoke to her? Can I call her now? God, I bet she's worried. Where is she? Will she be here?"

"Whoa, slow down." Chris chuckled. "She flew back home, so she won't be here. But Eddy can help you make a phone call... after you rest. Com'on."

I thanked Malcolm and Wallace before they disappeared through the living room, then followed Chris.

The brothers were right. I needed rest. I barely slept the entire way to Beaufort. If getting information out of them wasn't the reason, it was my fear of believing everything was a dream. I was afraid that if I went to sleep, I would wake up back in the condo.

"Here we are. I haven't seen it, but Kyle said he cleaned it up a bit."

Chris opened the door to a large room with a four-post queen-sized bed, a flat screen mounted on the wall, and a small balcony. The balcony was slightly open, and the curtains flowed gently with the wind cooling the room. Suddenly, my body felt exhausted and worn.

"It's perfect. Thank you, Chris. And tell Kyle thank you."

"No problem, sis. If you need anything, just holla. One of us, if not all, will show up."

Chris left me to soak in the room's comfort. I let the flowing breeze caress my face and inhaled the salt water smell. Tossing the duffle bag on the bed, I walked to the balcony. The massive oak trees, mixed in with the Spanish moss, made a beautiful scene against the still rising sun. I smiled and committed the image to memory as I whispered a silent prayer for Gregory's safe return. Chris let me know he was still in New York, wrapping things up with Eddy and the FBI. Still, none of them mentioned anything about Jake. Because Gregory orchestrated and gathered the evidence against him, they had to question him, too. He also spoke on my behalf and cut some deal with the Bureau.

I left the balcony and crossed the room to the bathroom. I stood breathless at the door, stunned by the exquisite view. The black and white swirls and spotted designs on the floor were made of marble and clearly handmade. A large black tub sat underneath a circular sunroof, allowing light to shine in that single spot. Directly across from the tub was a glass-enclosed shower room with multiple shower heads extending from the wall. A full mirror sat behind the double sink, with a marble countertop that matched the design in the floor. The entire space was jaw-droppingly gorgeous, and I wanted to know which brother was responsible. I was willing to bet on Wallace and his hobbies. I brushed my fingers over the edge of the cool tub. My lips formed into a grin as I took in the sight a bit longer. It had been so long since anything relating to design crossed my mind. But there I was. Feeling the art flow through my veins once again.

#

It was late in the evening when I retraced my steps. The aroma of herbs and Cajun seasoning caused my mouth to water and stomach to growl. Going through the family room like I'd seen Malcolm do earlier, I pushed through a heavy door that took more effort than I thought. On the other side was a large, modern style kitchen with a beautiful S-shaped island in the center, and six metal cushioned barstools surrounding it. On the stove were two pots and a skillet steaming, and I could just make out something in the oven. Everything smelled mouthwatering, and my senses led me straight to the stove. I lifted the lid on the pot, and the rising steam filled the air with an array of aromas that made me squeal.

"I knew the food would get you up. Opening the vent works every time." A masculine voice chuckled from behind.

I dropped the lid back down, making a loud clank.

"Didn't mean to scare you."

He strolled to the island and sat down a large paper bag he'd been carrying. I shook my head at the five handsome brothers that Carla had hidden away. For years I'd known her and hadn't met a single one. He, too, was tall, dark, and handsome like his brothers. But his build was slimmer, unlike the other Dunn brothers at all. It was him that favored Carla more than the others. In him, I saw her eyes, her nose, and her smile. I wondered if he had her personality, too.

"How'd you sleep? Aches and pains? Malcolm told me to ask. He thought you might feel post-pain from the crash and the attack on Wallace."

"So, has everyone heard the story? It was barely an attack."

"Pretty much. I'm Kyle, by the way." He walked around the island and washed his hands.

"I figured as much. I'm Nhoell."

"The one and only. So…" Kyle removed the lids one at a time, checking the dishes. "I saw you over here drooling in my food."

Kyle finished cleaning the two bowls and made his way back to the barstool. The food that I had been drooling in was as delicious as it had smelled. It made me think of home. But the house was too quiet with the others missing. Malcolm received a call from a patient, and Chris rushed off to another emergency on the other side of the world. Wallace had gone to pick up a package from Carla. She was sending more stuff.

I caught myself staring at Kyle now and then because of him and Carla's similarities. Not only that, he was so free-spirited and open that his presence drew me in and comforted me so easily. Carla's brothers had all taken me by surprise. Their different lives, their personalities. How she described them, if she ever, was all but charming. That had me wondering about what happened with them.

"Seriously, we're happy you made it out. For my sister's sake, and ours. Besides, you've helped us for years, we owe it to you."

"Years? I doubt that." I replied.

"Since Carla met you, yeah. Because of you, in this unfortunate situation, you brought us all together for the first time in years. We went through a lot, especially her. So, growing up, we were hard on her, but most times, she was tougher than us.

"I think, she felt smothered, so she left right out of high school. But once she split, everyone else sort of drifted. We each had our eye on her, though. When she met you, everything about her changed."

"Me?"

"Her routine, her studying, even her grades."

"I take it you didn't get permission to view those grades."

He smiled a mischievous grin. "She seemed more motivated and happier with you. A couple of months later, she finally reached out to one of us. She still kept her distance, probably scared we would run off whatever dude she was messing with."

I chuckled. "Nah, Carla does that well all by herself."

"Probably our fault, too. She just seemed to find herself with you, and from that, we're able to be with her, see her. So we didn't hesitate when she called Chris and Eddy asking for help"

That part of Carla's life escaped me. Deep down, there seemed to be an entirely different issue on why she ceased contact with them. Because that didn't sound like the Carla I knew. She didn't leave because they were hard on her. Because of me, my situation with Jake, Carla made a tough choice to call on all her brothers.

"In a way, I'm relieved that I didn't tell her as soon as everything started. From what I know about being with him, I know now he would have killed her if I had." I whispered as I looked out the window at the dancing trees. "No matter what threats he threw her way, she stayed by my side, though. If all of what you say is true, I have y'all to thank for that."

"I'm sure she would say the same about you. In some way, you saved her, too. So, if you need anything, don't hesitate to ask."

I pondered his questions.

"In that case... Chris told me you hacked Nora's records and found out Marilyn is the heir. You think you can look into something for me?"

Chapter 31

Malcolm entered with a duffle bag in hand. Kyle and I finished a second helping of dinner and just finished up a whole topic on the security system he had set around the perimeter and the tech he designed for Chris and Wallace. I guess it was another of Wallace's hobbies to go on missions with Chris.

"K, I'm about to head out." He sat the duffle bag by the table.

"Alright, it was nice seeing you, Crab. Next time don't stay away so long." Kyle replied and Malcolm flicked him off.

"Sis? It was nice meeting you. Car sent more things." He placed the bags down at the end of the island where Kyle and I sat.

"Thank you, Malcolm. For everything."

He nodded and strolled away. Over his shoulder he yelled out, "oh, your man's outside."

"Greg?"

But Wallace had already left.

"He does that. Just lays the most essential information on you so casually."

"I'm nervous," I admitted.

"You shouldn't be. You know him."

I looked at Kyle and felt the breeze coming through the open door of the back porch. I wrapped myself in my arms.

"And these?" I tilted my chin toward my bruises.

"He knows what you've been through. There's no way he would think you'd come through without scars. I mean that figuratively too. He'll love you with or without them. Trust me. Now get your ass out there."

I smiled at how much he was like Carla, then took my exit from the kitchen.

My heart drummed steadily in my chest as I made my way through the hall. I could feel the pounding vibration in my ears and each pulse in my fingertips. Gregory made me feel alive. And with each step I took toward the door, my body felt lighter. I didn't care how things ended between us in the past. I only cared about the man on the other side of that door.

I pulled it open and peered into the dark night. The taillights from Wallace's vehicle disappeared into the distance as I stepped onto the patio. With a suitcase in his arms, Gregory approached from the darkness. My heart raced, my stomach tightened, and I couldn't fight the tears that stung my eyes. He dropped the luggage and took long strides toward me and I lept down the stairs, crossed the lawn, and flung myself into his arms. His embrace wrapped around my body like a blanket as I gripped his back. Finally, back in his arms. In his embrace. And I couldn't do a single thing but cry from the happiness and relief I felt from having him with me. His chest pounded against my ear and he squeezed me tighter. It was the drumming of his heart that I felt. At the same time, I knew he'd felt mine too.

"It's over." He said.

#

The high moon illuminated the doors, casting a white tint in the room. The fresh air that came with it eased the heat building between Gregory and me. I hadn't wanted to take my eyes off him, but I couldn't bring myself to look him in the eyes for more than a few seconds. When I did, my entire body turned into a puddle. I stood by the balcony door as he faced me nearer to the bed. The ten-foot difference felt like an ocean between us.

"I'm sorry I couldn't keep you from getting hurt. And that I didn't get you out sooner. And for lying to you." He said.

"You have a lot of sorries. Look where I am now. Nothing else matters to me."

"I'm glad you're safe. The brothers and Carla were a big help," He closed the gap between us. "She's a great friend."

"Yes, she is."

When he reached me, he stroked my face with the palm of his hand and looked at the bruise that was left.

"No matter what, I will help you heal."

"You're a good man, Gregory." I nudged into the warmth of his touch.

"Did you mean what you said... about loving me?"

My heart fluttered and I raised my head. "Yes." I replied without hesitation.

He kissed me deeply as we stood in the moon's light. I engrossed myself in every sensual and erotic nibble he placed on me and cooed in delight. My back arched from the cool door frame and my legs weakened underneath me from the shivers coursing through my limbs. The place that Gregory took me to reminded me of the exploding stars from our childhood. They burst into my chest and exploded one after the other. When we broke our embrace, we panted as we stared hungrily for more. Hungry for more touches. I placed my fingers on my lips as they pulsed with the rhythm of my heartbeat.

Grabbing me by the hand, Gregory led me to the bathroom, and I waited on a small ottoman. Only the light from the moon lit the bathroom, casting shadows on the walls. He added oils to the tub and pulled out a few small packs that reminded me of the paste Malcolm rubbed on me. When Gregory turned on the faucet, the rippling water's reflection cast to the ceiling and mirror, giving it a dancing effect. My breath caught in my throat as I watched the dancing paintings surround me.

Gregory kneeled in front of me. "Nhoell, I can only imagine the things you've been through. I can only try to relate. From this day forward, I promise to protect you, heal every wound you have and provide you with security. Above all, I promise to love you." His hand moved up my arm where the bullet grazed. "Everything that comes with you, I'll cherish. Because that is only a reminder of the strength you have. I'll never let something like that slip from me."

Gregory moved his hands up my arms and traced his fingers over my collarbone, sending a flurry of vibrations through me.

"I want to take care of all of you. I'm gonna start by putting you in this tub."

I shrunk into the seat and turned my head down. He lifted it back up to face him.

"And I'll still love you. I'll see you every day for the rest of your life and still love what I loved years ago."

With those words, and internally debating, I rose and dropped my hands at my side. He undressed me and removed the bandages as the heat grew between my legs. But also the embarrassment and shame of what Jake had done to me. With ease, Gregory laid me in the tub. It wasn't until he rubbed me with a soft cloth that I became aroused. Any thought f being judges had dissipated. I tried holding in my whimpers of pleasure as the warm water soothed my aches and Gregory soothed my heart. I wished it would end and not end, all at once. As he washed my hair, I closed my eyes and fell into the rhythm he played in my head. Moonlight reached the top half of the tub and my breast and face glistened. The reflection from the water's movement shimmered on Gregory's dark tone like waves of shadows throughout his skin. The sight of him left me in awe.

After the bath, he took exceptional care of my entire body by rubbing me with oils and a concoction I was sure came from a certain doctor. That first night, he massaged me until I fell asleep.

#

"Everything?" I blurted out.

It was the next morning when Gregory shed light on what he thought would have been the deal sealer with Jake. We sat on the back patio, surrounded by whistling birds and the light ocean breeze. I felt calmer than I had in months. I felt the difference in my body and mind. Last night had been the first time I'd slept through the night without being haunted by one thing or another.

"Yes. I think he left Nora Vaughn a small house in the country." Greg replied.

"The country? There is no way she would move to the country."

"That's not all. She came from a Christian family who had churches all around the city."

"Yeah, I learned about that a couple of days ago."

"After Andrew Vaughn took his own parent's house, he foreclosed on her family's estate as well. Seems he had a grudge against both their families. It was that, or he didn't play about his money."

"Wait, I thought they went bankrupt from terrible investments."

"They did. Which led both families to borrow the money from Andrew. I don't think it's a coincidence that the investments and bankruptcy happened around the same time."

"I can't believe it. So why would he leave me anything? I never heard of the man." I pondered the question.

"Nhoell, I found nothing about you or anyone in your family connected to the Vaughns. Though I can't imagine him getting something like that wrong."

"I agree. So, how do we know for certain Jake isn't coming after me? Just because he's in jail doesn't mean a thing."

"He won't be released for a long time. With the amount of evidence implicating him, the FBI knows they've hit the jackpot. And, remind me never to cross Eddy Dunn, the guy is brutal."

I took a shuttering breath and hoped what he said was true. Still, it unsettled me. We were off-grid, and not being able to see what was happening was nerve-wracking. Jake was powerful, and with power came loyalty. Even after all the information pertaining to the Vaughns that came out, I still had no leverage in case he sent someone after me.

I told Gregory about what Kyle researched the day before. We dug up files on Andrew Vaughn and the entire Vaughn family. He pulled records on my mom, grandma, and even my father. Ethan Burke was his name. Born and raised in Virginia, the same place as me. He died on the job when I was three. Kyle didn't find any connections that were out of the ordinary. Apart from my family and Andrew Vaughn being in the same state before I was born, nothing linked our families.

After my dad's death, we moved two other times across state lines, then twice more before settling in Atlanta. What surprised me, though, was the origin of our last name. I always assumed that my granddad's last name was Sandbrook. My grandma was born Cordelia Reese. Her married name became Cordelia Doyle. My mama had also been Cortina Doyle, then later became Cortina Burke. After the death of my dad, our name changed to his mother's maiden name, Sandbrook. Why? Why did we take my grandmother's maiden name? Still, after all that, we were back to where we started. Nothing linked my family to the Vaughns. For the first time, I wondered if maybe Marilyn heard the wrong information. Maybe Jake decided to toy with me more. Maybe I was the wrong woman all along.

"Sorry for the interruption, you two," Kyle walked onto the patio. "Nhoell? Phone call."

My eyes shot open. "Is it Carla again?"

Kyle shook his head. "No, your mom."

My heart skipped a beat as I rose and grabbed the phone, excusing myself into the house.

"Mama?"

"Nhoell? Where are you? I've been trying to reach you." Her shaky voice blared on the phone. The signal went in and out as she shot question after question at me. It pained me to hear the worry in her voice and to know I was part of the cause. Mainly for not telling her before the media had.

"I'm sorry, I should have told you. I should have told you everything." I sat on the barstool in the kitchen.

"It's okay, baby. Can you come home? I need you to come home.

Where are you?"

"I'm safe. I'm with Greg."

"Great. I'm glad he is with you. Where are you? Can you come home now?" She sniffled into the phone and my chest ached. I pinched the spot between my eyes, holding back the tears.

"Not yet, Mama. Maybe in a little while. Things haven't calmed down yet. But I will call you no matter what."

She grew silent again.

"Nhoell, please, I need you here. I'm worried about you."

"You don't need to be worried. I promise I'm safe now."

"I love you, baby. Everything I have done has always been for you and no one else. You are my baby, my daughter,"

On the patio, Greg rose from his seat facing Kyle at attention. The veins in his neck and the tight-jawed expression he made sent a burst of movements in my stomach.

"And I will kill anybody that tries to hurt you."

The phone beeped then line went silent. The signal bar on the screen flashed green, displaying a perfect signal. Scrolling up to the dial pad, I dialed out her number to call, then remembered a separate phone Kyle used for outgoing calls.

"What's going on?" Greg asked, stepping into the kitchen with Kyle close behind.

I stared at the phone screen again. "She hung up."

"What did she say?"

"She's worried and wants me to come home. Is everything okay?"

Kyle interjected. "What was she worried about?"

My brows furrowed at both of them.

"She must've seen something about me on the news. Greg? What the hell is going on?" I stood from the barstool.

"You're not in the news, sis," Kyle replied.

Greg added, "My request to keep your name out of the media was granted. Some things can't be helped but, the focus isn't you, Nhoell. That was part of my deal with the bureau."

"How did your mom get this number?" Kyle asked.

"I don't know. I didn't think about that. Carla, maybe?"

"Carla probably gave it to her. Not intentionally." Kyle mused.

"What the hell is going on?" My voice rose. "Gregory?"

A pained expression crossed his face. "It's Nora Vaughn. She fainted and was rushed to the hospital. They don't think she's going to make it."

"Oh, my goodness." My hand flew to my chest, and it surprised me to feel saddened by the news.

"A judge signed off on Jake's temporary release."

Chapter 32

Cortina Sandbrook. A formidable woman. She looked so frail and tired when she opened the door. Although she was in her fifties, she looked well in her sixties, from stress and illness, I imagined. The guilt hit at me like a slap in the face. How much I'd stayed away from home. Away from her. Tears flowed down my cheeks and I rushed into her arms. It relieved me to see that she was alive and well. Especially since Jake was on temporary release.

After hacking the hospital security footage and seeing him heavily guarded and entering Nora's room, my fears of him coming after me eased. I was relieved to be home.

My mama's tight grip cupped my back, and I took in all she had to give. Even with the ache in my wrapped torso.

"Oh, baby. I'm so sorry. I'm so sorry," she repeated.

"I'm okay, mama." I pulled away long enough to let Greg know we were fine.

"It's nice to see you again, Ms. Sandbrook." He stepped up to the door and looked behind her.

"You are a good man, Gregory." The quiver in her voice turned my stomach.

"Thank you. I'm sorry it took so long to bring her back. Are you okay?"

Mama nodded her head and looked between the both of us.

"She's here now and so are you. There ain't a thing that can keep you two apart. Don't go far, ya hear me? Don't go far." The look she gave him was one I'd never seen before. Admiration, sincerity, strength, and a plea.

"I'm never too far."

Gregory grabbed my hands in his. "I haven't been back here in years. I'm not sure how they'll take it."

"You have to try, Gregory. Just talk to them. If they aren't willing to listen, then we will be here."

Gregory gave my hand a gentle squeeze, walked down the steps, then crossed the street to his childhood home. Once she and I were inside the house, my mother cracked, her face distorted in a tight grimace and her eyes filled with tears. My heart sank at her expression.

"Mama, what's wrong? What's happening?" I panicked.

She said, in between sobs. "I'm so sorry, Nhoell. There are so many things I haven't told you,"

"Like the type of whore, she really is."

My bones chilled, and the bile from my stomach rose to my constricted throat at the raspy sound of Jake's voice.

"Surprised to see me, Sweetheart?"

Looking at Mama leaned against the wall clutching her shirt pained me. But it was her expression of deep fear when she looked at Jake that crushed me. I couldn't stand there and watch her, but that would mean facing Jake. The only thing that stood between him and my mama, though, was me. And nothing was standing between Jake and me. I gave in and turned to see him in a nice fitted suit like he'd just come from a corporate event.

"Jake," I could barely speak his name.

When he began walking to me, I stepped back, closer to my mama and squared my shoulders. "What do you want? Why are you here?"

"You don't know? You have something that belongs to us, and I want it." He stopped ten feet away from us. It still wasn't enough.

"I have nothing that belongs to you, Jake. Just leave."

"Do you know the fucking strings I had to pull to get here? Do you know what I had to spend to get here? If one agent can't be bought, another one can. I'm disappointed that you thought you could get away from me. Nhoell, when will you learn you will never win?"

"Are you sick! I will not be your wife, Jake! You are not in New York anymore. This is Atlanta, and I will call the police on your ass!"

"Try it." His voice suddenly more intense. "Looks like he has made you forget your place. Once we're married, they can arrest me all they want. At least you'll be mine. Besides, I won't be there for long."

Jake came closer, and I took another step back, pinning my mama against the wall. I knew if he were to come at her or me, there would be little I could do except fight for our lives. And I would die trying.

"I don't have a place. If there is something you want from me, just take it. You can have it."

"I figured you hadn't told her when she didn't recognize my name. Or me." Jake placed his hands behind his back. "Nhoell, did she ever tell you of the affair she and my father had?"

"What?"

"As I thought. This whore was fucking my father right under my mother's nose. They made her into a laughingstock and he left us nothing because of it. Yet, he leaves his whore's daughter an estate. The estate that belongs to my mother. My family!"

"An estate? Affair?" Without turning to her, I said, "Mama? Is it true? You were with his father?"

Behind me, she sniffled. "It wasn't like that, Nhoell. It wasn't an affair."

"Lying whore! Tell the fucking truth!"

My heart shuttered at his commanding voice.

"I didn't have an affair with Andrew," she sobbed. "I was married, and he was married, too." Jake pulled out a handgun from his suit jacket. I backed into my mama, afraid, but ready to take any bullet that would come our way.

"Oh, if I wanted to, you'd both be dead already. You slut! You were the reason he didn't love us. You are why he came home beating her. You were the reason he treated us like shit. Say it! Tell the truth!"

"Jake, please, just put the gun away and we can talk. We can all talk."

"Oh, you just shut the fuck up! I will deal with you later. My entire empire is gone, because of that piece of shit. But he will get his soon enough. And those lying ass parents, too."

"Andrew and I didn't have an affair," my mom said from behind me. "I met him when I was fifteen. That was the only time we were together. He found me again after I had you, Nhoell. I was married to Ethan and I couldn't."

"You're lying!"

Jake rushed us as I shielded my mama. It wasn't her he was after, though; it was me. He grabbed me by the back of my neck and I fought him as he pulled me to the living room. The crashing pain hit at my stomach as Mama hit at his back. But none of it fazed him. He turned to her after pushing me onto the couch. In one swing, she hit the floor. I quickly rose from the couch to go to her when Jake hit me with the butt of the gun, knocking me back down. My vision blurred instantly.

"I'm sorry," I cried out. "I'm sorry, mama."

Jake crouched in front of her. "You have one chance to tell me the truth or I will kill you then take Nhoell with me. And, her life will be hell underneath my roof."

I stayed put as Jake trained the gun on her. Afraid to move in fear of him pulling the trigger.

"Tell the fucking truth!"

"Okay! Please. Don't hurt my baby. She got nothing to do with this!"

"She has everything to do with this. Now talk!"

"I met Andrew when I was fifteen. He was attending a college near where I worked part time. He knew I was young, but he didn't care and I didn't care. We kept on seeing each other. Ma was strict, Nhoell. More back then than when I had you. I could only go to school and work. I loved Andrew. But… I got pregnant and couldn't tell him. When Ma found out, she took me out of school, and I couldn't work. Beads of sweat appeared on her forehead.

"I didn't see Andrew the entire time I was pregnant. I gave birth in Ma's bed, and after two weeks, she took the baby and left. We moved that same day. It was the last time I saw my baby.

"Irrelevant. Keep going."

"Nhoell, I met your dad right after high school. We married shortly after and a few years later, we had you. I didn't think to tell him about my past. I couldn't. I should have. Andrew showed up about eight years after we moved.

"I thought it was a coincidence that we ran into each other. We talked, and he told me about this child he had. This little girl someone left at his campus dorm.

"It was my little girl. She had left her with Andrew. He wanted me to meet her, to see her, to be a family. But I couldn't. I had my own family. I had you, Nhoell." Mama sobbed.

"No. No, that can't be. She's dead. That woman's dead." Jake repeated. I also started to understand. A daughter. Given to Andrew. That didn't belong to Nora.

"Marilyn?" I said in a low whisper. Marilyn was my mom's daughter? My sister, my blood? I finally understood where I recognized her from. I saw my own face in her. I saw my mother's face in her when she smiled. A beautiful bright smile. It was because Mari looked like her mom, that's why he loved her more.

"He said he named her Marilyn. I couldn't go to her. Not without telling Ethan that I had another child out there. I couldn't do that to us, to you, Nhoell."

"This can't be. I checked her out. I saw the death certificate. How?" Jake repeated as he held his head and paced the floor.

Mama continued. "He became so angry when I refused to go to her. I'd never seen him like that. I'd never seen him so consumed with anger. We went our separate ways. The next day, your father was in an accident and was killed. I knew it was Andrew. I ran back to Ma, and we picked up and moved again. That was the last I heard from him. We moved until we heard he'd died. I promise that is it. Nhoell, I'm so sorry I didn't tell you. I'm sorry this happened to you, baby."

Jake switched the gun from hand to hand, looking in every direction but ours. I still sat in disbelief, not knowing what to say.

"No. No! You fucking whore! He said you were dead. I saw the death certificate. My mother told me all about how he planned trips for you. Then he would come back and kick her ass. I would hear it. It was you!"

"No, I spent most of my life hiding from Andrew. He wasn't the same man I knew as a girl. If he could kill my husband so easily, he could have killed my daughter. And now you, the seed of him," She spat. "coming back to haunt my family because I turned my back on my baby. But I won't let you hurt her. I won't let you take her down with you!"

Mama lunged at Jake, and I jumped to intercept her. Easily, he knocked her back down with his gun and she lay unmoving. I let out a penetrating scream and dropped to her side, praying the impact from the floor and the blow to the head didn't kill her. My hands shaking, I called out to her.

"It's time to go. Get up," he said.

"No! I'm not leaving with you!"

"Get up!"

Jake yanked me from the floor effortlessly and I jerked my body and beat at him to release me. The agonizing pain shooting through my torso didn't help. Still, it didn't slow him down. He pulled me through the dining room and kitchen towards the back. Approaching the basement door to my art studio, I got an idea, then prepared myself. I had only one shot. As soon as we stepped parallel to the door, I jerked my body against him rather than away and we both crashed through it. We'd both fell down the stairs, but Jake's body broke most of my fall whereas he hit much of the railing and stairs. As soon as we hit the floor, his grunts ceased and a surge of pain shot through my arm and ribs. The wind was knocked out of me along with the scream that manifested. I could sense him on the ground behind me, but the darkness didn't let me see any other part of the room. When I eased myself from the cold floor, Jake groaned behind me, intensifying my need to move quicker. Cringing with each movement, I held my arm against my body and I scrambled to my feet and limped to the basement door. Boxes on top of boxes blocked the exit. I cursed. Jake let out another loud groan, and I jetted to the stairs, my chest beating unsteadily. As soon as my foot touched the first step, I lunged up two at a time, feeling my body tear apart until I could not stifle my screams. Before I could reach the top, a loud bang deafened me. Another loud bang and I fell on the top floor screaming from the searing pain in my leg. I scooted down the hall into the kitchen, wincing at every movement as Jake's heavy footsteps marched up the stairs. The knife holder stuck out like a sore thumb and I lifted myself against the counter.

"Nhoell? Sweetheart? There is nowhere you can run. How do you think I found you? How do you think I was able to slip from the hospital? I still have connections Nhoell, so you'll never be safe if that's what you're looking for. I have eyes everywhere. Remember that."

It was terrifying how calm his voice was as he grew closer. Once his foot crossed the threshold of the door, I held my breath and stabbed blindly. The knife hit its mark and Jake screamed as I pulled it out and stabbed again. It was a miss. I took off to the other side of the kitchen and into the dining room. The next shot Jake let off felt like the bullet was only inches from my ear. I dropped the knife and collapsed, crawling until I made it to the living room. Mama was gone from the floor and the door was wide open.

"Where are you going?"

I turned around to see him standing in the doorway to the living room, his eyes black, his gun pointed at me. His white shirt blossomed red as I wheezed in pain but stared hard, refusing to give in to him. My mama was safe and that's all that mattered.

"Look at you now."

"If you're gonna kill me, Jake," I forced out. "Kill me. Because I'm not going with you unless I'm a dead woman, you bastard!"

He aimed the gun at me. I closed my eyes and seconds later, a shot blasted. Nothing. I opened my eyes to Jake's crimson shirt and his gun pointed behind me. Another shot rang out, and I covered my head and ears as a few more followed. No sooner than the bullets stopped flying, there was a loud crash. I finally lifted my head to see Jake and Gregory fighting on the dining room floor, knocking over chairs and crashing into the table. They both threw punches at one another as they each tried to gain the upper hand. Blood, I assumed from Jake, was trailing all over the carpet as they rolled around taking hits and giving them. Even with him being shot, Jake still matched Gregory in strength, and I imagined anger and humiliation kept him fighting. Gregory landed a clean blow to Jake's temple, knocking him flat to the floor. He kicked Gregory, knocking him back into the wall. In one motion, Jake was on his feet throwing blows at him, who took them all. But a knee to the groin caused Jake to double over. Grabbing him by the back of his neck, Gregory began thrashing him in the face. Using his weight, Jake slammed him back into the wall, sending them both crashing through to the other side.

I imagined they were both fighting to the death. The thought of Jake killing him then coming after me threw me into action. My leg and arm still ached and my body had felt light and tingling. My pants leg covered in blood, and its warmth made my entire body flush. I sat up and looked around for anything that would give Gregory the upper hand. Near the entrance to the dining room, the knife I'd stabbed Jake with laid on the floor. I crawled over wrecked furniture and bloody carpet to get to it. Glass broke from the other room and another crash shook the house. Grabbing the knife, I held onto it with a tight grip then pulled myself up on the doorframe. Using the wall to hold myself up, I limped to the hole in the hallway. I kept my fist tight and stood as solid as my body would allow. Adrenaline coursed through me, but I could feel myself getting faint by the second. I stuck my head around the door frame, and both men moved closer to the hall near the front door. My vision blurred, and I shook my head to steady my sight. Seeing Jake throw a powerful punch to Gregory's head, knocking him down, I made my move. He wouldn't get another chance to get Gregory down, and I knew I wouldn't get another chance to act. I tiptoed, the pain causing me to move slower than I wanted, but still, the gap was closing between Jake and me. He stood over Gregory, fist clenched. I was close enough to smell Jake's cologne lingering in the hall, and it turned my stomach. Just as Gregory lifted his head, Jake pulled his leg back, ready to give him an awful kick to the face. Before he could bring his leg forward to land the blow, I raised my arms as far as it would go. His beatings, his abuse, my hate for him, all came rushing through me. I brought the knife down with all my strength and lunged it into the top of his shoulder blade, then yanked down as hard as I could. He screamed out in agony and my body trembled at the sound. I yanked it out and repeated my attack. He doubled over and landed on his knees. Before I could pull it out and stab again, he swung his body around and knocked me hard against the table near the wall. Gregory kicked Jake, sending him flying back and landing hard on his back. Then there was silence. For the first time since being home, there was silence. I finally lost consciousness.

Chapter 33

The entire block surrounding my mama's house was in chaos. Not long after I stabbed him, the police arrived. Ten minutes after giving Jake's identity, dozens of squad cars, unmarked vehicles, and helicopters circled the block. News vans and crowds of people also swarmed the street. The paramedics saw to my injuries and recommended getting me to the hospital soon, but the police wanted answers. It looked like an earthquake hit and splattered red paint around the house. My clothes were covered in my and Jake's blood and I sat on the couch in a daze, ignoring their questions. Near the front door, Gregory talked to two other FBI agents, making heated gestures at them and pointing at me. They looked my way. Greg and I locked eyes. I was glad he was alive. Glad Jake hadn't killed him. Still, the only thing on my mind was Jake's gruesome scream when I stabbed him. So, I hadn't realized Gregory approached me until he spoke.

"We're headed to the hospital, now."

Two paramedics joined my side and began helping me onto the gurney.

#

"Why are you still looking at this?"

Greg entered the hospital room and my stomach growled from the Cajun seasonings coming from the bag he carried.

"I'm worried." I pointed to the TV, CNN on with a red bar scrolling at the bottom of the screen: NEW in Jake Vaughn Scandal. It wasn't long before they realized the connection between my mama's house, me, and Jake. And the press all over dove right into speculating on the chain of events.

"Exactly. So, don't drown yourself in it and worry more." He sat next to me on the bed, the food resting at the foot.

"How can I not? There is stuff out there people shouldn't know about. That's none of their business." Greg clutched my hand.

"We knew this would happen. And I know what you're talking about. Eventually, it won't stay hidden for long Nhoell. So," he leaned in closer to me. "when it does happen, I'll still be right here with you."

"I know," My shoulders relaxed, "I didn't foresee everything else though. The truth is, I don't know how to feel about Mama keeping so much from me. I'm angry at her, but I'm angry at myself too." I squeezed his hand. "Still, I don't want people hunting her down for answers about the past. I don't care what they say about me."

"You cannot protect her from the news, Nhoell."

I stared ahead at the TV again. "I can try."

My stomach growled, then we both burst into laughter.

"Well, how about you try later, and we can take care of this food now." He took out the food and placed them on the bed, then started flicking through channels. Already with a plate in my hand, I started eating.

Each news channel he passed reported on the same story. I didn't expect to be at the center of every single story floating around. Most of the incidents involving me led to weed out many of the people on Jake's payroll. Missing video footage from the plane had resurfaced and, they'd even dug up information on my business, only to learn Vaughn Incorporated owned it. Some media outlets speculated that I'd given it over to him in exchange for something, while others figured it was something he used against me. They got medical records from the hospital. So images of my bruised body were circulating across the internet. Other photos came from a closed case file in the police precincts. Some people called me a hero for killing him. Others called me lucky. But I didn't feel like either. I felt lost, broken and unsteady. Inside, I still felt afraid, and I didn't know why.

"We're gonna just turn this off." Greg interrupted my thoughts. The TV screen went blank, and I smiled with a mouth full of food. He leaned in and faintly brushed his lips across my cheek. I stopped chewing and held my breath, allowing the warm feeling from his kiss to wash over me.

"I knew we would cross paths again. Since the day I met you, there hasn't been a single day in my life where I haven't thought of you. Not one. That feeling you gave me. A boy wouldn't know what to do with it, but a man... he'll surrender himself. I waited for that day to come."

He pulled away a little to look at me. I stared at the features in his face. The way his eyes slanted, his arched brows and the fullness of his lips. I even took in the soft lines in his eyes and deep ones at the corner of his mouth.

"I tell you this now because you will be my wife, the mother of my children, the soul of my soul and always the drumming of my heart. I don't want there to be anything hidden between us. I will live with the regret of not looking for you. I could have prevented many things —"

"— Greg, stop," His head turned away from me, but then he looked back.

"Don't blame yourself for anything. If it weren't for you, Carla and I wouldn't be here. You don't know how things would have turned out. Eventually, I would have met him." It was my turn to stroke his firm jaw and clean-cut stub on his chin. "But we do know how things will turn out now."

"You're wrong about one thing. If it weren't for you, Carla and you wouldn't be here. It took strength and courage to ask for help again. Especially from me. That was you." He grabbed my hand and kissed the palm. "All you."

"Damn," I wiped my eyes. "you are making me cry again."

"Aww, com'on. You can cry. Nobody's watching."

"I am!"

I whipped my head up to Carla standing in the doorway with a vase of daffodils. Shoving the plate of food out of the way, I reached out my arms and she took long strides and embraced me in a tight hug. She buried her face in my neck and thanked God over and over for keeping her safe. Greg eased out the room and left us as we fought to see who can hold the other tighter. After a while, we broke our embrace.

"I'm so glad you're okay," I wiped the tears that escaped.

"No, I'm glad you're okay. Where did he disappear to?"

"Giving us privacy." I beamed at her. "I can't believe you flew down here."

"Ha, did you think I wouldn't? I'm pissed I couldn't get here sooner. I was seriously on lockdown. I can't believe their asses. One little shoot out and they confine me."

"I can't believe there is so much I don't know about you," I said in awe. Carla flopped on the bed and leaned back on her arms and raised her head to the ceiling.

"Every family has their secrets. Yours is stickier than mine though." She joked.

"You're right about that. Phew. But seriously, I hope one day you can tell me your story."

"Speaking of family, how is your mom?" She turned her complete body to face me.

"She's okay. A bit shook up. But she's holding it together. The house is a disaster, so she's staying at a hotel right now."

"That's good. How are you holding up? After what happened?"

"I'm not really sure yet. I can't stop seeing it. I'm relieved, but there is something else I feel when I think about it. I just don't know." Carla hugged me again.

"Make sure you talk to someone. To get this all off your chest and your head. I want you to be okay. Something like this can destroy you if you let it."

"I will."

There was an odd silence between us before she spoke again.

"So, about this sister of yours." She whispered.

I snapped my head to Carla and her dimples deepened in her cheeks.

"Don't play, Carla. It isn't funny." I swiped at her.

"I know it isn't. But are you guys going to say anything?"

I let my head flop on the pillow before replying.

"I don't think my mom wants to. I don't blame her. It's pretty much asking for the media to wreak havoc on her life. I want to keep a lid on this as long as I can."

"Now that you put it that way. I hope it works out. For all of you."

"Marilyn too?" I asked, not really expecting a reply.

"Yep. Her too. I can imagine what she's been through. But I'm glad she's going to take over the company, if there is even one left. It won't be easy."

Yeah, it won't be. But she's strong and smart."

I thought of Marilyn a bit longer. How she was so quick to risk everything to help me. How much she reminded me of my mama. Our mama. But I felt so guilty for agreeing to keep my mama's secret. I tried not to imagine what she'd gone through with her own family. But I couldn't help it. I couldn't help feeling like she was wronged. Like we both were. Still, none of that changed the fact that I would die to protect my mama from the media that reported non-stop on the Vaughn family scandals.

"Hey Car?" I pulled myself away from my torturing thoughts.

Carla faced me with those beautiful hazel eyes and that wild fiery hair. The soft expression on her face brought me happiness because it showed me a light in her I'd never seen before.

"Thank you for always being there. No matter what. I know it took so much to make that call, but I'm glad you did. I'm glad our forever still means forever."

"It always will. Blood or no blood. You are my sister."

"Thank you."

A knock sounded at the door. Carla and I both turned our head to Gregory entering.

"Sorry ladies," He held his hand up in surrender. "I'm only coming for the food. I'm starving."

I laughed out and shook my head. Carla stood up and embraced Greg when he approached.

"Thank you. You're a good one."

"So are you." He replied.

I smiled at both of them and my chest warmed.

"You both are good! Now get over here and eat." I picked up and started back on the plate I originally had. We ate on my hospital bed like old friends. Seeing the smile on their faces gave me the last bit of validation I needed to know it wasn't a dream. That I was truly free of Jake Vaughn. I turned to Greg and his eyes lit up at something Carla had said. My stomach filled with fluttering butterflies as his cheeks widened and he burst into a laughing cough. He was still the Greg I remembered. His authentic smile cascading in my memories reflected the one plastered on his face. My heart beat against my chest like a drum. Greg suddenly contained himself, then turned and looked at me.

#

Five days later, the chaos surrounding the hospital had calmed down enough for me to be released. After a couple of days of debating with Gregory, I agreed to stay with him in the guest house on his property. At least until I figure out my next move. I'd gathered the belongings I acquired during my stay. With my hoodie over my head, I met Gregory in the hall. Although I didn't think it was necessary, four officers walked with us until we reached the main entrance. There weren't as many reporters and cameras as it was the day everything happened. Still, there were people blocking the way and already yelling. Greg squeezed my hand and pulled me in close.

"You guys ready?" One officer asked. "The car is directly ahead and waiting."

"You're ready?" Gregory asked. I nodded my head, and we were headed straight through the doors into the flashing lights and reporters. The officers kept a perimeter around me as Gregory shielded me with his coat. Reporters yelled out questions about me and Jake, my business, the abuse and even Gregory. As soon as we got to the car, the police officers opened the door. A reporter from behind me yelled, "Nono," a name I hadn't heard since high school. I turned to him before Gregory helped me into the car.

"What's the real reason Jake Vaughn went through all of that trouble for you?" That reporter stared at me hard, waiting for an answer, then smirked right before the door slammed in his face. I continued to look at him through the tinted window. On the other side, he stared at the window too, as if he could see me. We pulled off, leaving the crowd and the one reporter behind.

Epilogue

Never did I imagine things would be this way. That things could fall in my favor after my father passed. I always knew he loved me. Every morning, he told me just how much I meant to him and my mother. I believed every word he said. Even now, I still believe that somewhere out in the world, my mother is still thinking of me. Praying for me.

Ever since the news broke that I was the successor in my father's company, my phone rang non-stop. Without a blink, I knew what I had to do. Jake was gone and his torturing could no longer hold me back. Nora was ill and still hospitalized. Holly's social status plummeted after scandals about the Vaughn's broke loose.

If what the FBI says is true, my brother had his hands full with more than I could have ever imagined. What I am grateful for is that he didn't use the company's funds for his illegal activities, though he used the name as a cover-up. The shit show he left me with had more to do with the companies he destroyed, the federal government looking into every one of our records and a target on my back. Someone underground had been sending me messages about money Jake owed and a contract he signed. I always ignore them. Apart from figuring out how to keep my dad's company from being seized by the federal government, there was a matter just as important I could finally deal with.

Sitting in front of my computer in my father's study on the south wing of the mansion, I reread the email in my draft's folder. All I had to do was press send. After that, it was only a matter of time before I had my answers. I checked the 'from' section to make sure I used my dummy account and the 'to' section to make sure the private investigator's email was correct. My fingers trembled over the mouse and sweat trickled down the sides of my forehead. A knock sounded at the door, breaking my concentration.

"Come in," I replied.

Eleanor, our oldest, longest working employee, entered.

"Just making sure you alright. I brought you some tea." She came in and sat the tea on the desk.

"Thank you, Elly." I picked up the glass and sipped from it. "Good as always."

"Don't stay up too late. One makes mistakes when they're tired. I'll see you in the morning, Mari."

She left right back out. I leaned back in my father's chair and sipped more of my tea as the computer screen stared at me. Lifting my hand over the mouse again, I dragged the cursor to the send button and clicked it. A sudden relief washed over me as I stared at the notification saying, 'Message Sent.'

Note from the Author

Pain, fear, anxiety, depression, loneliness, worthless, caged, torn, broken. From abuse these words become real. It isn't easy to deal with pain alone. Neither is it easy to face our fears alone. It is easy to feel worthless and caged and broken from the abuse that's given. It is never easy to leave. No matter the circumstances. But there is help. Even if you do not see it. There will always be someone there to help. But it starts with you, first. Speak up. Because we are here for you.

The National Domestic Violence Hotline – 1-800-799-SAFE (7233)
www.TheHotline.org

Domestic Shelter – www.domesticshelters.org

Contact, Reach Out, Speak

Website: www.machperson.com
Email: mperson@machperson.com
Facebook: Author Mach Person
Instagram: @mach.person

About the Author

I was born and raised in Atlanta, Georgia, and was adopted only a few months after my entrance into this world. The time I spent with my adopted family was more than I could ask for. There was joy, happiness, security, and more than anything; there was love.

Like many today, we faced hardship from many directions. Still, we overcame because of the formidable foundation my mother and father provided. From then, I was able to proliferate and learn quickly. I am now an adventurer in the world. Although some would say that I am lost. I call it exploring.

Through the art of the written word, I explore this vast world and the troubles, grief, pain, and love that it exemplifies. I operate as a vessel for my mother, whose mind is a beautiful thing. Like the planet I reside in, I am exploring it too.